Under a Falling Star

Also by Caroline Fyffe

Prairie Hearts Novels
Logan Meadows, Wyoming Territory, 1878

Where the Wind Blows

Before the Larkspur Blooms

West Winds of Wyoming

Under a Falling Star

The McCutcheon Family Series
Y Knot, Montana Territory, 1883

Montana Dawn

Texas Twilight

Mail-Order Brides of the West: Evie

Mail-Order Brides of the West: Heather

Moon Over Montana

Mail-Order Brides of the West: Kathryn

Montana Snowfall

Under a Falling Star

A Prairie Hearts Novel

Caroline Fyffe

Montlake
Romance

Text copyright © 2015 Caroline Fyffe

Published by Montlake Romance, Seattle

www.apub.com

Amazon, the Amazon logo, and Montlake Romance are trademarks of Amazon.com, Inc., or its affiliates.

ISBN-13: 9781503951044
ISBN-10: 1503951049

Cover design by Anna Curtis

Printed in the United States of America

Dedicated to my darling daughter-in-law, Misti Chanel,
who has filled our lives with love, happiness, and joy.

PROLOGUE

Union Pacific Rail Lines, Wyoming Territory, April 1883

Dalton Babcock lifted his .45 Colt from its holster and checked the chambers. As always, his weapon was loaded and ready, as was the gun that rested heavily on his other hip. Two loaded shotguns hidden on a bunk in the musty train car were extra insurance and within easy reach.

In three hours, the Union Pacific was due to stop at the Logan Meadows depot to take on water and exchange a few passengers. From there it would continue on to Seattle and then San Francisco, stopping at a dozen small, nondescript towns along the way. His journey was halfway complete.

Gazing out the small two-by-two window, Dalton took a deep breath and held the stale air in his lungs. The rough terrain, with the endless pines and large granite outcrops of rock whisking by outside, made a stark contrast to the three locked boxes behind him, filled with freshly printed one-hundred-dollar bills, said to total over a million dollars.

Thump, thump, thump. The knock at the door was right on schedule.

Grasping the heavy steel-enforced window guard, Dalton closed it, then threw the lock. He went to the door at the front of the car. "Yeah?"

"It's Evan, come to relieve you."

Dalton recognized his coworker's gravelly voice. "Echo, Echo . . ."

". . . river black," came the coded reply.

Each day of the week, the color of the code changed, in an effort to keep the First Bank of Denver's assets safe until they arrived in San Francisco. One million dollars was enticing to outlaws and law-abiding citizens alike. The guards had been instructed to protect the cargo at all costs.

Dalton unbolted the lock, and then lifted the bar. Evan slid inside as Dalton stepped onto the small platform between the connected cars, the rush of cool air brisk. The door was not to remain unlocked for more than a few seconds.

"Get some grub and hot coffee," Evan said. "Once we reach Logan Meadows I'll need both you and Pat"—he gestured toward the roof, where the third guard patrolled—"on high alert."

"On my way."

The door banged closed.

Dalton passed through the cattle cars, watching where he stepped, then through the luggage and cargo cars, the chugging of the train now so commonplace it went unnoticed. Once in the passenger cars he nodded to anyone who looked his way. Taking a seat at a table in the dining car, he put in an order and waited for his fare. Twenty minutes and three cups of coffee later, he felt the urgency within that always unsettled him right before a scheduled stop. He'd return to the money car and take his position on the outside landing.

Picking up the pencil, he signed the tag for his employer to pay, then stood at the exact moment a forceful jolt rocked the train, knocking him off his feet.

CHAPTER ONE

Logan Meadows, Wyoming Territory, April 1883

*S*usanna Robinson glanced around the newly constructed community hall, satisfaction warming her deep inside. Once construction had begun, the log cabin–style edifice had gone up in a month. It had several smaller rooms, as well as a kitchen. A stairway on the west side of the great room led to a narrow upper tier that ran the length of the building, allowing a person to watch the festivities from above.

A darn sight better than the large gray barn! As the caterer for the much-anticipated wedding of Brenna Lane to the town's schoolteacher, Greg Hutton, the Silky Hen Restaurant was responsible for today's shindig. The groom's family had ventured all the way from Pennsylvania, and everyone wanted Logan Meadows to make a good impression.

Susanna sighed and rolled her tired shoulders. She'd taken ten minutes to slip on an apron, freshly starched and ironed thanks to Tap Ling's laundry service. She ran a hand over her hair to make sure no wayward tendril had escaped. The bride and groom, as well as most of the town, would arrive any minute. Candles and lanterns amplified the late-afternoon light, glowing beautifully atop the long table covered in snowy-white cloth. Platters of seasoned beef, pork, and chicken, as well as an array of salads, would tempt the choosiest of eaters. Freshly baked rolls abounded by the basketfuls. At the end of the table, the decorated cake added the finishing touch.

Mrs. Hollyhock's quilting fairies had made white fabric flowers, which looked so real one was tempted to reach out and touch them, as well as streamers and doodads, which had transformed the open log room into something magical from a storybook. This would be a wedding to remember.

Susanna's boss, Hannah Donovan, breezed into the room followed by Tabitha Canterbury, Hannah's older cousin who'd arrived in Logan Meadows last November. Miss Canterbury, in her late twenties, had managed to persuade Frank Lloyd, her uncle and the bank's owner, to give her a loan to open a bookstore on Main Street—as if the task were no riskier than baking a cake. Susanna admired the business-minded, unmarried woman very much. As regally as a queen, Tabitha carried a tray filled with coffee cups and headed for the kitchen.

Hannah glanced around, nodding her approval. "The room is gorgeous, Susanna! Brenna won't believe her eyes when she steps inside—which should be in about five minutes. The ceremony was lovely. I'm still all aflutter." A dreamy expression crossed her face, making Susanna smile. "Church was just letting out when Tabitha and I snuck out to fetch the last tray of coffee cups at the Silky Hen. Is there anything else I need to do?"

Susanna placed a calming hand on Hannah's arm. "Yes. Take a deep breath and relax. Everything is ready. Daisy ran home to clean up and will be back any second."

Hannah exhaled a long sigh of contentment. "I couldn't have done it without you. You're more my right hand than this," she said, holding up her right hand. Susanna's boss smiled, then hurried away.

Would *she* ever be a bride? Susanna wondered with a smidgeon of uncertainty. *I'm only twenty-five, not yet a true spinster.* Since her arrival over two years ago, Albert Preston, the sheriff of Logan Meadows, was never far from her side. He took lunch daily at the restaurant where she worked, and sought her out more often than not for walks after Sunday service. She held their friendship close to her heart. It was the most special thing in her life. If she let herself, she would fall headfirst into his expressive dark eyes. And his laughter—he knew each and every way to make her smile, and did so often. But Susanna needed to play it safe. She'd rather have him as a dear friend than a used-to-be who needed to be avoided.

The sad truth was, *nothing* lasted forever. At least not in *her* family. If she never let them get started, then they'd never come to an end. Even if Albert might think he was in love with her now, the feeling wouldn't last. No, as much as she longed to be a wife, her fear of what might come after the vows was too much to contemplate. A cooling of their love, resentment, Albert walking out the door. Because of that, each time his tone turned serious, and she thought he might be veering toward a deeper relationship, she steered him to a safer subject, like the new people in town, what so-and-so was planting this year, how the weather had turned.

Besides all that, there was no easy way to tell him about her mother. Being a lawman, surely he'd think less of Susanna if he knew they had survived on the money men left behind after a visit to their house. Her mother always sent Susanna away when a suitor came to call, but it wasn't long before she understood the whispers the other children hid behind their hands.

Did Albert care for her? She believed he did—and deeply, if she indulged her imagination. He'd never kissed her, despite what her girlfriends thought. He'd been a perfect gentleman from day one. When she began to daydream of what might be, she reminded herself that his respectful actions extended to all the women he came into contact with.

Daisy Smith, Hannah's other employee, dashed through the door. In her black skirt, white high-collared blouse, and devoid of any eyeliner or lip color, she presented such a demure appearance that one would never guess she used to be a saloon girl at the

Bright Nugget. "Here they come!" she called in an excited voice. "They're parking the buggies. Everyone to their stations!"

Susanna plastered on a smile and hurried to the front door where she'd collect shawls from the ladies and hats from the men. She had a job to do—and it didn't involve mooning over Albert Preston.

CHAPTER TWO

*A*lbert Preston leaned his shoulder against the substantial hearth of the fireplace in the large log room and smiled as the wedding guests on the dance floor twirled past. He took a sip from his cup of bourbon-laced punch and swallowed, enjoying the view Susanna presented as she and the other woman cleared away the serving platters from the buffet table. Dinner had come and gone, and wine, as well as this tasty punch, had been served. The band—two fiddles and a guitar—filled the room with music.

Chase Logan, local rancher, lounged by his side. He gave a deep sigh and rubbed his stomach. "That was a darn good meal. I especially liked the braised sirloin tips."

Charlie Axelrose, standing next to Chase, laughed, then swilled down what was left in his cup. The newcomer who'd arrived in Logan Meadows last year looking for a safe place for his blind daughter smacked his lips. "That's because *you* supplied the beef, Chase. Modesty becomes you."

Chase looked at him askance. "Maybe. But Jessie and I thought it a suitable wedding gift for the new schoolteacher and his lovely bride. A party like this costs a pretty penny. Since we have cattle coming out our ears, we were happy to oblige."

Albert watched Charlie's gaze as it drifted around the room until it found Nell. He hid his smile at the newlywed's look of longing. Charlie and Nell had only been married a few months and worked side by side on their ranch.

"Why don't you go ask her to dance, Charlie?" Albert reached across Chase and nudged Charlie's shoulder. "Don't be shy. It'd be better than you standing here with that hangdog look on your face."

"She's busy with things."

Well, when Susanna was finished with her task, Albert intended to steal a dance or two, no matter how much she protested that her responsibilities came first. She looked exceptionally pretty in her soft indigo-colored dress, the wide sash accentuating her narrow waist and the color making her green eyes look blue. She was a beauty. *His beauty.*

Well, not yet, his conscience corrected—but soon, if all went as planned. There it was, that frustrating "if" that was always ready to dash his hopes. She *would* be his girl, he corrected. As soon as he was free to ask for her hand. Lucky for him, she didn't seem in any rush to make things official. Every time he'd mustered up enough courage to tell her about Floria, and the divorce he'd been trying to obtain, she'd diverted the conversation elsewhere. He wanted to rid his conscience of the burden it carried, and begin again with his past out in the open, as he should have from the start.

A surge of sadness rippled through Albert as it always did when he thought about the past. He hadn't intended for his marriage to last a mere two months, but overlooking Floria's dishonesty would have taken a better man than he was. He'd been duped, and badly. Blindsided by her beauty, and enticed by her charms, he'd proposed after only a week, unaware that was exactly what she had planned to get back at the man who'd jilted her.

Thankfully, his latest correspondence from his brother Corey, two months ago, had him optimistic. She'd agreed to go forward with the divorce. Corey would see that it was done and then forward the legal papers on to him, being his family home was only a few hours' ride from where Floria lived in Iowa. His brother Winthrop was the only one in Logan Meadows who knew his history. Keeping it from his friends hadn't been difficult. His shameful situation was his alone to shoulder. People had pasts. They came west to start anew—just as he had.

Albert had been watching impatiently for the papers for a good month, and was sure they'd arrive any day. Just as soon as he had them in his hands, and was sure Floria was not going to go back on her word once again, he'd have a heart-to-heart with Susanna. She was the only one he felt obligated to tell. Then it would be up to her if she could live with a man who'd kept such a secret from her for so long. A hopeful smile played around his mouth. She would. He felt sure of it. She was the most understanding woman he'd ever met. They were well suited.

He smiled when Susanna looked his way, a rush of warmth chasing away his gloomy thoughts. She had a way of lighting up a room. A man could only stand so much. He'd been patient long enough and needed to feel her in his arms. Just as soon as this song ended, he'd cross the room and collect on the dances she'd promised him last night.

Thom Donovan walked up to the group. "So this is where all the men are. I was beginning to think you'd gone home."

Albert gave his deputy a look of mock outrage, and then grinned. "Home before cake? That would be sacrilege. Besides, I like my spot by the fire just fine. As sheriff, my job is to keep watch on the townspeople, and that's exactly what I'm doing."

"We built this area with the men in mind," Chase added. "While the women like to visit and dance, we have ample room to sit back, smoke, and watch if we choose to."

Thom elbowed a place in between them. "Make room for one more. Mrs. Hollyhock keeps givin' me the eye," he said under his breath. "She's bound to ask me for a dance sooner or later. Just shy of eighty-seven, and she still has an eye for the men."

The bride and groom whirled by on the outside of the dancers, the melody of the waltz making Albert weave from foot to foot. Brenna's soft rose-colored gown looked sweet. Susanna had been especially excited about the garment, saying Mrs. Hollyhock and her friends had done a beautiful job, blindfolding Brenna for each fitting to keep the end result a surprise.

A loud crack sounded, and everyone turned to see what had caused the interruption. The music stopped.

Win, Albert's brother, had busted through the double doors of the community hall. His mouth gaped open as he struggled for breath, and the cranberry red of his face emphasized his fear-filled eyes.

"The Union Pacific has collided with a rockslide! People are hurt! We need every able-bodied man and woman to bring wagons and buggies to Three Pines Turn."

Albert headed immediately for the door. Three Pines Turn was about a half mile before the Logan Meadows depot.

Dr. Thorn followed in his footsteps. "Bring the worst to my office!" he hollered.

Albert stopped and glanced around. "Everyone else who needs tending, bring up here. Those of you who have cots, mats, extra blankets, or anything else that can be used as a bed, send somebody for them. And be quick about it. People may be dying."

CHAPTER THREE

*D*alton opened his eyes to a multitude of objects scattered around on the floor in front of his face. He ignored the searing pain in his head and blinked several times to clear his vision. The sounds of people crying and begging for help resonated through the air.

What happened?

He remembered signing his tab, then a loud screech ripping the air. He'd been thrown backward, where he'd struck his head against the hat rack. After which, everything went black.

He rolled to his knees. When he shook his head to clear away the cobwebs, a round of nausea almost made him retch. Somewhere a woman screamed, followed by the whimpering cries of a child. He needed to get to his feet. People were hurt and needed help.

The money car! Are we being robbed?

Grasping the dining car's nearest tabletop, he pulled himself up, then gave his legs a second to firm.

It was then he felt blood trickle down the back of his neck. Reaching up, he found a small gash. He extracted his handkerchief, folded it over, and pressed it to the back of his head.

Shattered dishes littered the area. Overturned chairs cluttered the aisle. It was a good thing the tables had been bolted to the floor.

He lent an arm to a porter who was lying in the passageway. "You all right?"

The man nodded as he stood.

"What happened?" Dalton asked.

"Don't know." The porter clenched his eyes shut for a second, then gripped his forehead. "Go, help who you can." He nudged some plates out of his way with his boot.

The passengers who were conscious began to stir. They climbed to their feet, moaning and crying. The porter raised his arm over his head and pointed toward the exit. "That way ladies and gentlemen. Make your way out of the car and help others as you go if you're able."

Urgency filled Dalton. He needed to get to the money car, check on Evan and Pat, but he couldn't turn a blind eye on so many who needed assistance. He stuffed his bloodstained hand-kerchief back into his pocket and clutched the door handle. About to jerk it open, he paused at the sound of a whimper.

Barely visible, and wedged in between a toppled chair and the wall, was a boy, maybe six years old. Blood ran down the side of his face from an angry-looking cut just above his temple.

Dalton dropped to a knee. "Here ya go, little tyke." He noted the child's frightened eyes as he uncovered him and gathered him into his arms. Standing, he set him atop a table, and with a knife he always carried, cut a long strip from the edge of the tablecloth. Cutting another square, he folded it up and pressed it against the wound.

The boy cried out.

"Now's not the time for tears—I need your help. Be a good boy and hold this for me."

He picked up the child's hand and showed him how to hold the bandage he'd folded and placed on his head. With nimble fingers, Dalton wound the other cloth strip around the boy's small head several times, then tied it off.

"There. That should stop the bleeding."

He glanced around for the child's parents. "Where's your ma and pa? Do you see them anywhere?"

The child shook his head.

"Fine then, you just sit still. I'm sure there'll be someone along soon to help you find them."

A shot rang out, then another. Dalton jerked up. *Outlaws?* Had they stopped the train?

When he turned to go, the child grasped his hand. "T-take me, t-too," he said through a voice clogged with fear and tears.

"It's too dangerous," Dalton said firmly.

"I'm scared."

Aww, hell.

He scooped up the bedraggled child, ignored a wave of dizziness, and jerked open the door. People behind him crowded his back in their hurry to disembark.

Soot and smoke filled the afternoon air, but there was no sign of fire. The townsfolk nearest must have somehow gotten word of the accident because a handful were already hurrying to and from the train, carrying injured passengers and Union Pacific employees. Dalton handed the boy to the first woman who ran forward. "Take him."

"Is he your son?"

"No. Couldn't find his parents."

Several more shots rang out.

She flinched but he pressed the boy into her arms anyway.

Now free, Dalton sprinted toward the back of the train, alarmed for the large treasury he'd been commissioned to safeguard, and the lives of the other guards. He weaved in and out of people sitting on the grass and the scattered luggage that had been tossed off the train. Adding to the confusion, several wild-eyed steers darted around him and ran off.

What was going on? Should he have been at the money car already? Guilt made him race faster. Was the money already gone?

Almost to his destination, another shot sounded. Dalton stumbled to a halt, his lungs hot with the effort of running. From inside the now-open cattle car, one of the porters glanced out at him, gun in hand. Several carcasses littered the floor. "Broken legs," the man hollered, his eyes filled with grief. "Couldn't be helped."

The money car looked intact. There was no sign of Pat Tackly, the guard who'd been stationed on top, but that didn't surprise him. Surely, the third guard had been pitched off the train when the engineer hit the brakes.

Dalton grasped the rail and pulled himself up on the bridge between the two cars. He banged on the door with all his might. "Evan! Evan, are you all right?"

No reply.

"Evan, can you hear me?" He pounded again. "It's Dalton Babcock. River black, river black. Open up!"

Dalton gazed toward the roof of the train and cupped his hands. "Pat Tackly!" he hollered. "Pat Tackly! You up there?"

Most of the action was taking place ten cars forward at the passenger cars. Men ran back and forth to the wagons, carrying people by their shoulders and feet. A fleet of wagons and buggies raced down the road toward the train. Dalton turned and scanned the top of the plateau that ran the length of the tracks on the opposite side of the train. In most places, the embankment was covered in trees.

Taking hold of the steely-cold ladder attached to the car, he climbed hand over hand to the roof of the train. He heaved himself up.

From here, he had a view almost to the front of the twenty-car train. Between the black smoke that billowed into the sky and the curve of the track, he couldn't see the first few cars, or the engine. He looked back toward the caboose. "Pat!" he hollered again through cupped hands. He scanned the terrain.

With his boot, he kicked off the hat-shaped bonnet that covered the air vent. Lying flat on the roof, he put his ear to the opening and listened. All was quiet. "Evan," he shouted. "Evan, can you hear me?"

A surge of sadness for his fellow guard squeezed his chest. Was he dead? The money car could only be unlocked from the inside. Accessing the car now would take manpower, as well as tools—and hours to break through the steel-enforced siding. Everyone was needed elsewhere. As was he—to save Evan might mean others wouldn't survive. And Evan might already be dead. Dalton had to keep a level head.

Certain the money was safe for a few hours at least, he jumped the short gap between the two cars and started for the passenger cars, searching both sides of the ground for the missing guard.

CHAPTER FOUR

On his third trip carrying injured passengers from the train to the wagons, Albert spotted a man running atop the cars toward the engine. He narrowed his eyes, wondering why the tall fellow was up there at a time like this.

"Albert! Over here!" Chase waved, distracting him. Chase, and Gregory Hutton still dressed in his groom's attire, stood beside a large man who lay unconscious on the grass. Women hustled here and there, toting cups of water and clean rags. How the men had removed the fellow, who looked the size of a small horse, from the wreckage was a mystery. "We need your help."

Joining Chase and Greg, Albert hunkered down and grasped an enormous arm and shoulder. Chase took the other and Greg grappled with the man's huge feet. They exchanged a doubtful look between them.

Chase glanced to the clearing where the wagons waited. "It's not too far. One, two, *three!*"

A groan escaped Albert's lips. Greg waited while he and Chase swung the giant's upper body around so they all could walk forward at the same time, enabling the trio to navigate the uneven ground.

"Stop before I drop him!" Greg said, fumbling with the man's legs, one worn-out boot in each hand. "I need a better grasp under his knees."

"Hold up, I can help!" someone shouted.

The stranger from the roof of the train ran over, his shirt splattered with blood. When he bent down to take hold, Albert noticed a gash on the back of his head still oozing. The stranger took one of the man's legs, and the foursome proceeded over the rough footing.

At the top of the rise, Thom Donovan pulled up in his wagon. "I see I'm just in time. Bring him this way." Thom climbed over the back of his seat into the bed of the wagon and hunkered down at the tailgate, lending a hand. Albert and the new fellow climbed inside to drag him forward to make room for a few others.

Albert nodded his thanks. "We appreciate the help."

"No problem," the stranger said. "Do you know what caused the accident?"

Albert glanced around at the confusion, wondering how they'd take care of all these people. "Boulders on the track."

He spotted Susanna from the corner of his eye. She extracted a crying baby from the arms of a badly shaken young woman and then they proceeded up the gradual rise to the wagons.

For a brief second, their eyes met, and held. A warm glow seeped through Albert seeing her strength. How he loved her, and wanted to make her his wife. The accident today proved every day was precious. He needed to tell Susanna the truth, and soon, if he didn't want to lose her.

"Albert, Chase, we need some help," Jessie—Chase's wife—called, waving her arms.

Albert slapped Greg on the back. "Come on, men, there's work to be done."

Two hours later, Susanna walked between her two rows of patients in the reception hall turned infirmary, checking to see if anyone needed more water. Twelve in all. She caught Brenna's gaze from across the room where her friend had twelve patients of her own. A tremor quickened Susanna's step. Everything had changed in the blink of an eye. The decorations that had appeared so pretty an hour ago looked out of place amid all the suffering. The cake had been pushed into a corner of the room, untouched and forgotten. Death was just a heartbeat away.

Susanna shuddered. With so many injured, the medication was stretched short. Dr. Thorn had yet to make it to the hall, having his hands full with the severely injured at his office. Susanna, along with Brenna and Mrs. Hollyhock were doing all they could to make these patients as comfortable as possible until the doctor arrived.

Julia Taylor, a young woman from the train, let out a low moan. Her arm, broken between the wrist and elbow, still needed to be set. That was bad enough, but she was still unaware her middle-aged aunt had been killed. Susanna knelt and placed her hand on the woman's clammy forehead.

Julia whimpered and opened her eyes.

"How're you feeling?" Susanna asked softly.

"Like I'm going to throw up."

The girl's badly bruised face contorted in pain. Scrapes and lacerations covered a good portion of her body. They'd stabilized her arm the best they could with a ripped sheet and two short planks, but Susanna knew the pain must be unbearable. The girl had been outside on the portico, watching for their arrival into Logan Meadows, when the engine had hit the rockslide. She'd sailed through the air and landed in an outcropping of granite.

Tears pooled in the corner of each eye, then ran down Miss Taylor's cheeks. "How're the rest?"

Susanna wished she could sugarcoat the truth, but Dr. Thorn had warned them all against that. They would learn everyone's fate soon enough. "The worst off, two men and one woman, are at Dr. Thorn's where he's performing surgery."

"Was anyone killed?"

"Yes, eighteen that I know of so far. Some passengers are still unaccounted for. The men are out searching as we speak."

At the train site, the row of dead bodies lined up on a grassy bank, their sightless eyes staring up at the clouds, had given Susanna a start. When she was nine years old, her stepfather, thinking it funny, had locked her in the parlor with his brother's corpse, prepared for a viewing the next day. She'd crept into the room in search of a misplaced book. Bare alder branches, moved by a violent storm raging outside, tapped eerily against the windowpane. When a ghostlike moaning emanated from the far side of the room, she'd dashed to the door only to find it locked. The harder she'd tried, the more terrified she'd become. The fifteen minutes it took for her mother to find her and let her out had felt like an eternity. Since then, bodies and storms always made her shiver.

Julia moaned, snapping Susanna out of her worst memory. The girl's eyes slid to the window. "It'll be dark soon."

"Just rest," Susanna said. "Everything will be all right."

"Do you know if Aunt Biddy has been here to check on me?" Her voice, a shaky whisper, was barely audible over the moans and whimpering cries in the room.

Susanna couldn't fathom the pain she must be in. Gabe Garrison, Chase and Jessie's adopted son, was due back any moment with some willow bark Mrs. Hollyhock had sent him to fetch from the Red Rooster Inn. Dr. Thorn's medications were stretched thin. The laudanum and morphine were allocated for the worst cases. Julia was in pain but wasn't critically injured.

"I'm sorry, I don't." She couldn't do it. She wouldn't be the one to tell her about her aunt. This young woman needed every ounce of will to stay strong.

"Where are the others? The ones who weren't hurt?"

"They've been taken to the hotel and the Red Rooster Inn. Every room is filled, and the rest have been housed with the townsfolk."

That brought a tiny smile to Julia's pinched face.

"Would you like a sip of water?"

Her lashes swept down to rest on her cheeks, colored slightly from the trauma. "No, thank you."

"You should try, to stave off a fever."

Gabe stepped through the door with a cloth bag clutched in his hands. Blotches of blood marred his once-white shirt, and his stern expression made him appear older than his nineteen years.

Susanna leaned closer. "The willow bark is here. Try to rest while I make the tea."

In the kitchen, Brenna already had several pots of water boiling on the stove. Mrs. Hollyhock straightened from the bucket she was rinsing in, a bloody rag grasped in her hands. She washed and dried her hands and reached for the willow bark.

Brenna's forehead glistened and her beautiful rose chiffon wedding gown, stained with blood and grime, was frayed at the hem from the trips she'd made back and forth between the train and wagons. "There's enough hot water for everyone to have a cup."

Mrs. Hollyhock began dicing the willow strips into small pieces. They'd need to steep for a good ten minutes.

"Your poor dress, Brenna," Susanna said, to break the heavy shroud of grief that hung in the air. Any topic was more welcome than the grim reality of what they were living through.

Brenna looked over her shoulder and smiled. "It doesn't matter— not really."

Susanna tried to smile back. "I know. You just looked so pretty today when you and Gregory were dancing."

"How's Missy Taylor?" Mrs. Hollyhock asked, stirring the water with a wooden spoon and pushing down the floaters. "I don't think I've ever seen an arm as misshapen as that poor girl's. Makes my toes curl jist thinkin' about it. And I've seen a lot in my many ol' years."

"She's in a lot of pain," Susanna said. "I wish we had some laudanum. At least then, she might be able to fall asleep."

Gabe glanced over, a boyish vulnerability in his eyes. "Albert's sent a telegram to Rock Springs to round up whatever supplies and medications they can spare. A courier will bring them as fast as possible, but still, that'll take a couple of days."

Brenna nodded. "That's the closest large town. What if they don't have any laudanum or morphine? What about New Meringue? It's closer."

"Thom's on his way there now on a fast horse."

Brenna touched Gabe's arm. "Did you happen to see my children when you were out? Penny is supposed to be keeping an eye on the little ones. I'm worried because there's so much confusion. I haven't seen them since Win made the announcement and everyone rushed out."

"They'll be fine, sweetie," Mrs. Hollyhock said, laying a shaky hand on Brenna's arm. "Penny won't let nothin' happen to 'em."

Gabe looked at Brenna over Mrs. Hollyhock's stooped form. "Sorry, Mrs. Hutton, I didn't."

Susanna smiled at Brenna. "I think that's the first time I've heard anyone address you as Mrs. Hutton since you said your vows. It sounds nice." She wanted to lift everyone's mood.

A dark blush crept up Brenna's face. "It did sound nice. I wonder where Gregory is, and what he's doing."

"I saw him goin' into the doctor's office," Gabe said. "On my way back from the Red Rooster."

Footsteps sounded, then Jake, the other cowhand who worked with Gabe at the Logans' ranch, poked his head in the kitchen door. He looked around until he spotted Gabe. "We need to round up the cattle that were released from the train. I have your horse outside."

"Go on, Gabe," Susanna said. "Thank you for your help."

She felt the weight of the world on her shoulders as the youth nodded and followed Jake out the door. Life could take unexpected turns in a heartbeat. She shouldn't keep putting Albert off. "I'll go make a quick round of the room," she said. "Make sure everyone is . . ." *What? All right?* What a stupid statement. No one in that room was all right. She wiped her hands on a cloth and headed out the door.

CHAPTER FIVE

$\mathcal{D}$alton and a few of the railroad employees made one final sweep of the train to make sure no one was left behind. He hitched a ride into town and went straight to the telegraph office, still open past closing time due to the circumstances, and alerted the bank about the crash. From there, he planned to elicit help from the sheriff's office but decided to take five minutes first to make sure the child he'd found on the train had been reunited with his parents. Something about that frightened little face pulled at his heart.

He pushed through the doors of the community center. Removing his hat, he glanced around. Streamers hung from the beams, and a cake sat in the corner. Musical instruments were laid out on a small stage, abandoned. The train wreck had interrupted a party.

Most of the patients, white-faced people in four long rows, were quiet, probably in shock, while others moaned, and begged him with their eyes as he walked by. He didn't see a doctor.

He proceeded halfway through the first row of cots and makeshift beds. The *clip, clip, clip* of boot heels drew his attention, and he dragged his gaze from the injured.

"May I help you? Are you looking for a loved one?"

He turned. It took a moment for recognition to register. *Susanna? Susanna Robinson?* Her deep-green irises constricted the moment she recognized him.

She looked down at his guns, then back up into his face. "Dalton Babcock," she said, taking a small step back.

She hadn't changed a bit, and yet she seemed different. Self-assured. A surge of pleasure bounced around his chest and up into his surprise-clogged throat. He hadn't gotten a chance to tell her goodbye before leaving Breckenridge, and had felt bad about it ever since. "Well, I'll be! I'm glad you haven't forgotten me, Suzie. It's been some time since we've seen each other." She blinked, perhaps startled by the use of her nickname. Seeing him after all these years must have been a shock to her system because her face became as white as the sheets under the patients, even though the sight of her warmed him through and through. She was the first ray of sunshine he'd seen today.

"Of course I remember you." Her tone held caution but he couldn't imagine why. "A thorn in my side every time we met."

Her expression softened her words and he realized she was joking. He chuckled. "Now, I wouldn't go as far as to say that."

She nodded, and crossed her arms. "Well, your sister was."

That was a fact. He'd been ashamed how his younger sister had treated Miss Robinson, always pointing out her threadbare clothes, and the fact her mother had a none-too-good reputation in their small town. He'd put Eloisa in her place for it more times than he could remember.

"I'm real sorry about that. I never could abide a bully—even when she's my own sister. I should have done more to protect you."

Susanna's gaze flickered away before coming back to rest on his face. "Well, that was a long time ago—and forgotten."

"That's generous of you. What're you doing this far from home?" He glanced at her hand but didn't see a wedding ring. "I didn't even know you'd left town."

"That's because you left town first, if I recall. You're not the only one who wanted to see more of the world than Breckenridge."

He chuckled again. "You have a point."

"You must've been on the train. Are you looking for someone?"

"Yes. A little boy. He has a cut on his scalp."

Her eyes widened. "Your son?"

He shook his head. "No. Just someone I found right after the accident happened. I wanted to make sure he'd found his parents."

She turned and started for the other side of the room. "There's a little boy over here, but I don't think he has a cut on his head, just an egg-sized lump."

She led him to a red-haired child asleep on a pile of blankets.

"No, that's not him. Would he be anywhere else?"

"He probably has been reunited with his mother and father and housed elsewhere. If it'll ease your mind, tell me what he looks like and I'll keep watch for him. If I learn anything, I'll leave you a note pinned to the bulletin board in the kitchen." She pointed behind her. "In case I'm not around when you check back."

"I appreciate that very much." He held out his hand waist high. "He stands about this tall. Has sandy blond hair and a good, long cut on this side of his scalp." He traced an imaginary line on his head. "I put a bandage on it best I could."

That seemed to soften her. The funny little crinkle he remembered so well formed between her brows. He gestured to the cake. "Special occasion?"

"Yes. A wedding. The bride is in the back room."

"What an anniversary date to have." He shook his head.

Now that the injured passengers were taken care of, his only responsibility was to the money, and keeping it secure until he could figure out how to get it safely to its destination. "I appreciate your help, Suzie," he said, feeling the need to keep moving. "I'll check back when I can."

He turned to go but she stopped him with a touch to his arm. "Dalton, your head! You've been hurt."

In the rush to help the others, he'd forgotten all about the cut on the back of his scalp. He wondered if he had blood matted in his hair. "It's not much."

"It most certainly *is* much." He pulled back when she leaned forward for a better look. "You won't be saying that if infection sets in. Let me douse it with iodine."

He shook his head. "I don't have the time right now. I have to get back to the train."

A woman carrying a tray filled with white porcelain cups came out of the side room, an older woman following behind her. He couldn't help but notice how fast Suzie stepped back from him, but before he could question it, a fella dressed in coveralls came through the front door. "Doc's on his way, says he'll be here in a few minutes."

"It's about time," the craggy old woman mumbled under her breath. She looked exhausted, her eyes dimmed with fatigue. Her messy hair could be mistaken for a beehive.

The young woman stepped toward the newcomer. "Win, have you seen Penny and Jane? I'm worried about them."

"Sure have, Brenna. Jessie Logan has them, along with your boys, her children, and a passel of others corralled in the lobby at the El Dorado. She's looking after the children so their mamas can help. Did you want me to give them a message?"

Relief washed over the woman's face. "No, thank you. Now that I know where they are, and that they're safe, I can relax."

Dalton glanced back at Susanna. "Just as soon as I have my business squared away, I'll come let you have a look." He gestured to the back of his head. "But like I said before, I'm sure it's nothing to worry about. I've been hurt worse."

"You're a doctor as well as a gunman?"

He couldn't stop a chuckle at her displeased countenance, as well as her sassiness. "No, not a doctor, just an old friend who has pressing business right now. In truth, I wouldn't mind a few minutes with you fussing over me." Her chin tipped up in surprise as he added, "Can't think of anything I'd like better."

CHAPTER SIX

$\mathscr{A}$lbert closed the door to room number fifteen and hurried down the narrow staircase of the El Dorado Hotel, stepping over a man who'd just plunked himself down on a step and fallen asleep, chin in hand.

Jessie Logan met him in the lobby at the foot of the stairs. "How's everything going?"

Shane was asleep in her arms. The full impact of what had happened wouldn't be felt until they laid all the deceased to rest in the cemetery by the church.

"As well as can be expected, I guess. Those three men were the last of 'em. Every room in town is filled, and I'm not just talking about the hotel and inn. There's not an empty bed anywhere. I even have a fellow that will be sleeping in the front room of my small apartment above the jailhouse."

"Don't forget about our bunkhouse out at the ranch, as well as in the house, Albert. We could support five or six, if need be. I hope Chase let you know."

"He did. Everyone I've dealt with prefers to stay in town, where they can check on each other and get the latest news on the train."

"That's understandable." She sighed and shifted the sleeping child in her arms. The lobby behind Jessie was filled with children. Her daughter, Sarah, played ring-around-the-rosy with several other misses. The circle of girls erupted in laughter and fell to their knees, and boys dashed here and there. "I wouldn't want to go too far if I were stranded in a strange town," Jessie said, raising her voice to be heard over the children. She fondled the baby hair on Shane's head.

"You look tired, Jessie. Now that we have the situation under control, the women will start picking up their young'uns and you can go home. Do you have a way to get there?"

She nodded, and laid her cheek against the toddler's head. "When Gabe and Jake are finished rounding up the loose stock, they're checking in here."

"Good."

"Did they find any of the missing passengers?"

He shook his head. "Not yet. Charlie, Chase, and a handful of others just returned for torches and lanterns so they can continue the search." He glanced out the window into the evening shadows.

"How could this happen, Albert? The train tracks are so new."

"I'd say the hellish amount of rainfall we've had the last few months loosened those boulders and they came down. I expressed my concerns to the Union Pacific when they were laying the tracks so close to the embankment." He shook his head, remembering the animosity that had arisen from that meeting. "I was instantly shot down."

One of the twenty-five children romping around the lobby let out a loud shriek. Jessie turned. "Boys, stop running!"

"We're hungry," a child he rarely saw in town whimpered. The boy dashed at the moisture in his eyes. "I want to go home. I want my ma."

"Danny Hall, your ma is needed elsewhere right now," Albert said, giving the boy a direct stare. "She'll be here as soon as she can. Help Mrs. Logan with the younger children."

Jessie smiled. "Thank you, Albert. They've been very good considering, but everyone's getting tired. I know I am."

Albert glanced through the door that connected the Silky Hen to the lobby of the hotel, now starting to thin out from its earlier crowd. "Everybody has their hands full, it seems."

"Yes. Logan Meadows needs a lot of prayers. For the poor souls suffering and for the people who have lost a loved one. It won't be easy."

"You're right about that, Jessie. You're certainly right about that."

"Doctor! You're here," Susanna gasped when Dr. Thorn came through the infirmary doors. He slammed into Dalton Babcock as her old acquaintance prepared to leave.

"Whoa, there." Dalton clutched the doctor by his shoulders to keep him on his feet, then pushed his own dark hair back as he straightened his wide, strong-looking shoulders. Soot and blood soiled his expensive-looking shirt, the garment attesting he was doing well. If she remembered rightly, he'd been twenty-four when he'd left their hometown four years ago.

Susanna did the introductions, all the while praying Dalton wouldn't let slip that they knew each other from before. The new beginning she'd built here in Logan Meadows—and loved so much—depended on no one knowing her past. She'd been judged plenty back home. Tainted by her mother's repute, they'd said. Cut from the same cloth, they used to whisper.

"It's fortunate you're here then, Mr. Babcock," Dr. Thorn said. "I need your assistance for a few minutes in setting a broken arm."

Dalton glanced at the door. "I have a pressing obligation of my own."

Dr. Thorn was resolute. "These women aren't strong enough for what I need. I promise I won't keep you long."

Dalton's gaze darted to Susanna. "Very well."

"Susanna, give Miss Taylor as much of this as she can stomach," Dr. Thorn said, pulling a bottle of whiskey from his leather bag. "Brenna, you and Mr. Babcock pull those two hat racks around and hang an extra blanket between them, so the others

28

can't watch. Her screams will be bad enough. Also gather the lanterns and bring them close."

He started for the kitchen, but turned back when everyone just stood there. "Go on. I have many people who need tending."

Brenna jumped into action with Dalton helping. Violet Hollyhock followed Susanna over to Julia's cot. Taking the cup from Violet, Susanna splashed in a good three inches of the brown liquid, knelt, and lifted Julia's shoulders. Mrs. Hollyhock stood on the other side of her cot.

"What's that?"

"Just a little whiskey. To dull the pain."

"I don't drink."

Mrs. Hollyhock reached out and ran a soft cloth over Julia's perspiring forehead. "It's all right, honey-pie. A little taste'll do ya fine." The statement wasn't casually delivered, and a deep crinkle formed between the old woman's eyes.

Susanna held the cup to Julia's lips, and the girl took a tiny taste, but came up sputtering. "Ohh, I don't like that! It burns." She coughed, then cried out from the pain the jostling had caused her broken arm. Her face blanched. "I think I'm going to be sick."

"Naw, honey, you're not. This is jist one o' those thing ya got t'get through whether ya want to or not. Take another sip for ol' Mrs. Hollyhock."

The girl's lips quivered, then her eyes widened. "Still no chloroform?"

"I'm so sorry," Susanna replied softly. "We must forge ahead without it so we won't have to start over later. If your arm begins to heal like this, the doctor would have to rebreak it. I wish it weren't so."

Dr. Thorn, back from the kitchen, had his head together with Dalton, whispering. They came toward the bed.

"One more large gulp, Julia," Susanna pleaded. "You can do it."

To her credit, Miss Taylor grasped the cup with her good hand and guzzled down the entire cup, then proceeded to cough and hack for a long minute. She lay back and closed her eyes, her jaw set in a hard grimace.

Dr. Thorn waited, giving the whiskey time to get into her blood. Five minutes passed without a word from anyone. The doctor sat by her side, carefully unwound the sling, then studied her upper and lower arm for a long time. Susanna forced herself not to look away from the badly distorted, purple-colored limb.

When Dr. Thorn probed the fracture, Julia moaned but she didn't open her eyes. He nodded to Dalton who was positioned at the girl's shoulder.

"Miss Taylor, we're ready to begin. I won't lie to you. It's going to hurt, but as soon as we align the bones, the pain will ease up some. The main fracture is down here, but there seems to be another smaller break between the elbow and your shoulder. We'll get this done as quickly as we can."

She didn't make a peep, or open her eyes, but the rapid rise and fall of her chest spoke volumes. Susanna inched forward and picked up her other hand, stroking the top with her thumb.

"You're to hold her shoulder as steady as you can, Mr. Babcock. I'll do the pulling."

The doctor gave one quick glance around. "All right, Miss Taylor, take a deep breath."

From behind her head, Dalton took a firm hold of Julia's shoulder. She screamed out in pain when Dr. Thorn slowly straightened her arm, increasing the force until Susanna thought she would faint and embarrass herself.

Julia never opened her eyes, but the shriek that came from her small frame was surprising. Mrs. Hollyhock plunked down into a chair, and shivers racked her frail body. Brenna huddled close by.

Dr. Thorn signaled Dalton, and they let up. Laying Julia's arm across her chest, Dr. Thorn inspected their work. "Bring that lamp closer, Susanna. Hold it over Miss Taylor's head."

As she fetched the lantern, Susanna met Dalton's familiar caramel-gold gaze. He looked shaken and stalwart at the same time. Dr. Thorn directed her aim. "Right there, so I can get a good look." The doctor's adept fingers gently palpated Julia's arm. Rising, he shook his head. "We're not finished yet. She has a small bump here where the bones are not in exact alignment." He pointed. "We can do better."

A low moan issued from Julia's mouth.

Dalton once again took hold. Dr. Thorn, with his own hold, pulled and manipulated. He lifted and slightly turned the girl's arm. Perspiration slicked his brow.

Julia screamed, and then her head rolled to the side. Dr. Thorn stopped, held her wrist with one hand, and examined the length of her arm with the other. "Good. That's all." He looked around. "I'll get a cast on this, and then we'll see to the others. I don't want Miss Taylor out of bed for a good five days. After about Wednesday, most her pain will be gone, and the bones will have a good start on knitting together. After that, she should be good to do just about anything she feels comfortable with."

He extended his hand to Dalton. "Thank you. It would've been much more difficult to get that set correctly without your help."

Anxiety ricocheted through Susanna's chest. It was as if she could hear his response before he opened his mouth.

"You're welcome, Doctor. I'm glad I was able to assist you. Any friend of Susanna's is a friend of mine. We're from the same small town in Colorado." He tossed her a fond look. "Isn't that something? It's a small world, to be sure."

She had no choice but to smile and nod, feeling as if quicksand were pulling her under. Only when silence filled the room did she realize they were waiting for her to respond. "That's absolutely correct," she said, forcing a smile and a shrug. "Dalton and I go way back. A very small world, I'd say."

CHAPTER SEVEN

$\mathcal{D}$alton strode away from the infirmary, focused on his next task. He needed to get into the train car he'd been guarding, but how, he couldn't fathom. The car had been constructed to thwart potential break-ins. A moment of wonder made him glance back, still unbelieving he'd run into Susanna so far from Breckenridge.

His last memory was of her eyes filled with shimmery tears as she walked away from the mercantile. His sister and a friend had been teasing her again, until he'd come and put a stop to it. With a defiant tilt to her chin, Susanna had told Eloisa just what she thought of her haughtiness, then she'd turned away, but not before he'd seen her face crumble. He'd wanted to tell her he'd gotten a job with Wells Fargo and would be leaving, but lost his nerve. His attraction to her had always been one-sided.

Maybe destiny had just given him another chance.

A disgruntled shout in the distance jerked him back to the present. What had happened to Pat Tackly? He'd sure like to know. The head guard had hired Dalton the day before the shipment of cash was scheduled to leave. Somehow, Pat's third man had gotten himself killed just hours before, and Pat needed another fellow good with a gun. Being Dalton had ridden guard for Wells Fargo for several years, he fit the bill. Dalton, pleased at the opportunity that had landed in his lap, had thought it over for a whole two minutes before accepting. The job paid more money in one month than his yearly salary riding guard on the Wells Fargo stage, and then some. Enough to send half back to his folks to help on the ranch. That was a pretty darn good return on his time.

Dalton strode down the alley beside the hotel, and stepped up onto the boardwalk. The sun had set, but all the buildings of Logan Meadows were alive with lights and townsfolk. With the train a good half mile from town, he needed a wagon and tools. But most of all he needed trustworthy men. He passed by the saloon. A skinny fellow at the piano tapped out a tune with one finger as the bartender poured drinks to a full bar. Looked like things were picking up now that most people were settled. He halted in front of the sheriff's office. He was under no obligation to inform the sheriff of his cargo, but he did have an obligation to protect the money. His best opportunity for help resided inside.

He took hold of the brass doorknob and stepped through the door. A large wolf-like dog lying in front of a potbellied stove lifted his head, looked him over, then lay back down. The sheriff sat at his desk, writing. He appeared none too pleased by the interruption.

"Yes?" The tone was curt.

"I'm a guard employed by the First Bank of Denver. I need some help."

"You and a hundred others."

"That may be so, but in my case time is of the essence. I need tools and manpower to break into a specially built train car that's bolted closed from the inside."

The lawman set his pencil down. "You helped with the big fellow today, isn't that right?"

"It is." Dalton put out his hand. "Dalton Babcock from Denver, Colorado." He extracted his officially stamped letter, stating he was an employee of the bank with authority over their cargo.

The sheriff grasped his hand. "Albert Preston. Why's it so darn important to break in? Can't whatever's inside stay locked up?"

"It's a guard who's not responding—if he were, he'd be able to open the door. I'd like to get him some help as soon as possible, in case he's still alive."

The sheriff nodded, understanding washing over his face.

"And there's also the small matter of a million dollars cash." Sheriff Preston gave a loud whistle and his eyebrows arched. "The longer it remains unprotected, the more enticing the treasure becomes. I saw your bank on the way over. It secure? I believe locking the money up there is the best option until management from Denver can arrange transport."

"Nobody's getting into Frank's vault unless he opens it. I've never seen the like."

"And it's large enough for that amount of money?"

"It's half the size of his back room—a joke until now when we need it."

"Good." Dalton glanced out to the dark street. "The other two guards and myself have been closed mouthed about the cargo, but information like that has a way of getting out. Somebody had to pack it and schedule its transport. People know it's en route. I'd like to get out to the abandoned train as soon as possible." He directed his gaze back to the lawman. "The head guard was on the roof when the train hit and is still among the missing."

The lawman stood. "Let's get moving then. I'll find you a horse and ride out with you. I have some fellas out there now searching for anyone who was thrown from the train on impact. They're my right-hand men. I'd trust any of them with my life."

"With a million dollars?"

"You bet." Sheriff Preston went to the gun rack, pulled out two rifles, and handed one to Dalton. He filled a saddlebag with bullets then headed for the door. "Let's go see what we got."

It took less than five minutes to lope to Three Pines Turn. The stars were bright in the sky. None of the men Albert had sent out, including Chase Logan and Charlie Axelrose, were close by. The engine, the only car off the track, sat kitty-corner and a bit tilted behind a pileup of large boulders. It was a horrific sight, even the second time around. He and Babcock rode silently down the side of the eerily quiet train toward the money car.

Albert pointed to several torches that shined like fireflies in the distance. "The searchers. The engineer hit the brakes when he came around the corner and saw the pileup directly before him, but couldn't stop completely. With the length of the train, survivors could be as far back as a quarter mile." He pulled out his sidearm and squeezed off a shot into the air to signal the others over.

Babcock reined up before a dark train car.

"This it?" Albert asked, glancing around.

Babcock nodded, then dismounted. He strode over to the train and pounded on the side of the car. "Evan, can you hear me?" he shouted. He pounded some more. "Evan, knock on the side, or the floor, if you can't talk." After a moment, he looked back over his shoulder. "Nothing."

Babcock's face was a mask set in stone. Death was never easy.

Albert dismounted and dropped one rein to the ground. He made his way to the side of the train and met Chase, Charlie, and a few others as they rode up. "You find any bodies?" Albert asked.

"Two. The undertaker's been out already and hauled them away," Chase Logan said, still sitting his horse.

Babcock straightened. "Either of them big, over two hundred and fifty pounds?"

Chase shook his head. He glanced at Albert and asked, "Whatta we have here?"

"Chase, Charlie, I need your help. The rest of you can go back to town and see what needs doing. If there isn't anything, go home and get some sleep. There'll be plenty to do for days to come."

Three men nodded and rode off.

"You're sounding awfully mysterious, Albert," Chase said, the stock end of the burning torch resting on his thigh. He looked Babcock over with a discerning eye. "The way you dismissed the others, I'd say you're about to share something interesting."

"You know me too well, Chase. We need to break into this train car, but not until morning."

Babcock took a step toward him. "We need to get inside now! By morning Evan could be dead."

Albert ignored the man's sharp tone. "I'm not risking the necks of these live men for someone who's most likely dead already. The only way in would be through the air vents on top, and that may even be a bust. Working with heavy tools in the dark is not worth the risk. That's my decision. We'll begin at first light."

Babcock cut his gaze away, clearly unhappy with the turn of events.

"Chase, I'd like you and Charlie to stay here and help stand guard until morning. Can you do that? Thom Donovan will relieve one of you after midnight, when he gets back from New Meringue, and I'll do the same at one. Right now, I need to get back to Logan Meadows and keep an eye on the town. Whiskey's flowing easy in the saloon."

He strode over to the men and handed over his rifle.

Charlie's brows lifted in speculation. "What's inside? Seems if we're risking our necks, we have a right to know. Can't just be a dead body."

"What I'm going to tell you goes no further. Mr. Babcock works for a bank in Denver and is moving some cash. One million dollars to be exact. One of their guards was thrown off the roof, and the other is locked inside, either dead or unconscious. After we get in, we'll transport the money to the bank until arrangements can be made to get it on its way."

Chase looked none too pleased. "What about our families? Jessie's still in town."

"I just spoke with her a little while ago. She said Gabe and Jake plan to take her, Sarah, and Shane home after the children she's watching have been picked up. What about you, Charlie? Where's Nell?"

"Helping out at the Red Rooster Inn. She has Maddie with her."

"If you're both agreeable, I'll stop by and let both your wives know you won't be home until sometime after midnight. I'll make sure Nell and Maddie have an escort home, and I'll send you out some grub."

The crickets were his only response.

"Guarding someone else's *money* don't sit well with me, especially when there're people in town who need tending, and a worn-out wife to look after." Chase's tone spoke to his displeasure.

"Everyone who needs tending has been taken care of, Chase. This is where I need you now. But, just say the word and I can find someone else. We'll begin work at first light."

Chase shifted in his saddle as he swiveled to look at Charlie. Charlie nodded. Babcock looked back and forth as the men talked, a frustrated expression on his face.

"Fine, Albert, we're in. You got yourself some guards."

CHAPTER EIGHT

$\mathcal{S}$usanna stood near the front door of the infirmary, listening to instructions from Dr. Thorn, a man of endless energy. The thirty-two-year-old bachelor had methodically worked his way through the patients, most suffering from minor injuries like lacerations and bumps on the head. Miss Taylor lay in a liquor-induced sleep, moaning from time to time.

Disbelief at seeing Dalton Babcock had pushed away all of Susanna's fatigue. His sister had been the bane of Susanna's existence, but Dalton had always been shy, hardly saying a word to her. Seeing his face here in Logan Meadows had brought a surge of bad memories—and a bushel of worries about what Dalton might tell someone about her past.

"It's time for you to go home and get some rest, Susanna," Dr. Thorn said. The doctor's usually combed, light-brown hair was mussed, and his intense green eyes that by now could easily be filled with exhaustion, burned with purpose. "You've been a huge help." He glanced across the room to the bandstand where Brenna and Mrs. Hollyhock were slumped in their chairs. With her eyes clamped closed, Mrs. Hollyhock's soft snores floated through the air.

An affectionate gleam lit his eyes. "You've *all* been wonderful. Widow Brown is on her way here to take over for you."

"I can't leave," Susanna whispered. "I want to be here when

Julia wakes up. She's bound to feel horrible from the whiskey, let alone the pain from her broken arm. I'm not going anywhere."

His brow arched.

"I'm not." She firmed her mouth. "You can talk until you're blue in the face, Doctor, but I plan to stay all night."

He chuckled and shook his head. "Some women are more stubborn than . . ." He snapped his mouth closed at her threatening look. "Fine then. At least take a break and get something to eat. How about I send the others home, and in the morning they can come back and relieve you?"

"Yes, that's perfect. I can—"

At that moment, Albert stepped through the door, cutting off her sentence. His concerned expression sent a surge of pleasure through her. He took one look and pulled her into an embrace. "You're exhausted," he said next to her ear. His warm breath sent tingles dancing down her neck. He leaned back and looked around the dimly lit room. "You're working her to death, John. I don't think I've ever seen her this tuckered out."

Dr. Thorn pointed to the others. "They've all worked themselves to death, but it couldn't be helped. And they aren't finished yet. Susanna has just offered to stay here all night."

When Albert opened his mouth to protest, Dr. Thorn went on. "I'm needed at my office, Albert, and I really do need someone here. She's good with the patients. I performed two surgeries that I must monitor. Now that I've seen to these patients, most just require nursing. Get her something to eat, and see that she gets off her feet for a good hour." The doctor glanced at Susanna, then back at Albert. "Go on, now."

"That's an excellent idea," Albert said. "The Silky Hen is closed, but you have the key. I'll fix you a plate of leftovers."

With Albert looking at her like that, and the doctor's expression of gratitude, heat crept into Susanna's face. "First, I want to take Mrs. Hollyhock home and tuck her in. If I don't, she'll get sidetracked helping someone else and forget about her own needs." She gave Albert a beseeching gaze. "Can we do that?"

"We can. Afterward, I'll get some warm food into you and tuck you in."

"Albert!"

He chuckled. "I'm just teasing. Go on and round her up, and Brenna too, if she's also coming. I'll find a buggy to borrow. There're so many sitting around town I'll have my choice. I'll be back in five minutes expecting you to be ready to leave."

Within a half hour, Susanna and Albert had dropped Brenna at her home and Mrs. Hollyhock at the Red Rooster. The minute they'd walked through the door of the inn, Beth Fairington had pounced on Mrs. Hollyhock with a hundred complaints and issues, as if she'd been waiting for the tired old woman to come home and solve all her problems.

Now, alone in the buggy, sitting close enough that their knees rubbed whenever they went over a bump, Susanna felt dizzy with happiness. Albert had come for her, to check on her, make sure she'd had something to eat. The Silky Hen was their next stop, and her empty stomach wouldn't let her forget she'd worked up an appetite indeed. Pulling the buggy to a halt, Albert helped her to the ground. She fished for the restaurant key in her reticule.

"Poor Brenna," Susanna said as she handed the key over to Albert's outstretched hand. He unlocked the door after a bit of a struggle, then stood back, letting her enter before him. "First her wedding, and now her honeymoon night. She and Greg had planned to stay at his rental since he has it until the end of the month and let Penny watch the children across the street. Now, with all the confusion, she's afraid the little ones might be frightened. She's staying at home and Gregory is at his place."

"That *is* a real shame. Everyone has been looking forward to them finally tying the knot. I'm sure they must be disappointed."

They walked through the quiet restaurant. Hannah and Daisy must have been swamped. The place, although straightened up, needed a good cleaning.

In the kitchen, Albert lit a lantern and glanced around, his bemused expression so unlike him. "Lord Almighty! Looks like a tornado went through here. I've never seen this place look such a shambles."

"Albert," she got out on a half laugh, her tone scolding. He knew exactly how to cheer her up. "But you're right. They'll need help tomorrow when there're more mouths to feed than plates to serve them on. I'm worried about running out of supplies, not just here but all over town. How on earth can we feed all these people?"

Albert turned her into his arms, his face alight with emotion. "That's not your concern, Susanna. You can't do everything. If you keep up at this pace, you'll make yourself sick, then you won't be any help to anyone." The tender look in his eyes belied his stern tone. It was then, in the quiet room with shadowy light, that the weight of his hands on her shoulders made her insides turn to mush. The shape of his lips curled up at the corners had the power to chase every coherent thought from her head. She'd never dared let herself imagine what being in love would be like. She couldn't, and shouldn't, be the one to speak her feelings first. She remembered her mother's cautionary words.

They'll love you and leave you as sure as there's a sun in the sky, Susanna. As soon as they know they have you, they'll throw you away. Don't repeat my mistake. Doing and caring for a husband, only to have him break your heart with someone else is something you'll never get over.

Susanna may have been just a girl, but she'd been smart enough to know most of the men her mother had told her to address as "pa" weren't married to her mother at all. And it seemed her mother had gotten over each abandonment quick enough

41

to take up with someone else. Susanna remembered their wolf-like eyes following her every move whenever her mother wasn't around. She couldn't even remember her real father's face in the blur of men that had paraded through their shanty.

Men don't mean to, but they crave what's on the other side of the pasture, Susanna. Mark my words or else you'll end up exactly like me, penniless and alone, alone, alone . . .

"Susanna?" Albert gave her a gentle shake. His gaze dropped to her mouth, making her insides feel feathery light. "You're asleep on your feet." He led her over to the small table in the corner and pulled out a chair. "You're going to sit down here and not say a word until I have some food in front of you." He gave her a stern look. "Understand?"

She didn't want to sit. She wanted him to kiss her—*finally*—to put an end to her wondering what it would be like. Seeing all this misery made her realize how fragile life could be—and just how fast things could change. Maybe her mother was wrong, and she should tell Albert how she felt about him.

"Susanna?"

She nodded, then lowered her aching body onto the cane-backed chair. She set her chin in the palm of her hand and watched as Albert marched to the cold box in the next room and brought out tonight's leftovers, a platter with a half-eaten roast. Setting it on the counter, he opened the oven and stuck in his hand. "Still hot." He sliced off several chunks of beef and set them on a plate, and then into the oven. Opening the stove's small lower door, he added some wood and stirred the coals.

"Albert, I can—"

"Nope!" He held up his finger. "I'm doing this all on my own. Now close your eyes and rest."

She did. And it felt good. The sounds of him clanging and banging around the kitchen brought a tiny smile to her lips. Even after two years of knowing Albert, she'd never seen him cook. Time passed and she sensed herself drifting in and out of sleep.

"All right," he said softly, close to her face. "You can open your eyes."

His voice was low, and the sincerity of his tone felt like a caress. An enticing aroma wafted up into her nose.

She opened her eyes. A plate of roast beef, a scoop of beans in sweet sauce, a slice of bread with butter, and a large pickle.

He gave her a sad look. "It was the best I could do on such short notice. And it's barely warm, but I figured it'd do. You must be famished."

She lifted her fork. "This will be delicious. I know, I made the beans myself yesterday." It didn't matter what was on her plate— she *was* hungry. The fact that Albert sat across from her, taking care of her, was more than she deserved.

He sat back, letting her eat for several minutes.

"There's something important I've been meaning to speak to you about for a long time, Susanna," he said, "but the time never seems right."

Susanna chewed quickly, then swallowed. She'd just contemplated telling him her own feelings, but now an overwhelming fright squeezed her throat so hard it hurt. She didn't want to lose him. She loved him too much. *Don't go there, don't go there.*

His smile wobbled. "Today's train wreck has me thinking. We don't know how long we have and—"

She gripped her forehead in her palm, ashamed for the small falsehood she was about to say. "Albert, the stress of today has my head pounding something fierce. Can we talk about this tomorrow?"

He looked taken aback. His eyes roamed her face, and something passed briefly in their depths, as if maybe he didn't believe her. "Can we? You never mentioned that your head hurt."

She cut a few more pieces of meat into smaller portions as she nodded. "Yes, of course, tomorrow. I never mentioned the headache because I didn't want you to fret." She smiled and held up a bite of the meat on her fork, trying to distract him. "This is good, Albert, thank you for taking the time out of your evening. You must be incredibly busy with everyone pulling you every which way."

"Never too busy for you, Susanna." Again, the look. He seemed undecided about something.

Once they know they gotcha, honey, they move on. You remember my words or you'll end up like me, like me, like me . . .

The same week her mother had passed away, one of her mother's male friends had come calling on her doorstep, expecting Susanna to take up where her mother had left off. She'd kept her wits about her long enough to send him packing and then stuffed the few items she owned into one little bag. Digging up the wages she'd saved from her earnings at the laundry house, she'd bought a ticket for the stage and never looked back. When she'd gone as far as her money would take her, she hired on someplace until she had more funds to keep going. She wasn't proud. She'd cleaned rooms, cooked for an army unit, even served whiskey in a couple of saloons. She kept moving, propelled by an emotion that demanded she put as much time and distance between her and the town she called home as possible. And now Dalton could spoil everything.

Albert made a sound in his throat. "I guess you're even more tired than I first thought. You keep slipping away to somewhere else. If there's something on your mind, tell me."

She brought her gaze to his, still lost in memories of arriving in Logan Meadows. She'd walked into a busy restaurant to find Hannah struggling to cook and serve at the same time. When Susanna offered to help, Hannah had almost swooned with happiness. They'd worked together ever since.

The clock chimed ten. She blinked the past away. A perplexed expression had replaced Albert's sideways smile.

"I'm sorry. Did you say something?"

His eyes wandered her face, assessing. "I guess you'll tell me when you're good and ready, and not a moment before." He looked at her empty plate and stood.

Still agitated, she pushed back her chair and followed. "I'm sorry, Albert. Right now all I can think about are all those injured people. I have to get back. Dr. Thorn probably thinks I've forgotten and fallen asleep."

"I doubt that." There was an edge to his voice that hadn't been there before.

How did one navigate such dangerous waters? Every time she thought it safe to speak her feelings, something surged up inside bringing back all the painful memories of her childhood. Albert knew she liked him; heck, he probably knew she *loved* him! Why did they have to spell it out to each other? Once that was done there wasn't anywhere to go from there but down. She wouldn't survive if his love cooled as the days went on, finally to die completely. That was a moment she never wanted to experience.

CHAPTER NINE

$\mathscr{F}$ive o'clock in the morning was much too early to be drenched in sweat. Dalton hefted the steel pry bar and rammed it down into the one-inch air vent on the top of the converted boxcar. His arms ached. Sweat ran down the side of his face and dripped from his forehead into his eyes, the salt stinging even as he blinked it away. Wedging a block of wood under his tool, he leaned over with all his strength, leveraging the roof up a tiny bit more. The collision had fractured the iron that ran the length of the roof, but at this rate, it would take the whole day to extricate Evan and the payload below.

"I'm ready to give it a go," Gabe Garrison said. Dalton and the young cowhand had been changing out at five-minute intervals. Still the access area had barely grown. Accomplishing their task would be no easy feat.

"One more minute, Gabe," he said, feeling the responsibility on his shoulders. It was demanding, backbreaking work. He lifted until his hands were over his head, then slammed down the steel bar, aiming for the hole. If you weren't careful, you'd miss the target entirely, which Gabe had once, sending the treacherous widow maker flying to the ground when it slipped from his hands. The plan was to enlarge the small ripped area by pulling back the thinner layer of iron that covered the top of the car until the hole was large enough to get a small man or boy inside to unlock the door from within. That was the only way.

Dalton glanced up at the morning sun shining in the cloudless sky.

"How's it going?" Albert called up.

As the sheriff had promised, Thom Donovan had shown up at midnight, relieving Charlie, and Albert had returned an hour after that, allowing Chase to go home.

Dalton stripped off his shirt and wiped it over his body. "Slow. Haven't made much progress."

"I've been thinking about that," Albert replied. The sheriff started up the ladder, a ray of sun glinting off the man's five-pointed star. He came close, walking carefully on the roof, and examined the small opening.

Dalton rested the tip of the pry bar on the roof and sucked in several deep breaths. The men of Logan Meadows were a fine lot. Especially the sheriff. Dalton hadn't expected him to pitch in and help with the extrication, but that was exactly what he'd done since he'd arrived with a wagonload of tools he'd borrowed from his brother's livery.

Albert knelt, then lowered himself onto his belly, one hand placed on either side of the small opening. He gazed into the dark chamber. "Hello? Evan Stone, can you hear me? Knock on something if you can't speak." He turned his head and pressed his ear firmly to the roof. After a moment, he climbed to his feet next to Gabe. "I think we could work away at this forever and not get in. I have an idea that will have this done in the blink of an eye."

"We've already decided against dynamite," Dalton said. "We can't risk it."

Albert lifted his hat and swished it several times in front of his face. Dalton had already learned that you couldn't rush the sheriff when he was about to say something important.

"We did decide that," Albert finally said. "But that was when we were talking about blowing the door. I say we blow this hole. It's above Evan, so the concussion will go up and away from the cash boxes. If your friend is alive, getting him out before much longer should be the main concern. The explosion can't cause him more harm than to leave him in there for days on end. Besides, most likely he was pitched to the front of the car when the train jerked to a sudden stop. I'll bet he's up against the wall, which is the best place for him now."

Dalton thought that over. He had a point.

At the sound of wagon wheels on gravel, all three men looked around. Dalton shouldered his way back into his shirt when he noticed a woman at the reins. Thom Donovan, still sitting his horse and guarding the car, waved, a large smile splitting his face.

"Must be your deputy's wife," Dalton said.

"That's right. Hannah Donovan."

Dalton watched the buggy approach. "A good woman would make everything easier to bear. You married, Sheriff?"

A strange expression crossed Albert's face. Maybe he'd overstepped.

"Me?" Albert grasped the back of his neck and worked his muscles. Seemed he was avoiding Dalton's gaze. "Have you seen a wife around that I don't know about?" His forced chuckle was strained. "I do have a girl that sets the moon and stars."

"Moon and stars?" Dalton said with a lilt of humor. "Talking pretty colorful for so early in the morning, aren't you?"

Albert shrugged. "Laugh all you want, but it's true. You'll see what I mean when it happens to you."

"A man can't ask for more than that, I guess."

Mrs. Donovan pulled the buggy to a halt. Thom rode forward and the sounds of their soft conversation floated up to where the men watched. She laughed at something Thom said, then turned and waved. She climbed out.

"Good morning, Albert, Gabe," she called. She momentarily glanced at her husband again, before going on. "And you must be Mr. Babcock." When he nodded, she continued, "Doctor Thorn said you were a big help yesterday. Are you making any progress with the train?" She gathered some things from the back of the buggy and made her way toward the money car, a tray with cups and a covered basket in her hands. Dalton hoped she'd brought some food.

"I have hot coffee and biscuits. No man I've ever known likes to go to work without something hot in his belly. Come down and take a short break. Refuel your energy."

Gabe was the first to hit the ladder. "Coffee? Biscuits? That's awfully kind of you, Mrs. Donovan."

"Don't mind if we do," Albert called down. "Thank you kindly, Hannah."

Dalton waited until Gabe's feet hit the ground before starting down himself, the thought of coffee more appealing than his mama's sour-apple pie.

Seeing Hannah Donovan reminded Dalton of Susanna. God's truth, he'd hardly thought of anything else through the long dark night. Her face and sassy words kept popping into his head at the oddest times. Actually, he owed her a glass of lemonade for keeping him so alert when fatigue would have had his eyes drooping. Once they had the money safely in the bank, he'd look her up again. He certainly wanted to know why she'd settled in Logan Meadows. She hadn't been wearing a wedding band, another fact that had played at the corners of his mind. But, that would have to wait until his other responsibilities with Evan and the cargo were resolved and he'd found Pat. Hopefully both guards were still alive and just needed doctoring.

Once on the ground and flanked by Albert, Dalton waited as Mrs. Donovan filled a white porcelain cup with fragrant, dark liquid. She handed it to Gabe, who already gripped a handful of biscuits. She glanced at Dalton. "Don't be shy, Mr. Babcock. Get some biscuits before they're gone."

Gabe's face turned three shades of red, but he kept on chewing at the rate of a racehorse. "I got out here early, Mrs. Donovan, before I had a chance to eat."

She smiled and nodded. "That's precisely why I'm here."

Dalton dipped his chin. "Thank you, ma'am. And we do appreciate it very much."

Reaching into the overfilled biscuit basket, Dalton realized he'd taken a shine to these townsfolk. He felt right at home.

CHAPTER TEN

$\mathscr{N}$ew light brought new hope. Susanna walked slowly down her aisle of patients, being careful not to let her heels touch the floor. The best medicine now, for most of them, was deep, uninterrupted sleep. At the end of the row, she looked out the front window. People milled around the back door of the El Dorado Hotel looking lost and still a little in shock, probably trying to make sense of the accident that had disrupted their lives, killed their loved ones, or placed them in the doctor's care.

Thoughts of Albert filtered into her mind. Things would work out, she told herself for the hundredth time since seeing him yesterday. He cared for her, and would probably do more if she'd get past this stupid fear of rejection. He'd been trying to express his feelings again last night until she changed the subject on him. The considerate things he did daily showed her how much he cared. He wasn't like the men her mother knew. He was honest and good. She was tired of her insecurities. She would put her trust in him, let him court her, and then be the next bride in Logan Meadows.

A thrill of excitement zipped through her and she couldn't stop her imagination from galloping off as she daydreamed about what it would be like to sleep in Albert's arms. The next time they were alone, she'd tell him so, she promised herself, still gazing on the scene out the window. After all the times she'd avoided the subject, he'd think she'd lost her mind. Still, he was going to be so happy. Perhaps she'd be married by this time next week.

What about Dalton? He knows the truth about Mother. If he says anything, will Albert still look at me the same?

She glanced at the clock. Almost six. Her gritty eyes burned. Her pillow was going to feel so nice when she finally made it back to her house and crawled into bed. She expected Brenna any moment. Mrs. Hollyhock was already in the kitchen preparing a large pot of mush for the patients' breakfast.

A long, shuddering moan brought Susanna around. She rushed to Julia's side just as the girl leaned over the side of her cot to vomit into the bucket Susanna had set there for that exact purpose. Twice during the night, she'd done the same, then sunk back into her misery.

Susanna crouched by the side of Julia's bed as the girl began to lay back, her uninjured arm cradling her fractured limb, now protected in a cast. "Let me help you," Susanna crooned. With strong arms, she lowered the ginger-haired beauty back until her head once again rested on her pillow.

Julia tried to smile.

"What can I get you?" Susanna asked.

"There's nothing," she whispered. "I just need to get through this the best that I can. I'm sorry for the mess."

"Nonsense. I'm sorry I made you drink all that horrible liquor last night. It was enough to set a horse on his backside. Your head must ache terribly."

The girl gave a small nod.

"I have a bit of good news. The doctor was just here. He's coming back with some laudanum. It'll help you sleep until the worst has passed." She didn't tell Julia that the doctor had a surplus of the medication because two of his surgery patients had passed away during the night. The girl had enough to think about without that gruesome news.

Julia smiled. "I'm glad. My arm does hurt something fierce." She glanced away for a moment, then back at Susanna. Her eyes pooled with tears. "I really want to speak with my aunt Biddy.

Can you please send word for her to come? I thought by now she would've found me. It's not like her to make me worry." *I can't lie to her any longer. Now that her arm is set, she needs to know the truth.* "Julia, I'm sorry."

As if the girl knew what she was about to say, her head began to rock back and forth in denial and a low keening vibrated in her throat. "No," she whispered. "It can't be true. Please tell me it's not true."

Susanna gently stroked Julia's clammy forehead. "I'm so sorry."

Several minutes passed with tears Julia's only movement. Susanna pulled her handkerchief from her pocket and dabbed at the outside corners of the girl's eyes.

"How?"

Susanna breathed in. "I'm not sure. She'd already passed when they found her. She must have hit her head. I wish I wasn't the one to have to tell you."

Julia blinked away more tears. "I guess I probably knew the truth all along, but didn't want to accept it. Poor Aunt Biddy. She was such a gentle soul."

Susanna just listened; a voice inside said that was what the girl needed now more than anything.

"She wasn't my real aunt, you know. She was kind enough to take me in when my mother died when I was only five. They were friends."

"That was a very caring thing for her to do. Where were you traveling to?"

"San Francisco. To Aunt Biddy's sister. I've never met the woman, but I could tell by her letters that she didn't really want us to come and live. But we had nowhere else to go. Aunt Biddy's employer died and the new owner laid off a handful of employees. I don't know what I'll do now. Where I'll go."

The sounds of the town coming to life filtered into the room. Mrs. Hollyhock shuffled through the kitchen door carrying a tray filled with bowls. Susanna needed to help her. Brenna came through the front door, and the doctor appeared as well.

"You need to go?" Julia whispered.

Susanna propped some pillows behind her back so she'd be able to eat. "Yes, I do. You're not to worry about your future; you're to concentrate on healing that arm." She smiled. "Things *will* work out, you'll see."

"You'll come back, won't you, Susanna?"

She nodded. "Of course. After breakfast, I'm going to run some errands, do a few things for the doctor, and rest for an hour or two. But I'll be back. Wild horses couldn't keep me away."

Julia braved a wobbly smile. "I'll be right here waiting." The young woman was stronger than she looked. Sometimes it took the worst of things to bring out the best in people. Julia strained to see the doctor. "Now, where's that laudanum? I want a nice big dose."

"Coming right up as soon as you eat," Susanna said, then winked. "I'll go speak with Dr. Thorn right now. We'll fix you up for a nice long nap."

Dalton insisted on being the one to set the charge. He wouldn't risk the life of the sheriff, or any of the others for that matter. This was his responsibility, and he'd see it through. Lifting the flap on his left front pocket, he felt around for the matches he'd put there not ten minutes before. Winthrop, Albert's brother, had come out an hour ago and relieved Thom, who'd gone back to town to alert Frank to the fact the money would soon be on the way, if all went to plan. The jovial livery owner sat his horse a safe distance away, with two other men, keeping a sharp eye out. If outlaws planned to make a play, the time of the explosion—and any subsequent confusion—would be their best shot.

Standing next to the wagon, Albert's eyes narrowed. "Don't be nervous."

"I'm not."

Albert pulled his hat lower to shield his eyes from the rising sun. "Then get a move on."

Dalton selected a stick of dynamite from the box in the bed of the buckboard and stuck it into his waistband, then gathered the spool of detonation cord. With an unsteady heart, he closed the distance to the train car and climbed the ladder while Gabe drove the wagon a good distance away. Nothing like a dangerous situation in the morning to wake you up and make you rethink your life. When had he last spoken with his mother? A small ache in his heart said it'd been a good long time. The only commendable thing about today was the strong breeze cooling his skin. He glanced up at the sky and noticed a few new clouds sailing along at a good clip.

On top of the train car, he hunkered down. "Evan, if you can hear me, try to get under the bunk. We're going to blow the top." He took a minute to listen again, but silence was his only reply. He wedged the dynamite into the hole they'd barely widened after four hours of work. He tied the cord to the fuse.

Albert stood below on the tracks, watching.

"Go on and get back with the others," Dalton called. The sheriff's keen stare was creating more jitters than he already had.

"Nothing doing. We'll go together."

"You're a jackass." The words surprised him. If he were to guess, Albert and he were close to the same age, a year or two under thirty. If this didn't work, and the charge was too powerful and killed Evan and blew up the money, he'd probably go to prison for robbery and murder by explosion.

His mouth was dry as sand. He willed his hands to be steady.

Finished tying a secure knot, Dalton slowly backed away, rolling out the cord. A gust of wind almost took his hat. He heard a chuckle from below, but didn't shift his concentration from what he was doing.

The plan was to string the cord across the roof to the ladder, then cut it about a foot past the edge. There he would light it, giving him plenty of time to finish the climb down and run to safety.

At the end of the car, he stepped over the edge and fished for the step with his boot. He climbed down several rungs, which left his head still in view of the charge. Withdrawing his knife, he made the cut and tossed the roll down to Albert.

"This is it. I'd feel better it you got back a few hundred feet."

"What are you so worried about, Babcock? Just light the darn fuse and let's get this over with."

Easy to say when you're not the one with the match. "Fine."

In three heartbeats, he had the thing burning. The hiss from the small flame as it slowly crawled up the fuse prickled his skin. Dalton went down two rungs at a time, but Albert caught his shoulder just as he was about to turn and run.

"What?" It came out in a bark.

Albert pointed. The flame had been extinguished after burning only a foot. The breeze played with the cord, moving it back and forth along the edge of the train car.

"Tarnation!" Dalton rubbed his moist palms down his pants.

"You want me to do it?"

"No. I told you that before. Now move back. I don't want to be responsible for killing the sheriff of Logan Meadows."

Dalton started up the ladder, knowing he could talk until he was blue in the face and the sheriff wouldn't budge. He quickly lit the fuse, and gave it a gentle toss. Problem was, at that exact moment, a healthy gust of wind picked up the string like the tail of a kite and it flew upward. A sick feeling clamped Dalton's chest. He poked his head over the top of the edge to see that the end of the fuse had doubled back on itself and landed on top of the charge. If he and Albert didn't get out of there fast, they'd be blown to smithereens.

"RUN!"

He grasped the sides of the metal ladder and all but slid down the rungs. His foot caught the landing when he went to jump, and he landed on his hands and knees in the rocks. Albert hauled him to his feet and they ran like lunatics alongside the train.

They hadn't gotten but ten feet when the explosion knocked them both to their knees.

CHAPTER ELEVEN

*W*hen a mighty blast rent the air, Susanna dropped the bundle of soiled laundry she held in her arms. Fear and confusion reverberated around her chest. Squatting quickly, she gathered up the pile of sheets and towels and glanced around Main Street at the other frightened people.

Heading straight for Albert's office, she hurried through the door to find Thom behind Albert's desk. "What on earth was that? And where is Albert?"

Looking up, Thom smiled. "Morning, Susanna." He stood and came around the desk, resting a hip on top. He looked as worn out as the rest of them were. "He's blasting a hole in a reinforced train car. If all goes as planned, they'll be here in fifteen minutes or so."

"What?" She thought she hadn't heard him correctly. "Why? That sounds dangerous."

He stifled a yawn. "It is, I guess. And since you'll find out the reason soon enough, I'll go ahead and tell you—being you're a close friend of the sheriff's."

Seemed everyone thought they knew where she stood with Albert, except her.

"Just what is it I'm not supposed to know?"

Thom filled her in, but when she left the sheriff's office, she was more concerned than ever. A million dollars was an unthinkable amount of money. Enticing to anyone. It would put Albert in danger, as well as Frank Lloyd, the bank owner. And Dalton. He'd always been kind to her back home—she wouldn't want to see him come to any harm.

Susanna crossed Main Street, her mind a whirlwind. She passed people without stopping to talk, anxious to rid herself of the burden she carried, and find out if Albert was all right.

Entering the long, narrow laundry house, she tapped the silver bell and waited. The clammy air felt good on her face. The familiar scents of incense and scorched linen were comforting after the last day and a half of uncertainties. A small sign on the back wall read WASHING & IRONING in big, bold print. Sounds in the back attested that Tap Ling, and his pretty wife, Bao, were hard at work as usual. Mr. Ling hurried out, his long black braid swinging from side to side beneath a small round cap.

When he saw her, a large grin split his face. "Miss Robin-*son*," he said with a polite bow over his hands. "Welcome." He drew a handkerchief from the pocket of his loose-fitting black pants and wiped his shiny forehead.

It was always a mystery to Susanna how neat and tidy Mr. Ling stayed through hours of hard, backbreaking labor. She couldn't get to work early enough to beat him, and he was usually there when she left the restaurant. Even if she came into town late at night, there would be a light burning.

"Hello, Mr. Ling," she replied. "I have some washing to drop off for Dr. Thorn."

Mr. Ling began sorting through the heap of white sheets and towels she'd set on his long wooden counter.

She looked toward the adjoining door. "Is Bao working? I'd like to say hello."

He looked up, his black eyes bright with fondness. "Took Lan home to eat." He smiled and rubbed his stomach. "That little grasshopper eats her weight in noodles."

"How is my darling little Lan? Still working hard on her letters? When she's through with the book I brought by, let me know, and I'll get you another."

The couple had the most darling little girl. She'd easily wrapped Susanna around her pinky finger from the moment she'd smiled up into her face. Her name meant "orchid," and the child was just as pretty as a flower, if not prettier.

Mr. Ling blinked several times, his face clouding with emotion. "Thank you. Means much that Lan learns English. Thank you—"

Susanna stopped his gratitude with a smile of her own. "It's no problem in the slightest, and I'm happy to do it. Next year when she's ready for school, the learning will be easy for her. And that makes it fun."

He looked uncertain.

"Now, when can I pick these up for Dr. Thorn?" There. They were back to surer footing.

"Monday. Day after to-*morrow*."

"Oh, I'm sure we won't need them that soon since several women have loaned us a good supply, and you have lots to do already by the look of things." There was a pile of laundry stacked on the end of the counter. "I'll be by Tuesday afternoon."

A relieved smile appeared on his face. "Thank you." He gave another small bow and she bid him farewell.

Back outside, the boardwalk was almost as cluttered as her mind. Between worries over supplies for the restaurant, what Julia was going to do now that her aunt Biddy was dead, and whether Albert was in danger—*and now Dalton*—she almost missed the man and woman walking toward her. The boy in the man's arms fit the description Dalton had mentioned. A bandage was wrapped around his head.

They were about to pass when Susanna said, "Excuse me." The woman wore a blue homespun dress, and the man's worn jacket looked several years old.

"Yes?" The man touched the brim of his hat. "Can I be of assistance?"

"I hope so," Susanna replied. "I'm helping out in the infirmary where most of the injured passengers were taken right after the accident. A man, Mr. Babcock, came asking around yesterday about a young boy he'd pulled from under a table in the dining car, and bandaged a cut on his head. His description fits that of your child. He was concerned, and wanted to make sure the boy had been reunited with his parents. Do you think he was talking about your son?"

The woman's face brightened. "Yes," she said, her tone heavy with appreciation. Her hand came up and smoothed the boy's sleeve, her hand lingering. "Terrence told us what happened, but didn't know the name of the man who had helped. We're so grateful, and we'd like a chance to thank him in person."

Susanna was sure it was not out of need of acknowledgment that Dalton had inquired, but she'd be happy to bring the four of them together, if that was what the woman wanted as well.

"Yes, that's exactly right," the man added. "We can't tell you how frightened we were to find Terrence missing right before the crash. We'd begun searching, and then the train hit, and everything was crazy. Seems he got hungry, snuck out of his seat, and went in search of food. We were so relieved when we found him in a wagon outside the doctor's office. Please, can you tell us were to find this fellow?"

"He's going to check back with me sometime soon. Tell me where you're staying and he will look you up."

During the conversation, Terrence had lost a bit of his shyness. He squirmed and his father set him on his feet but kept a tight hold on his hand.

Being an only child in the home she'd grown up in, Susanna wasn't sure how she felt about being a mother. Her heart longed for the experience, but she'd never want to let her child down as her mother had her. Could she do a better job? What if she didn't know how?

"For now, we're staying at an inn on the outskirts of town called the Red Rooster. Do you know the place?"

Susanna smiled. "Yes, that's one of Logan Meadows's oldest

establishments. We're quite proud of the dwelling. You know Mrs. Hollyhock then?"

"Oh, she's a dear," the woman said. She glanced at her husband as if she expected him to say something more.

He didn't disappoint. "It's the other woman who's hard to abide."

"Wallace." His wife's tone was cautioning.

"Well, she is," Wallace said. "If she doesn't want to be known as a sourpuss, she should act accordingly." He looked apologetically at Susanna. "We're Mr. and Mrs. Sadler. Please, have him look us up."

"Thank you, I will. I'm Susanna Robinson. I usually work at the restaurant, but for the next few days, I'll be splitting my time between the Silky Hen and nursing at the town hall we've turned into a makeshift infirmary."

Perhaps there was a silver lining to be found amongst all the pain and confusion of late. Logan Meadows would get past this trial, and be the stronger for it. It was remarkable how the town had pulled together in their time of need.

Terrence took a handful of his mother's skirt and gave a pull. "I wanna see the buffalo."

"Yes, *honey*, we're going there right now."

Mr. Sadler touched his hat once again, then placed his hand on his wife's back, still keeping hold of his son's hand. The three soon disappeared in the sea of unfamiliar faces as they made their way to the livery to see Maximus and Clementine, the town mascots. It was times like these that Susanna hungered for what the three of them had. Family was good, and precious. She had to believe a marriage like that would last. She just had to.

CHAPTER TWELVE

*A*lbert cradled his head in his arms as debris rained down on his back. Rocks and sticks jabbed into his belly. Then the air went silent.

"Preston?"

Albert scrambled to his knees, then took the hand Babcock offered. The guard looked as disheveled as Albert felt, and his hand was bleeding from landing on some rocks. Albert stood and brushed at the front of his shirt, which had taken the worst of his careening fall. His ears rang painfully from the discharge.

Funny, at that last second before the dynamite went off, all he could think about was Susanna, and how much he'd miss her if he accidently turned up dead. Morbid thought, but a thought just the same. Was he a fool to keep thinking Floria would give him the divorce? Just because that's what he wanted, didn't mean it would happen. Or that Susanna would still want him. He wished he knew what was bothering her, besides all the trouble of late. There was something, he was sure.

"You all right?" Albert asked, pointing to the cut.

Babcock gave a mirthless chuckle. "What was that?" He pulled his earlobe, his face scrunching in pain.

Albert nodded. "Yeah, I can't hear a thing either. What about your hand?"

"Just a scratch." Babcock stepped out of the smoke and waved the others over. The men took off toward the train at a gallop, and Gabe followed more slowly in the wagon.

He and Babcock started back to the train car.

Albert retrieved the coil of rope they'd laid close and started up the ladder, not sure what he'd find on the top, if there was a top to the car left at all. He poked his head over and gave a long whistle, then looked down at Babcock. "That did the trick all right. I can see your man. Looks dead from here. The money trunks are intact." He finished the climb and made room for Babcock.

Susanna looked down the street at Albert and Dalton as they made their way on horseback. Her heart surged as she took in Albert's rumpled appearance, the hard lines on his face, and his slumped shoulders. He was exhausted. They were two of four armed riders surrounding a wagon that must be carrying the money. Win drove, and Gabe road shotgun.

Since the blast, the saloon had gotten even rowdier, if it were possible. Some hard-looking characters stood outside and watched the convoy approach. One tossed back the contents of his glass, then threw it into the alleyway with a crash. The guns strapped to his thighs sent a shiver of dread up Susanna's back.

"Sheriff Preston!" he called. "When's this town gonna get some food? We're hungry!" He sneered and looked around at his cronies, who nodded and waggled their heads. A few more men stepped off the boardwalk and strode toward the oncoming wagon, making Susanna's internal alarms go off. Was this some sort of distraction?

"Stay where you are," Albert called back calmly. He nudged his dun, the agitated animal's sweaty coat most likely a reaction to the disquiet in the air. "The eateries will have more beef soon, as well as other foodstuffs. The proprietors have been hit hard with the extra mouths to feed. They're doing their best to put out large quantities of grub and keep up with all your appetites." Albert narrowed his eyes. "You come in on the train?"

The man glared back and Susanna stepped forward and grasped the post in front of her, laying her face against the cool wood. She couldn't drag her gaze away. *Don't look for trouble, Albert. Wait until the money is locked up. Wait at least until your hands are free.*

"What difference does that make?" the man sneered.

"Not a thing. Now, step back onto the boardwalk and give the wagon room. I don't want any trouble from the likes of you. This man needs a doctor!"

He's alive!

Albert's tone had changed. He wouldn't be defied. Susanna realized shamefully that she hadn't asked Albert one question about his day when they'd talked last night—not how he was holding up or what troubles he was dealing with since the Union Pacific accident. She'd been wrapped up in her own petty hurts and worries. Humbled, she let her gaze travel over his face and body. The lines around his eyes and the grim set to his mouth attested to the stressful situation.

The cantankerous man didn't budge. He'd had just enough whiskey to feel invincible.

Albert straightened in the saddle. "Get back! All of you. If you're looking to get locked up, just stay where you are."

Thom Donovan, walking on the boardwalk, hefted the shotgun he carried in his hands. The men stepped back and the wagon continued forward, coming to a halt in front of the bank.

Dalton looked edgy, too. His gaze bounced from the roofs of the buildings to the bystanders who lined the street. The whole scene playing out would have been fascinating if Susanna weren't so worried for everyone's safety.

"What do you think it is?" an unknown woman standing next to Susanna asked the man at her side. "It looks mighty important."

"It's a million dollars," her companion answered. "Heard talk of it on the train, but thought the person telling the story was making it up. Now I see it's true."

The woman gasped. "A million dollars!" she said at the top of her voice. Faces turned to look at her.

Frank Lloyd hurried out, hefted one of the trunks from the back of the wagon, and then disappeared inside his bank. He repeated the process twice until he had the three trunks safely inside. He closed and locked his door. Dalton dismounted and looked around.

Their eyes met. Susanna looked away but not before she saw him nod in recognition.

Oh, why hadn't she shared her past with Albert before this? He would've understood she'd not had any power to change her mother's ways. Now, if and when the truth got out, surely everyone would think differently about her, especially Albert. He'd feel duped. He'd shared amusing stories of his early life back on his parents' farm, the trouble he and his brothers had caused—and the punishments they'd received. Shame had kept her quiet about her past. Now, she just might pay the price with her whole heart.

CHAPTER THIRTEEN

$\mathcal{W}$ith Evan Stone in the care of the doctor, and the money now locked in the bank's safe, Dalton released a sigh of relief, but he couldn't let down his guard. He nudged his shoulder against the wooden siding next to the bank's front door to get comfortable and struggled to keep his eyes open. The fact that Evan was still alive had been a shock—but a good one. His fellow guard was in critical shape, but Dr. Thorn had given him a slim chance of recovery—the one saving grace of the day. Blowing the roof had been the right plan of action.

He dragged his hand over his whiskered jaw, stifling a yawn. He hadn't had a wink of sleep since his short nap before the calamity yesterday. Necessity and excitement alone had kept him on his feet, but now that he was stationary, he had little hope of staying awake much longer. As soon as Albert sent a replacement, he planned to flop down in the bed that had opened up in Frank Lloyd's guest room.

Dalton lifted a heavy hand and touched the brim of his hat in acknowledgment of a buggy filled with women passing by. He felt like a wooden Indian on sentry outside a smoke shop. Everyone was interested—or maybe it was talk of the million dollars. Either way, every man lingered in the doorway to the saloon next door, gawking.

"The Union Pacific has a crew on the way to repair the track."

Dalton turned to Albert, who'd appeared from the opposite direction. The sheriff held several telegrams in his hand. "Preston," he said in greeting.

"That, along with several stagecoaches to begin the dispersal of passengers. And here's a reply to the telegram you sent yesterday." He handed one of the brown slips over to him.

Dalton scanned the words. "Good. They'll pay anyone we trust to stand guard until they arrive. They'll get here as soon as they can." He looked up at Preston. "Does the Union Pacific have a timetable of when the train will be moved and the track repaired?"

"It's too soon for any of that, but I'm sure the representative will get here as soon as he can. I also sent a telegram to Fort McKinney asking for a dozen soldiers to come and stand guard. I don't like asking the men of Logan Meadows, many who have families, to put their lives on the line."

Dalton straightened, stretched his back muscles, then let his hands fall down to rest on the hilts of his guns. "I'm still puzzled. There's been no sign of Pat Tackly. No one has found the head guard's body have they?"

"No," Albert said. "I've been wondering about that myself." He nodded to a woman hurrying past. "Ma'am." He smiled and doffed his hat.

"I'd like to send out more searchers," Dalton said, nodding to Win, who had just arrived. "I'm not ready to give up on him yet." He also wanted to dispel his growing suspicion that his fellow guard might have had something to do with the wreck.

"Go get some sleep, Babcock. You're about dead on your feet. The money'll be safe for now. I have a man across the street watching from inside our newest establishment, Harrell's Haberdashery. With him, Win here, and myself, you needn't worry. I'll also see what I can do about rounding up some more men to keep searching for Tackly."

On the hill across the way men worked in the cemetery, their shovels glinting in the sun. "In all honesty, sleep sounds darn good. As much as I'd personally like to stand guard all the time, I can't."

"When you return, I'm headed up to the plateau where the boulders came loose and started this trouble. There's just something niggling at the back of my mind."

Dalton cut his gaze away from the grave diggers to look at Albert and Win. "You suspect foul play?"

"Anything's possible. With a cash shipment this large, it wouldn't be unheard of to have men here waiting for the train's arrival. It's not a far stretch for them to assume we'd bring the cash to the bank rather than leaving it in the train car. What better cover for a heist than a calamity on a grand scale?"

Susanna spotted Dalton on the boardwalk before he saw her. Between his rumpled clothes, bloodshot eyes, and slumped shoulders, he looked exhausted. He went along slowly, as if each step were a chore. His gaze halted the moment their eyes met. She guessed it wouldn't serve any purpose to try to avoid him now that he'd told the doctor, as well as Brenna and Violet, that they were old friends.

"Here you are, Suzie," he said, his friendly tone warming her. "I've been thinking about you. And Miss Taylor," he added quickly. "How's she feeling?"

"About how you'd expect after what she's been through, poor thing." His smile appeared and she remembered that even though she didn't know him well back in Breckenridge, she'd thought him attractive. Imagine, he'd defended her against his sister. She hadn't known that about him. "I just got off at the infirmary and am doing a few errands before I head home for some sleep." Taking his arm, she turned him around so she could see the back of his head. "Are you free now? Since you've not lifted a finger to take care of yourself, come with me to the doctor's office just down the street. If Dr. Thorn's not there, I'll get this disinfected myself. It'll only take a moment."

He chuckled and held his ground. "I appreciate your concern, but I'm about to fall asleep on my feet. I'll doctor it as soon as I get to Mr. Lloyd's house. He just offered me a room, and told me the same thing. He has a new bottle of iodine in his medicine cabinet."

She arched a brow. "Frank has a nice place. You'll be comfortable." She couldn't miss the gleam in Dalton's eyes, and wondered if it was the prospect of the nice house or something else. He seemed interested in her, but then why wouldn't he? She was the only one in the town that he knew.

"Where do you live, Suzie?" he asked, and glanced up the street. "Is it close?"

"Yes."

His smile widened. "In the same direction as Frank's?"

She nodded.

"You're going my way, then. Let me walk you home for old times' sake. We never really got to know each other very well. You were always so shy."

I was the girl from the wrong side of the tracks. At his intense gaze, she looked away.

"I'd like to remedy that right now," he said. "You haven't told me much about yourself."

"We've hardly had a chance." She couldn't stop a nervous laugh from escaping. Since coming to Logan Meadows, Albert was the only man who'd paid her any attention, in a more than friendly way. Walking with Dalton felt odd. She remembered seeing him around Breckenridge, washing windows or doing other small jobs to earn money when he was young, always polite and kind when their paths crossed. Once when he'd seen her, he'd backed up so fast he'd tripped over his water bucket and fallen into the street, his face turning a painful shade of red. Years later she recalled him opening the door to the dry goods store when he'd seen her coming. She'd thought at the time someone else must be behind her that he was trying to impress. Now she wasn't quite sure. "Only if you promise me you'll clean and dress your cut as soon as you get there."

A tired smile creased his face. "It's a deal, Miss Worrywart." He held out his elbow and waited for her to take hold.

CHAPTER FOURTEEN

$\mathcal{E}$arly the next morning in the sheriff's office, Albert bit back a curse when he smashed his finger feeding the cast-iron stove. Pain radiated up his arm. He gave it a good shake, all the while remembering the picture Babcock and Susanna had made as the newcomer escorted her down the street.

She's my *girl.*

A flash of uneasiness passed through him. Had the two just met, perhaps in the commotion of moving the injured passengers? A mite reserved, especially with newcomers, Susanna usually kept to herself. Even the prospect of the divorce papers arriving any day couldn't lessen Albert's concern. He should have insisted she listen to the truth, one of the more than fifty times he'd tried to broach the subject. Then she'd understand why he never made any advances to let her know what was in his heart. He would if he were free.

He latched closed the door to the iron stove. As much as he'd like to attend to the matter now, he had pressing business to discuss with Chase Logan and Charlie Axelrose as soon as they arrived. He'd already discussed the situation with Thom at length, and they'd decided to bring Chase and Charlie in on it as well—and Babcock to a certain degree. At the moment, Win and Babcock were on guard at the bank, as was Frank Lloyd. Since the money had been stored in the vault, the banker hardly left the premises.

The door opened. Chase and Charlie arrived together. Chase went straight to the stove only to turn and regard him with a confused expression.

"Sorry, we're out of coffee," Albert mumbled. "Thom went down to the mercantile to buy some—if he's lucky."

"That's a fine how-do-you-do," Chase said, none too happy. "I've never been in this office when there wasn't a pot brewing."

"That may be, but since yesterday, supplies have been flying off the shelves. You may as well get used to it until we're back to normal."

"Don't I know it," Charlie said. "I could hardly get past the stage office with all the people crowding in trying to get tickets."

Albert glanced out the window and down the street to the rumpled folks, jammed in the stage office. The line flowed out the door and down the walk a good ten feet. There was still so much to do to help them on their way.

Thom came through the door empty-handed.

"No luck?" Albert asked.

He shook his head.

Albert handed him a piece of paper. "Before I forget, I'd appreciate if you'd go to the undertaker's and compare this list of passengers with his list of the deceased. Match names as best as you can. One of the porters dropped the names by this morning and I don't have enough hands to do all the things I'm supposed to do. We'll start sending out telegrams to the towns, and their sheriffs can deal with finding their next of kin."

Thom folded the paper and put it in his pocket. The three men pulled up chairs.

"Fort McKinney has soldiers on the way," Albert began. "Until they get here we'll have to have guards at the bank and across the street twenty-four hours a day. I took a ride to the top of the bluff yesterday afternoon where the boulders came loose. It's hard to tell with the rain and mud, but it's possible that someone has been up there recently." His three right-hand men watched with serious eyes. "That doesn't mean the accident was planned, but, it does have me thinking. These last few months have been overly wet, making this part of the country a prime target for landslides. If anyone knew how close the tracks are set to that embankment those few miles around Three Pines Turn . . ." He shrugged. "It's a far reach, but not impossible."

Charlie sat forward. "So, you're saying we have outlaws hanging around here in Logan Meadows?"

Albert swiped a palm across his stubbled face, reminding him that he needed to shave the first spare moment he got. "Could be. We'll have to be vigilant. Maybe the guards were in on it." He let that sink in. "Maybe they thought they could stop the train and make off with the money in all the commotion. Perhaps whoever was up on the hill dug out the base of the boulders and was waiting with horses, but when the inside guard got knocked out and they couldn't get the door open, they had to scramble for another plan."

"Babcock?" Chase asked. "You think he's involved?"

"It's crossed my mind." The thought had kept him awake long into the night—or maybe it was the thought of the man cozying up to Susanna yesterday. So many problems pulling him in every direction.

Charlie uncrossed his ankles. "And the missing third guard? Why would Babcock be concerned about finding him, and alert us to his presence, or lack of it? I'd think he'd keep his mouth closed if he were involved and they were waiting to make a play."

"He had to tell us about Pat Tackly in case one of the passengers or porters mentioned him. It would seem strange if he didn't. I just hope Evan Stone eventually comes around. He might shed some light."

Albert had been so deep into the explanation of his theory he didn't hear the door behind him open, or Susanna's footsteps until she was standing alongside, a basket in her hands. The sight of her brought a rush of joy. "Susanna!"

He'd lain awake all night conjuring up the worst about her and Babcock. Now here she was. Maybe the divorce papers would come today. He'd be happy to cast his single status away again as soon as he could, if Susanna would only say yes. He rubbed his whiskered cheek, a bit embarrassed, wishing he'd taken a second to clean himself up. "I'm not fit—"

"You look fine." Her gaze reassured him. "I've brought you some breakfast. With all you're doing, I'm sure you're not taking care of yourself—or taking time to eat. I thought you might come to work this morning without anything in your stomach." She glanced at the others. "Morning, Chase, Charlie, Thom."

"Mornin' Susanna," the three chorused.

"That's exactly what I've done and I'm plumb starved." Albert lifted up a corner of the blue-and-white checkered cloth covering the fare to see a jar of milk, a loaf of bread, some apple butter, and a few slices of beef. He reached in and felt the bread, right after he gave her a meaningful gaze. "Thank you. It looks real appetizing."

She gestured to the others. "I'm sorry to interrupt. I know your day must be busy as well."

"It is, but never too busy for you. Are you on your way to the infirmary?"

"Yes, but after I stop by the restaurant to see if Hannah needs anything."

She'll have to pass by the bank and Dalton Babcock. Albert's fortunate feelings faded.

"I'll walk with you."

"Albert?" It was Chase; probably thought he'd lost his mind. Well, he had. Any sleep he could have gotten last night had been robbed by thoughts of her and Babcock walking down the boardwalk together.

Susanna smiled, and a soft little laugh escaped her mouth. "You have a meeting going on, Albert. But there *is* something important I want to talk to you about. When you have a few minutes. I promise we won't get sidetracked this time." Her gaze dropped boldly to his lips, and lingered. As if she knew he couldn't take much more, she glanced around him and smiled at his friends. "Good day."

The peanut gallery replied and she turned to go after she'd placed the basket of goodies on his desk.

He turned to the men. "Give me a minute."

He opened the door for her and they stepped out onto the walk. "Susanna," he said quickly, keeping his voice low. "Thank you for thinking of me." He glanced past the saloon, to the bank, where Dalton stood watch. Win was across the street, stationed inside the haberdashery. He could feel Chase, Charlie, and Thom watching him and Susanna through the window. "You be careful passing the saloon."

"It's seven in the morning, Albert; I think I'll be safe enough." Again, her gaze touched his face affectionately. "What's gotten into you anyway?"

Gathering his wits, he glanced across the small bridge in front of the livery where Clementine and Maximus were already in the front enclosure, munching on a pile of hay. If only he could blurt out the reasons he'd held back over the past two years. He'd profess his love—and she'd be overjoyed. But still, he couldn't help but believe his best course of action was to wait for the official papers to arrive, setting him free, then court her for all he was worth.

He gave her hand a small squeeze. "I just miss our lunches together. Everything feels off, since . . ."

She nodded. "I know what you mean. Maybe if we're not too tired tonight, we can take a walk. Like I said before, I have something important I want to tell you—but not now." Again her gaze wandered to his mouth, and he realized she was longing for a kiss. How he'd like to accommodate her—if he were free.

"It's a deal. Now go on and I'll watch until you pass the Bright Nugget."

She started off, and he couldn't help but feel that not just Susanna had changed, but he had as well. Since taking the sheriff's job in Logan Meadows, his life had been one of structure. And security. Get up, make the rounds, take lunch at the Silky Hen, and visit with his girl. More rounds, check all the doors, and turn in. Floria and her waffling about the divorce had been the only dark spot in his life. The gentle sway of Susanna's skirt made his heart pick up tempo. Change was in the air or his name wasn't Albert Preston!

Past the saloon, Babcock brightened when he saw Susanna approach. She stopped to talk. Had that been her aim all along? Albert scowled when her laughter reached his ears. All his good feelings evaporated like steam. Floria's letter couldn't come quick enough to suit him.

CHAPTER FIFTEEN

onday came and went with agonizing slowness. Violet Hollyhock closed the gate to her chicken yard as the first rays of the new day peeked over the distant ridge. Being mindful of the eighteen fresh, still-warm eggs nestled deep in the dishtowel of her basket, she stepped prudently. Buttercup, one of the older hens Thom Donovan had graciously given her for her birthday almost two years ago, ran up to the gate, followed by eight scampering chicks, little fluff balls of chirps and cheeps.

Using the fence post to steady her, Violet squatted, unable to keep a wide grin from her lips. She stuck a finger through the chicken wire and the hen sidled up close, letting her scratch her neck. "Go on, Buttercup. I can't stay out here all mornin' playing with ya, no matter how much you'd like me to."

Every so often, out of guilt for stealing their eggs each morning, Violet let one of the founding matriarchs of the flock keep her clutch until it hatched. This had been Buttercup's turn, a sweet-natured chicken, and Violet's favorite. Violet's flock had grown to twenty-five hens, which gave her plenty of eggs to feed herself and any guests she might have, as well as supplying the mercantile and Hannah's restaurant. Pansy was the only rooster she kept. The others were sold or butchered.

Violet turned and gazed at the inn nestled in the trees beside the road that led to Logan Meadows. Her life had been full since coming here.

Thank you, Lord.

Her heart lifted at the simple prayer. Another day to enjoy the things and people she loved. She'd gotten into the habit of praying herself from one celebration to the next, last being Brenna's wedding, and in a few weeks it would be the May Day social. Each day she opened her eyes in her soft, cozy bed was a gift. Sometime soon, those gifts would stop. She was ready, and yet she'd miss so many people. A tiny prick of sadness made her heart thump against her ribs. *Will I ever see my boy Tommy again? I always believed I would someday, but now that I've grown so old. . .*

She pushed away the disquieting thought. It wasn't for her to question God's ways. She had people to look after, and she'd best get moving.

Several days had passed since the terrible train accident, and the town was finally settling down into a halfhearted routine of sorts. Thank heavens, two of her guests, one being a giant of a man who ate his weight in food, had departed yesterday, leaving in her care only two adults, their child, and Beth Fairington, the woman who'd followed her to Logan Meadows from their old home in Valley Springs. As temperamental as her old mercantile clerk was, Violet was happy to have Beth's help—even if it wasn't much. This calamity had taken its toll on her decrepit old bones. For the first time ever, she was feeling every day of her eighty-six plus years.

Crossing the yard, Violet went to open the back door, but one of her guests beat her to it. "You should have told me you were going to the chicken yard, Violet. I'd have been happy to collect the eggs for you." Laine Sadler carefully took the basket from her hands. "You go sit by the fire. I'm taking care of breakfast this morning."

"I can't let ya do that, Laine. You're my guest. You're supposed ta be enjoyin' yerself."

Laine gently took Violet by the shoulders and guided her into the living room, already toasty from the fire in the hearth. She sat her in her favorite chair, then placed her knitting needles into her lap. "You can, and you will. Besides, Beth will be up soon—or should be—and she can help me. You've been cooking and cleaning and keeping up with this houseful of unexpected visitors." Laine looked deep into her eyes. "There, how does that feel?"

"Like I'm luxuriatin' when I should be workin'."

Laine laughed, the delight going all the way up into her eyes. Violet liked this young woman a lot. Reminded her of herself when she was in her twenties. She'd shared with Violet that they were on their way to look after her father, who was old and feeble, after her mother had passed on. It was a homecoming for her, and her father would finally get the chance to meet his grandson for the very first time. Laine was a worker, and a doer, and had a heart as large as the moon. She didn't sit around for someone else to take up the slack, not like Beth. Sadness squeezed her chest at the disparaging thought of her dear young friend, still asleep when she should be up greeting the day. *What will become of her once I pass on? Ain't likely any man here'll take her on. Kinda hard to warm up to a prickly pear.*

The rooster crowed again, and one of the bedroom doors opened and closed none too gently. Footsteps tromped toward the living room.

"Violet! That rooster has got to go!" Beth screeched from the hall. "No one can get a bit of peace with it crowing every few minutes." Her dingy nightcap topped her head like a giant mushroom. She clutched a small lap robe firmly around her thin frame, and her bare feet were exposed beneath her too-short gown.

Behind her, Laine laughed, making Beth's eyes widen in surprise. "It keeps crowing because it's time to get up. You wouldn't want anyone to think you're a lazybones, would you?"

Beth whirled around, having missed the guest in the kitchen when she'd made a beeline for Violet.

"Go on now and get dressed," Laine commanded. "We're going to whip up some breakfast before the others are up."

Violet sucked in a breath and prepared for the explosion she knew would follow.

Beth sputtered at the direct order. Laine was much more forceful with Beth than Violet dared. There was just something about their guest that Violet couldn't put her finger on. A look in her eye, or the way she carried herself with authority. She got things accomplished.

Beth straightened as if preparing for a fight. "What time is it?"

"Five-thirty."

She looked down her long nose at Laine. "I don't rise until seven."

"That's ridiculous and no never mind to me. And I'm sure it's because Violet's been carrying the load around here for far too long. Today dawns a new schedule at this inn. It's you and me, Beth, so just get used to the idea."

It was all said very calm and controlled, and in a nice tone. Violet almost laughed at the determined smile on Laine's face.

"I work at the mercantile today, at nine. That doesn't leave me time to—"

Laine stopped drying the bowl she held in her hands and arched an eyebrow. "There's plenty of time if you quit your caterwauling and get a move on."

Violet imagined the red line creeping up into Beth's face, the one that appeared on the rare occasions she met confrontation.

"I can't cook, dress for my day, and be to work on time. It's just not possible. Violet usually—"

"Yes, I know," Laine cut her off. "But starting now, things around here are changing. You *can* help, and you *will* help, even if you have to rise two hours early every day to do it. The inn will be your first priority, and then your job. If you can't do both, quit the mercantile. Do I make myself clear?"

Beth's eyes narrowed to slits. "I'll *not* be ordered around by the likes of—"

"Do. I. Make. Myself. Clear?" Laine stood as straight as any soldier Violet had ever seen, not in the least bit cowed, and actually more than a bit intimidating. Violet wouldn't want to take her on.

Violet set her knitting aside and straightened her creaky bones. Much to her surprise, Beth, completely white faced with anger, held her tongue. She stomped down the hall, her footsteps sure to wake up everyone clear to Logan Meadows.

Wallace Sadler passed Beth in the hall as he pulled his suspenders up over his thick shoulders. He turned and watched her disappear into her room.

Turning back, he gave his wife a long look. Although he'd washed his face and combed his hair, he still looked half-asleep. "What in blue blazes is going on out here? Sounded like rabid squirrels grappling over the last pine nut." He nodded friendly like to Violet.

"Never you mind, husband," Laine said, placing a mug of hot coffee into his hands. "Just as soon as you have some hot vittles in that belly of yours, would you please chop some more wood? That stack out back has been dwindling since our arrival."

He leaned forward and pressed a kiss to his wife's cheek. "I'll be happy to, dear." He took a long guzzle, then winked at Violet. She'd miss this nice couple when they left, as well as their darling little boy. That was a day she hoped would be a long time in coming.

CHAPTER SIXTEEN

$\mathcal{D}$alton approached the Red Rooster Inn on a horse Win had generously offered. He had one hour before he was scheduled to relieve Chase at the bank, and decided to follow up on the information Susanna had given him. Smoke from the chimney filled the air with a woodsy scent, and the sounds of someone chopping wood echoed from the back of the dwelling.

He dismounted, tied his horse to the hitching rail, and walked up the stairs to the porch. He gave a sturdy knock on the front door.

"May I help you?" a young woman asked after opening the door, a dishtowel in her hands and a smile on her face.

"Yes. I'm looking for a couple with a small boy who is staying here. Their names are Mr. and Mrs. Sadler."

The woman's smile grew. "You must be Mr. Babcock. My husband and I want to thank you for what you did for our boy. Not everyone would have taken the time to bandage his head and soothe his fears in the midst of all the confusion, as you did." She held the door wide. "Please come in and have a cup of coffee. We've just finished with breakfast but have leftovers if you're interested."

"No, thank you, ma'am, I've already eaten." A mouthwatering aroma lingered in the room. "But I'm sure it was tasty. The scent alone is making my stomach rumble."

She nodded appreciatively and preceded him into the kitchen where a dour-faced woman who looked vaguely familiar glanced over her shoulder from the sink, her hands deep in a wash bucket. The old woman he'd seen at the makeshift infirmary sat at the kitchen table with a cup of coffee.

Her face crinkled into a mass of wrinkles when she smiled. "Mr. Babcock, it's good ta see ya."

Mrs. Sadler's face all but glowed. "Mr. Babcock is the man who tended to Terrence during the accident." She glanced back and forth between him and Mrs. Hollyhock. "Let me fetch Wallace, Mr. Babcock. He's out back at the woodpile with our son." She hurried off, leaving him with Mrs. Hollyhock and the woman at the sink. Drying her hands, the familiar but nameless woman took a few tentative steps in his direction.

"Mr. Babcock, is it?" Her uncertainty made him feel uncomfortable. "You're the man from the train who's guarding all that money. Am I right?"

"You are. Difficult to keep something like that a secret."

She stepped a bit closer, her avid gaze taking in his every detail. "My name's Beth Fairington," she said. "I work at the mercantile on Main Street and I've seen you out front. We're right next door with just the small appraiser's building in between."

That's where he'd seen her. "Ah, yes. I've noticed you sweeping the boardwalk."

Her sharp features softened. She smiled, her thin lips stretching almost across her whole face. "Yes. That was me. When Maude leaves at noon, I run the place until closing. It gets mighty lonely. Perhaps you can stop in sometime and say hello?"

Mrs. Hollyhock cleared her throat. "Beth, why don't ya get Mr. Babcock a mug of coffee? That's the least we can do fer the kindness he showed our little Terrence."

Miss Fairington all but flew across the room. With shaky hands, she took a mug off the shelf and sloshed some coffee inside from a pot on the back of the stove. Her polite smile did little to calm his growing discomfort at all the attention she was showing him.

She handed him the cup. "I s-suppose you've heard about the social the town is planning on May first. It's going to be a festive day."

"I haven't. But I doubt I'll still be in Logan Meadows by then." The quickness at which she batted her eyes almost made him dizzy.

"I hope you are."

"I wonder if they'll even still have it, with all the tragedy that's befallen us?" Mrs. Hollyhock said from her seat at the table.

Beth shot the old woman a look of irritation. "It's a way to make everyone feel better, Violet. Maude was speaking about this exact subject in the store yesterday. Plans are still underway."

Thankfully, the back door opened. Mrs. Sadler entered, followed by her husband and the boy he instantly recognized. The bandage was gone and the hair around the wound was clipped short. The boy ran to his side lickety-split.

Dalton set his mug on the table and hunkered down. "I'm glad you found your parents." The boy's inquisitive gaze made him chuckle. "How's the head feel?" He took a moment to look over the healing gash.

"Sort of better. Hurts some still when I touch it."

Mrs. Sadler cleared her throat, then placed a hand on his shoulder. "I told you not to touch it, Terrence. We want to keep it clean."

"Well, it looks good. I think you'll mend just fine." Dalton smiled at Terrence, and then stood.

The boy's father reached out his hand. "We can't thank you enough, Mr. Babcock," he said as the two men shook hands. "Those frightful moments will stay with us for a good long time." He glanced at his wife and a look passed between them. "We'd like to reward you for your kindness."

This couple looked like their every penny was precious. Besides, he'd never take money for doing the right thing. "No thank you.

My reward is seeing that Terrence here is doing fine. I just wanted to stop in and say hello."

A pleased expression warmed Mr. Sadler's eyes. "That's very kind of you. How's the fella you brought in on the buckboard, the other guard? Poor man looked in bad shape."

"Don't know if he'll make it," Dalton replied, a bit discouraged. "Hasn't come around at all."

She shook her head. "Such a shame."

Miss Fairington looked bored with the whole conversation now that it had shifted from her to other topics. Without a word, she turned and made her way down the hall, much to Dalton's relief.

Terrence pulled on his hand.

"Can I see your horse?"

The boy's inquisitive eyes were impossible to deny. Besides, Dalton still had a few minutes to spare. "Sure can. I'll even give you a ride."

Feeling hopeful, Albert stepped into the mercantile and let his eyes adjust, determined to keep his thoughts positive. The important papers from Floria would unquestionably be in his slot today. This torture had dragged on long enough. Surely she had come to her senses, and wanted to be free of him as much as he did her. If there was nothing from her, then there would be something from Corey, updating him on the situation.

Maude was at the far wall helping a group of women who were examining her shelf of footwear. A few others meandered around the store aisles, which looked uncommonly bare. He started to the back counter where the mail slots were bolted to the wall. From halfway across the store, he could see that his box was empty.

Damnation! Disappointment gripped him hard and all his positive thinking fizzed like a drop of rain on a hot stove. Would the letter *ever* arrive? Would he never be free of Floria's manipulations and falsehoods? Not even a letter from his brother. He fisted his hands and tried to remain calm. There was a small possibility Maude had been busy and hadn't gotten around yet to putting it out.

Susanna didn't deserve this! He'd done his best to make Floria happy—that was, until he learned she'd only wed him to spite the man who'd jilted her. When he stumbled upon them kissing in his own house, he'd been blindsided. The interloper had actually laughed in his face, saying he didn't want to give her up, just didn't want to marry her. Said he didn't mind sharing. Albert had packed that day, and never looked back. Floria had promised him a divorce, but since then, a game of cat and mouse had ensued. He was tired of her lies. She'd only held on to him for the money he sent home.

At the mail counter, he drummed his fingers in frustration. She had gone back on her promise again!

"Do you need something, Sheriff?"

He pivoted. Deep in thought, he hadn't heard Maude approach. Her gray hair was styled in a bun on the back of her head and a plethora of wrinkles grooved her face when she smiled a welcome. "Have you put out today's mail?"

She gave him a curious look. "I'm surprised, you know it's too early for the stage. And you were just in yesterday. Something special must be on its way."

"Just a letter from my brother." *Or from a lawyer. Someone!*

"Is there trouble back home?"

"Nothing like that." He tried to smile but his emotion felt forced.

"Well, good. You know if you do get mail, I always walk it down to you in case it's important—I won't forget. But, I'm glad you came in. I've been wanting to tell you what a fine job you're doing in the face of all this misfortune." Her scanty brows pulled down in concern. "Do you know when those poor people will be laid to rest?"

"Later today. Pass the word to anyone you see that we'll be having a group service at three o'clock."

Maude shook her head. "Such a shame."

"Yeah. I'm getting pretty sick and tired of all this death."

She nodded. "I agree. But I'm mighty proud at how well Logan Meadows has pulled together during this tragedy. How's Susanna? I haven't had a moment to look her up. That girl of yours is a hard worker. Hannah told me she and Brenna have done a fine job looking after the injured. Thank goodness for that. Not everyone is cut out for nursing."

"We've both been busy—" At that moment, he remembered Susanna's request about their walk Sunday night. He'd been so involved with making sure they had enough coffins at the undertaker's, guarding the money, looking for Pat Tackly, and finding someone to send to New Meringue for supplies, he'd completely forgotten. And now this business with Floria had him ready to holler.

"I just couldn't believe the news when I heard it. It's a small world indeed."

Albert had no idea what she was rambling on about. "What?"

Maude's eyes popped open. "Susanna and that bank guard, Mr. Babcock, are from the same town. Went to school together. It's remarkable, if anything." The bell over the door sounded and Beth ambled in.

"I need to go, Maude."

She patted his arm. "Of course."

Albert made his way toward the door in a state of shock. They were old friends? Had a history? It suddenly felt as if ten-pound weights had been nailed to the bottoms of his boots. There was a real possibility Floria would never release him. She'd flip-flopped so many times he'd lost track. Anger rolled in his gut. Had he been kidding himself for five years, believing she'd someday relent and come around? Now that he thought about it, the way Babcock and Susanna had been walking down the street, it seemed the man had taken a shine to Susanna—or was he rekindling an old flame?

Albert stepped out the door and looked down toward the bank, where Babcock stood guard. He seemed like a good fellow—that was, if he wasn't planning a bank heist.

As much as Albert wished it different, the truth was, he himself was a married man. Where did that leave Susanna? She couldn't wait for him forever. Nor should she have to. Pain ripped through his chest as if he'd been run through with a lance. At least one of them should be happy. If he loved her, should he release her now, especially when she had a chance with an old friend?

CHAPTER SEVENTEEN

Susanna picked up her pace as she headed up the street, a few early blooms clutched in her hand. Since Julia was still under doctor's orders to stay off her feet, Susanna had promised she'd attend her aunt's funeral and place a flower on her casket before it was lowered into the ground. A shiver slipped up Susanna's spine at the thought of all those bodies stiff and cold, but she was determined. As much as she wished she could forgo the funeral, she'd told Julia she'd do this small favor for her, and she would. If she didn't hurry, she might miss her chance to say goodbye to Miss Biddy.

"Now, don't I look cute!"

Across the street, two rough-looking strangers had snatched the round cap from Mr. Ling's head and were tossing it back and forth out of the small man's reach. The taller of the two placed it on his own oily hair and proceeded to dance around mockingly. A handful of people she didn't recognize had gathered to watch. Nobody in the timid group seemed inclined to step in. Mr. Ling stood between them, his face a stony mask.

Furious, Susanna dashed over, and going up on her tiptoes, plucked the black fabric from the man's head before he knew what she was about.

He turned around so fast he almost tripped, his face twisted in anger that someone had dared to put a stop to his fun. The aroma of whiskey all but enveloped her.

"Give it back," he said, scowling. He reached for it, but Susanna stepped back out of his range.

"Give it back?" she replied in mock innocence. "I'll give it back all right—to its rightful owner!" She stood her ground, annoyance making her blind to the dangerous situation. One punch from either of the men would seriously hurt her. "You should be ashamed of yourselves!"

She glanced at Mr. Ling. He looked as if he was about to say something, so she quickly shook her head. It wasn't unheard of for a Chinese immigrant to be shot dead for no reason at all. She'd read newspaper articles from other towns, but not here in Logan Meadows. Albert would never stand for stone-cold murder like that.

"We was just havin' some fun. Now give it back, 'fore I get annoyed . . ."

Fast as a snake, he grasped Susanna's arm and yanked her close. Dropping her flowers, she tried to wrench her arm back, but he held firm. Fear blossomed in her chest.

From out of nowhere, Dalton pushed through the crowd of people that had grown larger with the commotion, clamped one large hand on the back of the perpetrator's neck, pushing him forward, then wrestled his hold off Susanna. When he jerked him up close, the bully yelped in pain.

"Stay away from this woman!" Dalton growled, without taking his glower from the man's face. "And stay away from this gentleman."

"He ain't no gentleman. He's one of those little—"

"Mr. Ling *is* a gentleman," Susanna interrupted. "He conducts his affairs with dignity and manners. More than I can say for you." She took Mr. Ling's hat over to him and placed the dark piece of fabric in his hands. When she tried to smile her lips trembled.

"Get out of town if you have to walk!" Dalton barked at the two. "Unless you want Mr. Ling to file a complaint."

The men laughed again as if this was nothing but a joke. "Imagine that. That half-sized clown against a civilized white man." Tap Ling's wife, Bao, watched from the doorway of the laundry shop. Susanna hoped their daughter wasn't anywhere near.

Dalton took another step, his face livid with rage. "I meant what I said."

The men exchanged a look, then the one who'd been the instigator shrugged. "Let's go, Fred. I'm sick of this town anyway." They stomped away.

Rattled, Susanna gathered the blossoms scattered on the ground. Now that the men were gone, she couldn't keep her hands from shaking. Dalton led her to the boardwalk and she didn't resist when he laid his arm across her shoulders. As a matter of fact, it felt good and safe. With a finger under her chin, he tipped up her face and gazed into her eyes.

"Are you all right?" he asked, his voice deep with concern.

She nodded, wondering why she couldn't control the trembling that had taken over her body. She had to get a hold of herself and get to the cemetery. "Yes. Thank you for coming to our rescue."

"What were you thinking getting in the middle of that?"

That reminded her of Mr. Ling. She looked for him over her shoulder but he was gone. Before she turned back, she saw Albert standing in front of the undertaker's door. Their gazes locked. Before she could step out from under Dalton's arm, Albert turned and walked away.

CHAPTER EIGHTEEN

$\mathcal{L}$ong strides took Albert up the hill toward the cemetery, his mind reeling from the sight he'd just witnessed. Susanna in Babcock's arms. Susanna gazing into the man's eyes, her words inaudible, as if they were the only two people on earth.

He was breathing hard by the time he crested the hill. Not from the exertion of the climb, but more the fact that he'd waited too long. Susanna had slipped away and there wasn't one darn thing he could do about it. He was hobbled, and cuffed, as well as if he'd been arrested and thrown in a cell. In the dark tunnel of his thoughts, he cut a direct path through the cemetery and arrived at the area where everyone had gathered. It felt as if every eye was on him.

Reverend Wilbrand stood on the far side of the open graves with a Bible resting in his hands and the long tails of his frock coat moving in the breeze. The grief-stricken congregation stood opposite, their eyes red and swollen, with the long row of six-foot deep graves in between. Small groups waited in quiet conversation for the service to begin, while others stared off into the distance, at the graves, or at nothing at all.

Feeling like a fool for how he'd turned away when he'd seen Susanna and Babcock together, he wondered if Susanna had followed him up the path. The picture of her standing in Babcock's arms, regarding him thoughtfully, was too much to contemplate.

Albert slowly shouldered his way into the gathering, feeling the need to be just a part of the crowd. Logan Meadows citizens

CAROLINE FYFFE

were interspersed with the newcomers. He glanced at the path, needing to see Susanna.

As if his desire had called her forth, Susanna crested the hill and hurried toward the assembly. She looked pretty and soft. She held a small bunch of flowers in her right hand. Her strong determination, mixed with an innocent vulnerability, all the things he loved most about her, stood out against the vibrant blue sky. Memories of them together tumbled through his mind as he took in her glistening hair and the hem of her skirt as it swirled around her feet. He remembered the time she'd ventured out on a winter's day to join him in the sheriff's office. She'd stepped through the door covered in snow, with a basket of goodies on her arm. They'd sat by the window, in the glow of the woodstove, and watched the snow fall for hours. Or the time he'd been sick in his apartment upstairs, unable to get off his back. Unmindful of her own well-being, she'd brought him bowls of chicken soup, and tended him with care, making sure he had all he needed until he was better. Dancing a waltz at the annual Christmas party, church picnics in the green of the meadow. So many memories. So much love.

She nudged her way into the crowd, stopping beside Hannah, Thom, Brenna, and Greg. Violet Hollyhock was there, as was Dr. Thorn. Susanna had briefly glanced around before joining them, and he wondered if she'd been looking for him.

The reverend cleared his throat. "We're gathered here together to celebrate the lives and deaths of those killed in the train accident a few days ago. No one can make sense of such a tragedy. God works in mysterious ways. We can't guess the why of such suffering. We can only accept and pray that our loved ones are now content in the bosom of Abraham. We must pray for their loved ones left behind, for strength to go on and lead full lives in the face of their grief."

He lifted a sheet of paper off the page of his opened Bible and brought it closer to his eyes. "Mr. Harvey Bettencourt, Mr. Larry Carver, Mr. Herold Green, Mr. Joseph Martin, Mr. Scott

Olson, Mr. Joseph Moyer, Mr. Simon Nobel, Mr. Tyler Levine, Mr. Homer Rumi."

A woman cried out. When her knees gave way, the man standing close swept her into his arms.

The man next to Albert pulled a handkerchief from his pocket and wiped his eyes as Wilbrand continued, "Mr. Oliver Smith and his wife, Harriett. Mr. Jerry Hill and his wife, Lolita."

Reverend Wilbrand turned the page over. He drew his own handkerchief from his pocket and swabbed his forehead. "Mrs. Mary Chaucer, Mrs. Floria Brooks, Mrs. Nancy Merts, Miss Marcy Merts, Miss Biddy Lafont, Miss Joyce Kinkaid, and Miss Robin Rocha."

Albert held his hat in his hands, watching Susanna across the expanse of people. It took several moments for what he'd just heard to sink into his occupied thoughts. *Mrs. Floria Brooks?* He cut his gaze to the preacher. *Floria?*

Albert's heart slammed against his ribs so hard it made him cough. Shock and grief stunned him. With all that needed attending to in town since the accident, he hadn't checked the identity of every single deceased person. The Union Pacific railway was responsible for that. Still, he'd had Thom double-check their work and keep a list. Now he wished he'd done it himself.

Had he imagined what he'd just heard? Had Floria been on her way to Logan Meadows? Why on earth? And if she had, why had she used her maiden name?

At the far end of the row of graves, four men with ropes, Win being one of them, began lowering the first coffin down into the six-foot-deep pit. There were gasps, and cries, then the sounds of soothing. Murmured words.

The shrill cry of a hawk overhead rent the air. The large bird rode the wind on strong outstretched wings and hovered above as it watched the proceedings below.

Albert struggled with what he'd heard. Could it be somebody else? Floria hated Wyoming, at least that was what she'd told him when he'd given her his address.

He may have wanted his freedom, but he didn't wish death on anyone, especially not his wife. Albert took a deep breath, and slowly let it out. All these questions wouldn't tell him a thing. He needed to make sure, but there was only one way to do that, and he didn't have a moment to spare. "Hold up, Win!" he called out.

Reverend Wilbrand's head snapped around to see who had spoken. The men with the ropes halted their movements, the first casket halfway to the floor of its grave.

Albert closed the ground between him and Wilbrand. He put his arm across the preacher's back and turned him away from the crowd.

"What on earth is going on?" Reverend Wilbrand whispered, his gaze searching Albert's eyes. "These people can't take much more. We need to get this day over and done with, and help the affected survivors grieve."

"I agree with you, Reverend, but something has come up. Something I never expected. I need to open one of the coffins."

The reverend gasped. "Sheriff! That's impossible! You should have taken care of this business, whatever it is, before the service. Any such action, as you suggest, will traumatize everyone." Both Albert and Reverend Wilbrand glanced over their shoulders at the silent crowd straining to hear what the sheriff and preacher were arguing about. "There are children here, Albert! Burying one or both of their parents. Think about what you are asking."

That was true. Albert wished there was some way around it, but he couldn't think of a thing. "I'm sorry, but it can't be helped. I wasn't aware there was a problem until right this moment when you were reading the names of the deceased. If I don't identify the body now, I'll have to exhume it later. But I will check, and I will be sure."

The preacher's astonishment seemed to ebb away, and he clamped down on Albert's arm with a grip that belied that of a man of the cloth. His clenched jaw and crimson face were a testament to his fury. "Sheriff Preston, I have no idea what this is all about. It's highly unprincipled to open a coffin at this point. Surely this can't be as urgent as you think."

Albert stepped back and shook his head, at the exact time the hawk hovering overhead gave another sharp cry.

"My *wife* may be among those you're planning to bury today."

Wilbrand's eyes bulged. He snapped closed the Bible and clenched it to his chest. "Your w-wife? Did I hear you correctly?"

"You did. Am I supposed to go through life wondering if she's dead or alive?"

CHAPTER NINETEEN

$\mathscr{S}$usanna set her hand on Thom's shoulder and went up on tiptoe, trying to see between the heads of the men in front of her. She was thankful for any distraction to take her mind off all those clay-cold bodies sleeping in their coffins. If Julia hadn't asked her to come, she wouldn't be here.

Albert and Reverend Wilbrand were having some sort of intense discussion right in front of everyone. No, it looked more like a quarrel. The reverend pulled back and Albert leaned toward him. One shook his head and the other nodded. What on earth? What could possess Albert to stop the service?

Susanna let her gaze wander over Albert and the fine figure he cut. His long legs and strong chest were the personification of a western man. His black leather vest hugged him like a second skin. Shoulders broader than a header beam in a barn could carry any weight, no matter how heavy—and the people of Logan Meadows knew that well. They trusted their safety to him, but more, he'd earned their respect and love. He'd worried her today, when he'd all but stormed off after seeing her with Dalton, but once she explained the situation, and why Dalton had been comforting her, he'd surely understand.

Hannah leaned close to Susanna and whispered, "What do you think is going on with those two? I've never seen Reverend Wilbrand look so, so—dumbfounded. Or Albert so determined." She felt Hannah's inquisitive gaze. "Do you know, Susanna?"

Susanna shook her head. "I have no idea. I'm just as surprised as you are. Look at them; it actually looks like they're arguing."

"They're arguing all right," Thom added. "Whenever Albert rubs his jaw like that, I know I may as well give in. I should go see what it's about. See if there's something Albert wants me to do."

Susanna grabbed Thom's arm just as he was about to walk away, stopping him. "No. I just have the strangest feeling about this. Let them be." An eerie sensation pushed away her ponderings about Albert's good looks. What *was* going on? "Look. They're turning around," she mumbled more to herself than anyone else. "Reverend Wilbrand is about to make a statement."

The reverend held up his hand until everything fell silent. "Brothers and sisters, our sheriff needs to conduct some business that cannot be helped. Please, if you all would just turn around for a brief moment, we will deal with this swiftly, and then be on our way with the service. I assure you, if it weren't of the utmost importance . . ."

An uneasy murmur rippled through the crowd. Then whispers turned into weeping. Some did as Reverend Wilbrand asked and turned their backs to the coffins, but most of the men watched with narrowed eyes.

Albert and the preacher headed down the row of coffins, counting as they went. The reverend looked at his list as he walked, then stopped in front of the sixth from the far end. Susanna saw Albert swallow. For a fleeting second, he looked up, searched the crowd. Their gazes met and held, and a look of uncertainty, unusual for Albert, passed over his face before he dropped his gaze.

This is important to him. Personal.

A moment of panic made her breath catch. What was going on to make him act so strange?

Win, who stood close, handed Albert the hammer he had hanging off his belt. In exchange, Albert passed his hat to Win to hold while he made quick work of pulling the nails. The breeze ruffled his hair, reminding Susanna of a particular Sunday last month when they'd eaten a fried-chicken picnic down by the riverbank with their friends. They'd walked by the creek and enjoyed the sunshine. Talked about spring, and the May Day celebration. How had everything gotten so muddled? Pretty much everyone had turned back around and now watched with emotion-filled eyes.

A woman on Albert's end of the congregation, with a small boy in tow, began edging closer to where Albert and Reverend Wilbrand stood. Albert slid the top of the coffin to the side, and leaned over to look inside.

Floria's once-flawless white skin was chalk-like and dull. She looked peaceful—and for that, Albert was glad. Grief he hadn't known he could feel for her swamped him. He hoped she hadn't suffered. She was still, even after five years and all that had transpired between them, one of the most beautiful women he'd ever seen.

"Reverend? Sheriff?"

The middle-aged woman who'd called out to them stood just a few feet away. She held the hand of a small boy about four or five years old.

"Albert," Reverend Wilbrand said softly, as if he already knew the outcome. "Is she . . . was she—"

He wiped a hand across his face. "Yes."

"Mrs. Floria Brooks," the unknown woman said softly, gesturing to the coffin. "Is she kin of yours? She was seated one row ahead of me on the train, and this is her son. Since they were traveling alone, the porter asked if I'd look after him for the time being until they figured out what to do."

Her son! A tidal wave of sensations crashed through Albert's mind. The boy looked to be the correct age if he'd been conceived before he and Floria had separated. She'd been spiteful in all aspects of her life, so why wouldn't she keep such an important fact from him?

His heart swelled as he took in the lad's stoic expression that said he'd been carrying the weight of the world on his shoulders for far too long. His oval-shaped face and light-chestnut hair were two giveaways, but his wide, intelligent eyes, the same sandalwood color, dark brown with slivers of amber, just like his and Win's, removed any doubt. Above those were the distinctive Preston eyebrows.

His son. His and Floria's.

The woman straightened her shoulders. "Sheriff?" she asked, her tone hopeful.

Albert nodded. "Yes, ma'am, it's the Floria Brooks I know. I'm her next of kin."

A tentative smile appeared. "I'm so relieved to hear that. I'm traveling to California and wasn't sure what I should do with the child. He must have a father or other relatives back wherever they're from. Now you can see that he gets safely home. These clothes are all he has, until you retrieve his belonging off the train." She leaned in close so only he could hear. "He's been crying for his mother every night, saying she's lost in the train. I explained the best I could that she was dead, but he keeps saying we need to help her."

She led the child forward, intent on handing him over then and there. Bending, she kissed his forehead. "Here you go, Nate. Didn't I tell you everything would work out?" She tenderly placed her hand on his cheek. "You be a good boy for the sheriff and mind your manners." Just as she was about to retreat, she stopped. "How did you say you're related? An uncle or cousin?"

Albert couldn't stop himself from hunkering down to the boy's level to look him in the eyes. He wished he could soothe away his grief-stricken expression. "No, not an uncle." Albert smiled to put the boy at ease. "Is it Nate or Nathaniel?" he asked quietly. The redness of his eyes tore at Albert's heart.

"Nate," the child responded.

"Sheriff?" the woman asked. She wasn't handing Nate over to just anyone, not even a lawman. Her protectiveness touched him deeply.

Albert looked up at her with a nod. "I'm the boy's father. You needn't worry over him any longer."

Even though Albert knew Susanna was too far away to hear any of the conversation, the people next to them could. It wasn't more than half a second before a surprised murmur rippled through the ranks. Well, he'd found out what he needed to know, and so much more. He put out his hand and his son placed his small, warm one inside.

CHAPTER TWENTY

*I*t's the sheriff's son!" the man standing in front of Susanna said to his companion. "Don't that just beat all. Thank goodness they found him or the boy could'a ended up in an orphanage." Another murmured word caught her attention several times. Wife, wife . . . wife?

Susanna blinked. What? She stared at the scene playing out before her eyes. Hannah reached over and took her arm, pulling her close. "Wait until you hear all the facts, Susanna," Hannah said softly. "Maybe they overheard it wrong. I'm sure there's a logical explanation."

Susanna turned to face her friends. "Did you know Albert had been married?" She searched their faces. "Did you know, Thom? You work with him every day."

"No, this is the first I've heard," he said. Hannah, Brenna, and Greg shook their heads no.

Reverend Wilbrand took up his place, and said a few words Susanna didn't hear. He gave the signal, and Win and the men took up the rope and began lowering the coffins into their graves.

It was impossible not to watch Albert and the boy. He was darling, an exact replica of the larger man. Her heart ached with want, which only confused her more. After all this time, Albert had never said a thing about a wife, or a child! Why? She felt duped and embarrassed. So deep in thought she almost forgot about the flowers she held, and the promise she'd made to Julia.

Rattled, Susanna hurried forward just as Win and the other men slipped the ropes beneath Miss Biddy Lafont's coffin. Susanna glanced at Reverend Wilbrand. "May I?"

"Of course."

She laid the blooms atop the pinewood box at the exact moment the breeze caught one blossom, dropping it into Miss Biddy's grave. Susanna watched it go. *How strange. How strange life is. Here today and gone tomorrow. And Albert? What about him? He has a son—and a wife? What else about him don't I know?*

With a pounding heart, and head held high, she turned and met the pitying gazes of her friends. She kept her eyes trained far away from where Albert and the boy stood. Walking back, she glanced down the hill to the bank on Main Street where Dalton stood guard. A swell of melancholy rocked her. In shock, she took up a new spot on the fringe of the gathering and ignored Mrs. Hollyhock's sympathetic gaze.

The service continued. The men worked steadily, lowering each coffin. The cloudless sky looked the same as it did five minutes ago, but everything else had changed.

Finished with their arduous chore, and amid the wailing of the people, Reverend Wilbrand began a prayer. "Go forth, Christian souls, from this world in the name of God the almighty Father, who created you, in the name of Jesus Christ, Son of the living God, who suffered for you, in the name of the Holy Spirit, who was poured out upon you. May you live in peace this day, and may your home be with God in Zion from this day hence."

He began the first notes of "Amazing Grace" and soon other voices joined his deep baritone and others began to disperse to the graves. Women hid their faces in the shirts of their men, or cradled their children close, their grief a living, breathing entity. Susanna hadn't lost a loved one to death, but felt as if she'd lost Albert in another way. He appeared out of the crowd with the boy in his arms, the child's small face turned against his neck.

"Susanna?" His gaze searched hers.

Whatever she was feeling at the moment, she couldn't stop herself from reaching out and placing a comforting hand on the boy's back. "What's his name?"

"Nate."

"And the woman?" She hadn't been able to stop the question. Maybe she was an aunt, or guardian.

"His mother."

"Walk with me—us," Albert said, wanting to keep Susanna close. Who knew what the next hour would bring? Her clouded expression as she struggled to hold back tears sliced him to the quick, knowing he'd put it there. "I know I have some explaining to do, but I hope you'll agree to wait until we have a little privacy."

Her gaze flicked over to where their friends watched. She nodded.

"Thank you." He turned and ushered her toward the trail that led down the hill. Nate trembled, and Albert thought he must be terrified in the arms of a stranger, his mother dead, far from their hometown. They began their descent on the path to town, the rich, dark soil beneath their feet sprouting with new growth. Signs of spring were everywhere. A dark contrast to what so many were feeling after burying their loved ones.

"What will you do with him? Where will you live?" Susanna asked softly.

"I've been thinking about that since the moment he took my hand." He rubbed his son's small back, needing to comfort him. "I guess Nate and I'll just have to talk about that."

Susanna gave him a sideways glance. "Above the sheriff's office is no place for a child being it's next door to the saloon."

He shrugged. "I agree, but what else can I do?"

They were almost to the bottom of the hill, approaching the

bakery, the small clapboard building on Main where the path to the church came out. Dr. Thorn's office was opposite. Lettie must be frying donuts today because a delicious aroma filled the air.

"Now that Greg has moved in with Brenna, why don't you see if Maude has plans for her small rental," Susanna said. "It would be perfect for the two of you."

But I want it for the three of us, Albert thought, aware she was avoiding the obvious topic of discussion. The last time they'd talked, she'd said she had something she wanted to tell him. She'd gazed at his lips. Had all that changed? "That's a good idea."

The smile she gave wasn't real. She was hurting, and needed answers, but he couldn't go into it with Nate huddled in his arms. He veered for the front door of the bakery. "Come on, I think we all could use some cheering up."

"I should get back. Julia will want to know that the service is over and how it went."

He couldn't let her go when they were on such unsteady footing. "It'll only take a few minutes. Please."

When she nodded, he pushed open the door and then stood back, letting Susanna lead the way. Inside, the air heavily scented with sugar and cinnamon made moisture spring into his mouth. He removed his hat.

Nate picked up his head and looked around.

Albert smiled. "Smell good?"

The boy nodded, but kept his eyes trained far away from his own. Nate must wonder why his father had never come to see him. How could Albert explain without damaging his mother's memory? What kind of lies might Floria have told him? He set him on his feet.

Lettie, with her usual friendly smile and flour-covered apron, hustled around behind the counter, gathering up several donuts for the woman in front of them. The baker wrapped her creations in paper and tied them up with a string. The transaction was completed and the woman left.

"Hello, Sheriff, Susanna, sorry to keep you waiting. I've hardly had a chance to breathe since opening today. There was a lull in business for the funeral, but we're picking back up again. This is the first time there hasn't been a line halfway to the door. " When her gaze dropped to Nate, her smile ebbed. "An orphan from the train?" she mouthed to Albert.

"No, this is my son, Nate Preston."

Lettie's eyes popped open. "Your son?"

A hundred questions flashed across Lettie's face but Albert wasn't about to go into great detail until he had a chance to explain things to Susanna.

Nate looked up at Albert for a few seconds, then through the glass case at Lettie. "Nate *Brooks*."

Seemed the boy didn't say much, but he wasn't hard of hearing.

"I see," Albert said. "Fine then, we'll get to that later. For now, we need three donuts please." He gazed into the case. "It's looking pretty sparse."

Nate stepped forward and put his hands on the glass. "Slim pickings at best."

Albert exchanged an amused look with Susanna as Lettie sputtered, "I'm sorry, but these are all I have until I fry some more." There were eight donuts to choose from. "I've been running nonstop all day. The mercantile is almost out of everything I need."

"There should be a buckboard coming in soon with supplies from New Meringue," Albert said. "That should help."

Relief moved Lettie's face. "That's good to hear, Sheriff. Now, which one would you like, Nate?" she asked, directing her question to the child. Albert could only see the back of Nate's head as he tried to make a decision.

He had a son! It was still so hard to believe. He regretted that he'd missed his early life, and just hoped they could forge a strong bond henceforth. Had Floria loved him, been kind to him?

Nate pointed to a dark-chocolate donut drizzled with a white glaze.

"A fine choice, young man," Lettie said with a smile. She took it out and put it on a plate. "Susanna?"

"I'll have the same."

"Me too," Albert agreed. Amazement washed though him as he realized he was smiling. It was impossible not to as Nate's gaze followed Lettie around like a bird watching a bug. Both tables were vacant, so they settled at the clean one. Before he knew it, Nate's donut was gone and his cheeks were puffed out like a squirrel gathering nuts for the winter.

"Susanna, I'm sorry about missing our walk Sunday night. It totally slipped my mind."

"I understand. Everyone has had more than his share of things dumped in their lap. Especially you."

"Will you come by when you're off your shift today, so we can talk?" he asked. If she said no, he didn't know what he would do.

"I'm more interested in seeing that this little man is settled in properly. Everything else can wait."

So, she was playing it safe. He couldn't blame her in the least. "I agree. But our talking is important too. I promise, I won't keep you long."

He didn't want to beg, but their relationship was at a critical turning point. The image of her with Babcock was still fresh in his mind. Could her reluctance to talk stem more from that than her shock over the recent revelations?

"Susanna?"

She watched Nate lick his finger, then dab at the crumbs on his plate. She lifted her gaze to his. "Yes, I'll come by."

"What time?"

"Six o'clock."

CHAPTER TWENTY-ONE

*T*ired after standing guard since nine this morning, Dalton watched Albert come down the path that led from the cemetery with Susanna by his side and a child in his arms. The three went into the bakery across the street from the bank. He settled his shoulder against the porch post, his gaze on the bakery door, recalling the way Susanna had felt wrapped in his embrace after the incident with the Chinese launderer.

Had she sensed the connection between them, or had she been too rattled by the rough encounter? For him, the years since he'd seen her melted away like magic. She'd stirred his blood, and his thoughts for the remainder of the day had been about her.

A man exited the saloon, crossed the narrow alley and turned, intending to enter the bank.

"Hold up," Dalton said.

The man turned to him. "What?"

"You'll have to leave your sidearm out here with me."

The cowboy's eyes narrowed. "What're you talking about?"

Dalton pointed to a sign Albert had written and posted next to the door.

NO GUNS IN THE BANK BY ORDER OF THE SHERIFF.

Dalton held out his hand. The cowboy was lean and a bit windblown. Dalton hadn't seen him in town before today. "You'll have to hand it over."

The man's hand dropped possessively to the handle of his .45 Colt. "I'm not giving you my gun."

Dalton clenched his jaw. He'd been nice and polite, just as Frank had asked. No one else had taken offense at the request, knowing the sheriff was only looking out for the large amount of money locked up in the vault, as well as everyone's safety. Why should this fella be different? "Then you won't be banking today." Dalton took a small step forward. "Period."

"Thanks again, Mr. Lloyd." A gravelly voice from inside wafted out followed by an older gentleman.

"My pleasure. Taking out a loan is as easy as that. I look forward to seeing you each month." The farmer-type secured his dented hat on his head, then smiled politely at Dalton. Frank Lloyd stepped out after him.

Frank shuffled to a stop when he saw the fellow Dalton had stopped. A big grin split his face and he clapped the man on the shoulder. "Seth Cotton, it's good to see you. How're things out at the ranch?"

The angry tilt to Seth Cotton's face morphed into a knowing satisfaction. He thought he was about to have his way. "Just fine, Frank. I've been busy, so this was my first opportunity to get to town in two weeks. A shame about the train, and all those people dying." His gaze darted to Dalton, then back to Frank.

"And your cough?"

"Seems to be easing up some. Doc has had me drinking an awful-tasting elixir for the past few months. Nell's plenty happy about it."

"Ivy, too?"

Seth chuckled. "You bet."

Dalton relaxed, listening to the conversation, absolutely sure Mr. Cotton was just going to try and amble his way in on the shirt-tails of his friend. That wasn't going to happen on Dalton's watch.

Frank glanced his way. "Have the two of you met?"

Dalton smiled. "Not officially."

"Well, let me do the honors. Seth, this is Dalton Babcock. Came in on the train and is guardian over the money I'm sure you've heard all about. Dalton, Seth Cotton is Charlie Axelrose's brother-in-law. You know Charlie."

So, he was almost family. "Sure I do. Nice to meet you, Mr. Cotton."

The fella smiled, but it didn't reach his eyes. He wasn't finished yet either.

Frank turned on his heel and began to enter. "Have you come to make a payment?"

"That's right."

Frank didn't notice the tension in the man's voice, but Dalton caught it.

As he stepped forward to follow Frank, Dalton reached out an arm. "Your gun?" He couldn't keep the irritation from his tone.

Frank turned. "Dalton, Seth's a trusted friend."

"I'm just following the sheriff's orders. Besides, you want to set an example for everyone else to argue? It's not a good idea."

A staring match ensued.

"He has a point, Seth."

Five minutes later, Seth Cotton stepped out of the bank, followed by Frank. Dalton handed the man his gun and he strode away—without a word being said.

Frank cleared his throat. "So, how's the watch going?"

"Besides Seth Cotton, haven't heard a peep. I'm starting to think we don't have a thing to worry about. That said, I'll be a happy man when the soldiers finally show up."

Frank looked up and down the street. "Agreed. And the representative from Denver. I've always dreamed of what it would feel like to have a million dollars in my bank, and now I know. I'd just as soon be a small bank again."

Dalton nodded, still a bit put off by how Frank had tried to get around the new ordinance for a friend. He decided to shift his thinking to a more pleasant subject. "Can I ask you a nonbusiness question, Frank?"

Frank snapped his gaze from the hill where men worked filling in the graves, and a few mourners still lingered in the cemetery. "Of course. What is it?"

"I'd like to know more about Susanna Robinson. We grew up together. I'll admit, I liked her back then, and seeing her again has made me realize I've never stopped. Running into her now, out of the blue, almost feels like a sign."

"A sign?"

Two doors down, Beth Fairington came out of the mercantile, and smiled at him, something she'd been doing for most of the day. Frank chuckled.

Dalton ignored the amusement at his expense. "Sure. A sign that maybe I was supposed to meet up with her after all these years. Is she seeing anyone seriously?"

"I'm surprised you don't know," Frank said. "She and Albert have been a couple for some time." His brow scrunched thoughtfully. "Well, not officially a couple, I guess. But it's a known fact around town that they're sweet on each other."

Albert? Susanna and Albert?

Strange he'd not picked up on that at all. Since he'd arrived, he hadn't seen the two together until today, and her name had never passed Albert's lips. Or vice versa.

"A word of caution—Susanna isn't up for grabs. If I were you and looking to settle, I'd set my sights on someone else, someone attainable." Frank glanced down at Beth who'd just reappeared. "Albert and Susanna are as solid as they come."

That almost sounded like a challenge. Dalton was surprised the news didn't bother him more. Maybe because he couldn't picture the two together.

When Frank turned to leave, Dalton stopped him. "Something else. Around noon, the strangest thing happened. I turned around and found a little cloth bag tied off with a ribbon sitting on my chair. It was like it appeared out of nowhere."

"Let me guess . . . cookies?"

Dalton laughed. "How'd you know?"

"Logan Meadows has a secret do-gooder. Consider yourself christened."

"It's not . . ." He let his gaze move left to Beth strolling up and down on the mercantile porch, fingers threaded together behind her back, as if she didn't have a care, or chore to do, in the world.

"No," Frank said emphatically. "The incidents began before Miss Fairington came to town. That one wouldn't know how to do a kind deed if she tried."

A rush of relief flashed through Dalton. Perhaps the do-gooder was Susanna. He could easily see that of her. Maybe, just maybe, she was trying to get his attention, too.

CHAPTER TWENTY-TWO

*A*stounded over the events of the last hour, Albert walked down the boardwalk with Nate by his side. The fact that he was no longer married kept beating the drum of his heart. Still, poor Floria. He allowed himself to think kindly of her since she was dead. For Nate's sake, he'd do his best to forget all she'd put him through, how she purposely set out to wreck his life with no thought to his feelings. But now, there were more pressing matters. Somehow, he had to convince Susanna he had never purposely lied to her, and that they should marry right away. That would be tough. He'd seen her expression. Her hurt. She didn't understand at all.

He smiled when he felt Nate's wary gaze on him. Most of all, he needed time to become better acquainted with his son—that word still brought a flutter of wonder whenever he said it, even to himself—and make sure the boy didn't feel frightened, as Albert was sure he must.

Albert opened the door to the sheriff's office and held it wide. "There's someone in here I want you to meet," Albert said, gesturing for his boy to enter.

Nate didn't see the dog lying by the stove because his gaze went straight to the two jail cells. He shuffled inside and stopped by Albert's desk. "Who?"

"You missed him. He's over there."

With a brow scrunched up in bewilderment, Nate looked around. He spotted the dog watching him through interested eyes, his chin resting on his outstretched legs.

"A dog!" He hurried forward and went down on his knees in front of Ivan, but kept his hands to himself.

"That's Ivan. He's nice. Go ahead and pet him."

Nate regarded Albert over his shoulder for more than a few seconds, as if he didn't believe him. "I'll get in trouble when my mama comes back. He might bite me."

Shocked, Albert wondered if he should correct Nate's thinking, or let it go for now since he'd been through so much today. The funeral and then meeting a father he didn't know he had. He decided on the latter. "That's good advice about strange dogs, but I know Ivan. He loves children."

Albert came over and sat down on the floor next to the two. He scratched Ivan behind his ears, making the dog's tongue flop out the side of his mouth in pleasure.

Nate watched him stoically.

"He's just being polite and waiting for you to make the first move," Albert said. "If you do, from now on he'll be the first to greet you when you come in."

Still Nate held back.

Maybe it was best to show by example. Albert leaned over and put his cheek to the dog's back, his fur tickling his nose. "Come on, I wouldn't lead you wrong. His coat is soft. I'll bet you'll like it."

Nate placed his palm on Ivan's head and gave a little scratch. Albert sat up, pleased Nate was beginning to trust him. Ivan crawled forward, and lowered his head into Nate's lap.

Thank you, Ivan. You're just what he needs right now in a strange town, with strange people.

Thom came through the door, stopping when he caught sight of the three of them sitting on the floor. Albert climbed to his feet.

"I see ya met my dog," Thom said jovially, a wide smile stretching across his face.

Nate whipped around and snatched back his hand as if he'd been caught doing something naughty.

"No, go on," Thom encouraged. "Ivan loves attention. He never thinks he gets enough."

When the boy turned back to Ivan, Thom sent a censorious look Albert's way.

Well, now it had started. His friends felt duped. He'd have a lot of explaining to do, but not before he spoke with Susanna. She deserved to get the facts first.

"I'm Thom, by the way. Thom Donovan, your pa's deputy." He strode over and hunkered down, putting out a hand to Nate, who understood and shook his hand like a man. His boy had nice manners.

"I'm Nate Brooks. My ma is trapped in the train wreck and we need to get her out. She's scared. Will you go with me?"

How did one make a grieving five-year-old face the reality that his ma was dead and buried, and she wasn't coming back? Albert's chest squeezed painfully. He'd take his boy's hurt on himself if he could.

Thom cut his gaze away, surprised. "I, ah . . ."

Albert ran his hand down Nate's hair, Ivan still resting his heavy head in the boy's lap. "He knows about your ma, Nate. Things are going to be fine."

Nate kept his gaze on the dog.

Albert stepped away, challenging Thom with a direct gaze, who tipped up his chin. "Nate and I were just on our way upstairs. He's tired. I think he'd like to settle in and maybe take a nap."

The child quickly looked up, his eyes narrowed. "I don't take naps."

Albert glanced at the clock, then back to the pair on the floor. "Or not. Let's go upstairs anyway. I'd like to show you around and get better acquainted. I have a guest staying for a couple of days, so it's going to be a bit tight, but we'll manage."

Reluctantly, Nate climbed to his feet. When he did, Ivan followed suit.

"Mr. Springer came and collected his things about fifteen minutes ago," Thom said. "He was lucky enough to get a room that had opened up at the hotel. He told me to thank you for your hospitality."

Albert nodded. "Well, that's one problem taken care of. I was wondering how we'd all fit." He went to the door. "The stairs are outside around back. Follow me."

"It's my shift to stand guard in a half hour, so I'll be heading out soon," Thom said stiffly.

Albert felt a bit awkward under Thom's unwavering gaze. He hadn't been around children much, being neither of his brothers had taken a wife. His experience lay with the children of the townsfolk here in Logan Meadows. He held the door for Nate, then took his hand, which the boy allowed. The child's palm in his own conjured up a nice, homey feeling, reminding him of his own pa on the farm. He and Nate went around the building to the staircase leading to the apartment. Ivan's nails clicked on the wooden steps as he followed behind.

Inside, Albert moved a handful of papers off the chair by the front window where Nate would have a view of the comings and goings on Main Street. "Have a seat here while I pick this place up."

In ten minutes, most of the clutter was stuffed away, and he had a nice glass of cool water to offer his son. He took the seat opposite, feeling uneasy, and studied the child's profile as Nate kept his attention trained outside. Ivan lay beside the boy's boots, which hung halfway to the floor.

Where to begin. "So, Nate, I'm happy to meet you. I'm your pa."

Nate glanced over, blinked, looked back out the window.

"How old are you? I'd guess around five."

Nate nodded. "Yes, Pa," he replied dutifully, never taking his gaze from outside where he seemed to feel most comfortable looking.

Was it too soon to ask if he knew why they were coming to Wyoming? Or, maybe, they weren't coming to Logan Meadows at all, and this was just a peculiar coincidence that the train had crashed here and they'd met. He wondered if his brother Corey had any information that could help him sort this out. He'd send a telegram just as soon as he was able.

"I'm sorry I haven't gotten the chance to meet you before now," Albert went on, the strain of the silence hanging over their heads. "What do you like to do for fun?"

Nate fussed in his chair, getting comfortable, then turned to Albert. "I like to make puzzles, shoot my slingshot, or draw my letters." Releasing a deep breath, his shoulders slumped and his eyelids shuttered to half-mast. Albert wished he would lie down. "But mostly I like to hunt for frogs in the creek." He made a face. "Nana doesn't like it if I get my pants wet."

Nana? Albert wondered if Nate was referring to Floria's mother, a true force to be reckoned with. To the best of his recollection, Floria's father had died long before they'd ever met. But, he couldn't trust anything he thought he knew. "Women usually don't like boys to get wet or muddy," he agreed. "I used to like to go frogging myself when I was a boy. I'd dip the frog legs in egg and then roll 'em in corn batter. They fried up mighty tasty. You ever have them that way?"

Nate shook his head.

"Your uncle Win enjoys 'em, too. Did you like seeing the livery after eating your donut?"

He nodded.

"Do you know if you have some trunks on the train? Can you remember?"

He nodded again, and opened his mouth in a wide yawn. His lids dipped, and momentarily stayed closed. He rallied. "We had three."

Three trunks? That was a lot. Was Floria coming to stay? He had so many questions he'd like to ask Nate, but not if it brought up bad memories, or got him thinking about his ma and that she was dead. He'd have to watch what he said. "Men are retrieving the trunks off the train today. We should have some of your things here by tonight, and if not then, tomorrow."

Ivan let out a loud whine and stood up, again laying his head in Nate's lap. That brought a small smile to the boy's face, a smile that resembled Floria's.

Albert's heart lurched. So much had gone wrong, more than he even knew. Shame for abandoning the son he didn't know existed warred with his fury at Floria for keeping him in the dark. But even that emotion was placated by the astonishment and love he felt when he looked into Nate's eyes. And what about Susanna? His heart skipped a beat when he thought of their upcoming talk. Would she, *could she* understand his silence on the whole matter? Would he forgive her if the tables were turned? He didn't like to think it, but bad news might be on the horizon.

CHAPTER TWENTY-THREE

Hannah Donovan hurried through the doors of the Silky Hen, her thoughts crashing around like a handful of marbles in a tin can. She passed several occupied tables, and several that needed cleaning. So much for sneaking out for the funeral; her absence had put them all behind. Besides serving the multitude of hungry customers, she and Daisy were responsible for preparing food to deliver to some of the homes housing other folks. It was no easy task feeding so many people for such an extended period of time.

How could Albert have kept such information from Susanna? From all of them? She felt hurt, and even angry. She had advised Susanna to wait until she'd heard the whole story, but that didn't do anything to stop her own wayward thoughts from conjuring up all sorts of reasons for Albert's wife, ex-wife, whoever she was, coming to town with a son in tow. At the thought of the child, Hannah softened. He looked around Markus's age. He was a cute little dickens, with serious, dark eyes that reminded her all too much of Albert's.

She pushed open the swinging door to the kitchen to find her mother huddled close in conversation with her best friend, Mrs. Brinkley. Every time Hannah saw the woman she was reminded of the time her mother had planned to buy an expensive bolt of fabric out from under Mrs. Brinkley's nose. Thankfully her mother had changed a lot since then. Roberta's apron was spotted with gravy, and it seemed she hadn't looked in the mirror for some time, since she had a streak of flour across her forehead.

The two women snapped up straight when Hannah entered the room. Daisy glanced over from whatever she was mixing, a relieved smile playing at her lips, and Markus, seated at the round break table in the corner, was too engrossed in what he was doing to even look up.

"Hannah, you're back." Her mother's guilty expression stirred her anger. Thinking about Albert was one thing, gossiping quite another.

Hannah crossed the room and kissed Markus on the top of his head. "Yes, I am. Looks like you've been busy out there."

Mrs. Brinkley patted Roberta's hand and hurried toward the door.

"Don't leave on my account," Hannah called.

"I just stopped in for a second," she said. "I have supper to see to myself." The matronly woman waved and was out the door, but popped her head back in a moment later. "You have a new table out here."

"Thank you," Roberta said. She turned to Hannah. "I just heard the news!" The excitement that tinged her mother's voice set Hannah's teeth on edge. "I can't believe my ears. Albert has a son! And what about the boy's mother? Why was she on the train coming to Logan Meadows? It's such a mystery."

"And *none* of our business, Mother. Out of respect for Susanna and Albert, I hope you won't speak of this to anyone. It's going to be difficult enough for Susanna without wondering what everyone is thinking—and saying."

Roberta cocked her brow and darted a look at Daisy's back, as if embarrassed to be scolded in front of her. Lifting her chin, she started for the door.

"I'll see to the new table," Hannah said, feeling a bit contrite for her actions. "You've worn yourself out again today. Sit with Markus and have a cup of tea."

Her mother reached out and ran a hand down Hannah's arm. "I commend you for your loyalty to your friends. I promise I'll be more careful with my words." She winked. "All that said, I do think I'll have that cup of tea now that you're here. I haven't had a break since early morning."

"Good, you do that." Hannah plucked her apron from the wall pegs and tied it around her waist as she proceeded into the dining room. She took a moment to scan the room, spotting a lone man at the table by the window who hadn't been there a minute ago. Albert's table, she thought with a wry smile. The one he took every day to eat his lunch and talk with Susanna.

As she approached, she recognized Mr. Babcock as the man she'd met when she brought biscuits and coffee to the train. "Welcome to the Silky Hen," she said, trying not to notice his broad shoulders and rugged good looks. "I'm glad you decided to stop in."

"Good day, Mrs. Donovan. I just got off my shift at the bank—as a matter of fact, your husband took over for me."

At his engaging smile, she felt her face heat up.

"Gabe Garrison spoke so highly of your fried chicken with all the fixin's, I just had to come give it a try. I hope you haven't run out."

"Of fried chicken? Never. Would you like a cup of coffee with that?"

"Please."

Hannah practically twirled in her shoes and hurried off. Strange he'd come in today and sit at that particular table. She'd heard the talk around town, how Mr. Babcock came from Susanna's hometown and how he'd helped Dr. Thorn set that poor girl's arm. Seemed he and Susanna got along very well indeed. Ashamed for the direction her thoughts had strayed, Hannah went straight to the china cabinet without looking at her mother. She was doing the same thing her mother had been doing when she arrived. Speculating on things that weren't her business.

"One fried chicken, Daisy," she said over her shoulder as she gathered the items.

"Anyone we know?" Roberta asked, stirring the silver-plated tea infuser around in her cup of hot water.

"Well, sort of. It's Mr. Babcock, the man—"

"—responsible for all that money in Frank's bank! I've yet to meet him. Is he alone?"

Hannah was ready to push out the door, cup and saucer in one hand, the pot of hot coffee in the other, but stopped. "He is, but I don't know if it's such a good idea to intrude on his privacy."

"Oh, pooh. This is Logan Meadows not St. Louis. We don't hold to all those silly rules. I'll only say hello."

With a sinking feeling, Hannah preceded her mother through the door and across the room. She set the cup and saucer on the tablecloth in front of Mr. Babcock and filled it, hearing her mother's approaching footsteps.

"Mr. Babcock, I wanted to come out and meet you."

He was just lifting his cup to his lips, and set it back down and stood. "Ma'am?"

"Yes, I'm Roberta Brown, and Frank Lloyd, the owner of the bank, is my brother. I'm also Hannah's mother. I've heard about the shipment from Denver you're guarding, and how you had to dynamite the top of the train to get that poor guard out, as well as the money."

Before Hannah could stop her, Roberta pulled out the chair opposite Mr. Babcock and sat down with her cup of tea. "I hope you don't mind a little company . . ."

As Mr. Babcock was taking his seat, Hannah was heralded by a table who wanted to pay their bill, and then another who needed a refill on water. She wanted in the worst way to get back to Mr. Babcock's table and draw her mother away before she had a chance to interrogate him about Susanna and their past. She hurried into the kitchen for a tray to clear the dirty tables, then made a beeline back to the table next to Mr. Babcock's. As she approached, the two let out a round of laughter. What was going on?

"Your supper will be ready shortly, Mr. Babcock," she said, sending her mother a glance. "Mother, give Mr. Babcock a little time to unwind from his stressful day."

Mr. Babcock shook his head, then smiled. "I'm enjoying something else to talk about besides trains, guards, and the like."

Roberta beamed.

"Your mother is quite entertaining."

"Yes, I know."

"Order up," Daisy called from the kitchen.

Hannah just stood there.

"Go on, Hannah," her mother said. "I'll be right in." She graced Mr. Babcock with a smile. "There is one thing else I'd like to know."

CHAPTER TWENTY-FOUR

*I*t was five minutes until six, and Susanna had more than a few jitters inside at the thought of seeing Albert. She wanted—*no, needed*—to speak with him, but every time she imagined the confrontation, a burning pit of anxiety pinched her stomach and ignited a flash of anger at his deception. Nothing felt right since that moment at the funeral. Why had that woman been on the train? To reconcile? Now she was buried in one of the coffins, and the boy whose head barely reached Albert's belt buckle was his son.

Why hadn't he told her about his boy? Surely he must have known. Thank heavens she hadn't had a chance to follow through on her self-proclaimed promise to speak her heart to him. To tell him she loved him. Let him know she was ready to make a lifelong commitment. *Oh, heavens above!* The humiliation then would have been unbearable. It was bad enough now.

And what about that poor woman he married? Had the circumstances played out for her in just the way her mother said they would for Susanna if she ever gave her heart to a man? Maybe for Albert, the romance had been all about the chase, and as soon as they'd consummated their love, his ardor had cooled, and he'd left her with child. She wouldn't be the only woman in the world to be fooled in such a way. *Thank you, Mama. You were right. I'm so sorry I ever doubted you.*

Finished with the cup she was washing, Susanna set it on the towel she'd laid out on the counter and fished in the bucket for another. A handful more of the patients had left this afternoon, bringing a measure of relief. Some families had bought wagons from anyone willing to sell and were setting out on their own.

Brenna entered the room with a tray holding more dishes. "Dr. Thorn said you should take tomorrow off, Susanna. I can easily manage this on my own now that more of the patients have gone. And from now on, we're to rotate our days. The infirmary won't be needed much longer."

Since the funeral, Brenna had hovered over her like a mama cat.

"Actually, that sounds good," Susanna responded. They stood looking at each other, the undiscussed topic heavy in the air. "How could he do it, Brenna?" Susanna said, finally giving in to her need to talk. "How could Albert lie to me like that? I'm shamed and humiliated. As well as embarrassed and hurt." She gave a deep sigh.

"And angry?"

She nodded. "Yes. Exactly. That's why I'll take tomorrow off. I think I could sleep for a whole day and a half, and still not feel rested."

Brenna came forward and rubbed Susanna's back. "Say no to anyone who asks for your help. You have dark circles under your eyes. If you don't get some rest soon, you're going to get sick and end up in one of these beds."

Susanna smiled. "I don't know about that."

Brenna stepped back and gave her a stern look. "Well, I do. And I insist." She paused. "Are you going to see Albert tonight?" she asked as if it were the most natural question in the world. She was trying to figure out what was going on, as much as Susanna was.

"I promised him I'd stop by as soon as I was off." She glanced at the wooden pendulum clock and her stomach gave a nervous squeeze. "I should probably get going. Will you please keep a close eye on Julia? Losing her aunt has been traumatic for her. She doesn't have a home to return to."

"Of course I'll look after her. I've become quite fond of that young woman myself."

"By tomorrow, Dr. Thorn said she'll be able to get outside for some fresh air. Maybe sit in the sun and read."

"Don't say another thing. I'll fix up a nice place for her in the rock garden outside. And I'll even bring one of my books from home, just in case she's run out of reading material."

Susanna went to the shelf that held their personal items and gathered up her shawl and reticule. "By the way, do you know what Maude intends to do with the rental now that Greg has moved in with you? Is it spoken for?"

"She hasn't said anything to me. Why?"

Susanna didn't want to discuss Albert's plans until they were firmed up a bit more. "Nothing important."

Understanding moved across Brenna's face. "Say no more. Just remember you're one of the strongest women I know. Everything will work out, you'll see."

"Thank you. I'll keep that in mind. Now, I better get a move on." She glanced at the clock as she passed into the main room. It was ten minutes after. She hadn't meant to linger for so long.

Passing through the alley, Susanna stepped onto the board-walk between the mercantile and the El Dorado Hotel at the same time Dalton stepped out the door of the Silky Hen. His face lit with pleasure when he saw her.

"Suzie, you're the exact person I was hoping to see. Are you finished with your shift?"

She liked his gentle camaraderie. With Dalton, she didn't have to face the troubles at hand. He knew her past, and still accepted her. She didn't have to think of the embarrassment of being hoodwinked by someone she thought loved her. His expression reminded her of the time they'd come face-to-face in the livery in Breckenridge, both in their early adulthood. She'd been dropping off a neighbor's horse who'd thrown a shoe, and surprised Dalton shirtless in the forge. His chest and arms shimmered in sweat and the sight had made her blush painfully.

Remembering how self-conscious he'd been that day brought a smile. Now would be the perfect time to ask him to keep what he knew about her to himself. She glanced in the opposite direction toward Albert's office, then back at Dalton. "Yes, I just left."

He strode up to where she stood. His gaze touched her lips briefly, making her look away. "Then can we take a little walk? I haven't had a chance to thank you for helping me find Terrence and his parents. I appreciate that. The Sadlers are very kind. Funny though, how Mrs. Sadler seems to rule the roost out at the inn."

"That was nothing. With your description I spotted the boy right away."

Beth Fairington pushed through the mercantile doors, a feather duster in her left hand. Turning, she spotted them, and her mouth momentarily pulled down into a frown.

"Susanna, Mr. Babcock," she said. Her tone was the most pleasant Susanna had ever heard her use.

Susanna had tried to like the woman, she had. But the way she looked down her nose anytime Susanna had business with her made that utterly impossible. "Hello, Beth," she replied. "How are things in the mercantile?"

Beth smiled at Dalton when he tipped his hat. "Better now that emergency supplies have arrived from New Meringue. But what a chore keeping the accounting straight between the borrowed items. It's given me the most atrocious headache." She rubbed her temples as she gazed up at Dalton through her scant lashes. "Thank goodness Maude doesn't mind doing most of it."

Susanna snuck a peek at Dalton. It wasn't hard to see that Beth had her sights set on him as a possible suitor.

"How is the guarding business going, Mr. Babcock?" Beth asked.

"Fair to middlin'. I'll feel better when the soldiers arrive. I don't like putting everyone out. Once they do, I'll have a little more time to get reacquainted with Suzie—that is, before we load the cash and move it out."

Beth was fingering the feather duster in a poor attempt at seduction. At his words, she fumbled the implement and shot a calculating glance at Susanna. "Suzie?"

Susanna had just started thinking that perhaps the hard-edged woman was changing her ill-mannered ways. The malicious light in her eyes said different.

"I was sorry to hear about you and the sheriff," Beth chortled, unable to hide her glee. "Were you as shocked as the rest of the town? Keeping a wife and son under wraps must be a mite difficult. I'm just so sorry things didn't work out. If there is anything I can do to help, please let me know."

Susanna tamped down her ire. "You'll be the first one I come to, Beth. I so appreciate your kindness. Thank you."

Beth's nasty expression turned into a pout when she realized Susanna hadn't taken her bait. "I was only stating the facts. You must know everyone is talking about you." She waved her hand in front of her face as if to clear away what she'd just said. "I'm sorry. That just slipped out."

Serves me right for engaging her. I certainly know better.

Dalton tipped his hat. "Good day. Suzie and I have some catching up to do." He placed his hand on the small of Susanna's back to usher her away.

Beth's face turned stony. "I merely offered my condolences to my friend Susanna in her hour of need. Anyone with a heart would do the same."

"Your comments were meant to inflict pain more than anything else," Dalton said. "It would do you well to mind your own business and tend to your own heart. Perhaps you'd have more friends."

Beth's face flushed crimson. "Haven't you heard, Mr. Babcock? I don't have a heart, just a hard chunk of granite in my chest."

Dalton didn't miss a beat. "People can change, if they want

to." He looked down at Susanna, and she felt a blush creep into her cheeks at his affectionate gaze.

Beth turned and marched into the mercantile, slamming the door so hard the windows rattled and the bells over the door sounded like a symphony.

Susanna watched with dismay. Poor Beth. It must be lonely not having any friends.

They walked a few steps until they were out of view from the store, then stopped. The sheriff's office was only three buildings up and Susanna felt a burning need to get there. She was already quite late.

"How did you know?" she asked softly. "About Albert's past and his son?"

He gazed up the street for a moment. "I heard about it in the restaurant. But don't let that bother you. You need to hear Albert out. Give him a chance to explain."

She should have known the men would stick together. "So, you're on Albert's side?"

He took both her hands into his own and waited until she looked up into his eyes. "No, I'm on your side. But I don't want you making any important decisions without taking the time to think them over. I want your heart free and clear."

As much as she wanted to pretend she didn't know what he was talking about, she did. A woman could get lost in his eyes if she let herself. "Dalton. I don't—"

His gaze wandered to her lips again, and this time he deliberately let it linger. "I think you know. It was a moment of fate that brought me to Logan Meadows and us back together. I'll not pretend that doesn't mean a lot to me."

She dropped her eyes to their still-joined hands. What was she doing? Discreetly extracting them, she glanced up to see Win watching from his guarding post at the haberdashery. "I need to be going, Dalton. Thank you for everything you've done."

She started to turn away and then realized she might not get another chance alone with him. "I wonder if I can ask a favor of you."

His brows rose. "Anything."

"No one here in Logan Meadows knows my past." She didn't want to say any more.

"Your past?"

Surely he understood what she was referring to. He looked at her so long she began to wonder, then said, "You mean . . . about your mother?"

Was he playing dumb on purpose? "Yes."

A look crossed his face—not pity, but understanding, and conviction. "You don't have a past. Your mother may have, but not you. I'm sorry you've been carrying that around with you all these years. You have nothing to be ashamed of. On the contrary, I've always thought you one of the most honorable women I've ever known."

She looked away, unable to meet his eyes. Honorable?

"Look at me," he said softly. "Please."

She did. His sincerity moved her deeply as an invisible warmth wrapped around her. She pulled away, fighting back her feelings.

"Your past is safe with me. Now and always."

CHAPTER TWENTY-FIVE

*A*lbert paced across the small room of his apartment, the room closing in on him. He wasn't doing a very good job of entertaining Nate. The boy sat at the window with his chin in his palm as if this were some kind of prison. He hadn't said a word for the past ten minutes.

It was twenty past six. Susanna wasn't coming. Surely the people of Logan Meadows were peppering her with questions she didn't have the answers to. He was about to suggest they go out when footsteps on the back stairs brought him around and Nate to his feet.

Albert crossed the room and pulled open the door. Charlie Axelrose stood on the upper landing with a large traveling trunk in his arms, a sheen of sweat glistening his brow. Chase Logan waited below with the remaining two trunks Nate had spoken about. He held something in his hands. Albert stepped back, allowing Charlie to enter. "Thanks, Charlie, I'll get the rest."

Charlie glanced across the room to Nate. "I can bring 'em up."

Albert bristled at the censure he heard in Charlie's voice. He ignored his comment and descended the steps, hoisting the second trunk into his arms.

"Food from the women." Chase lifted the plate in reply to Albert's curious look. "They thought you might be hungry."

"That was nice of 'em," Albert said, then started up the stairs. When he came through the door, Charlie was showing Nate something, Ivan standing at his side. It was the first time Albert had seen his son smile, and a prick of jealousy, mixed with sadness, jabbed him in his side. He wanted to be the one to relieve Nate's sorrow.

"What's that?" he asked, unable to stop himself.

"Pocketknife," Charlie responded. "Every boy I know likes looking at 'em. Your boy's no exception." He smiled down at the top of Nate's head.

Albert harrumphed, and headed for the door. He skimmed down the stairs, a million thoughts prickling his mind, and hoisted the last trunk up onto his shoulder, thinking that would be a little easier than lugging the cumbersome item out in front of him.

Chase gave a smile. "Thanks. We've been delivering these all over town. I'm just taking a breather."

And here Albert had thought—

On his trip down for the food, he found Susanna in conversation with Chase.

He pulled up short, his heart painfully striking his ribs. He'd always believed a pounding heart was an old wives' tale; now he knew better.

He went to remove his hat before he remembered he wasn't wearing one. He dropped his hand feeling like a fool. "Susanna."

She smiled and her eyelids lowered briefly. They hadn't been so shy around each other in ages.

"Albert, if this isn't a good time, I can stop by tomorrow."

He put out a hand. "No, it's fine. Chase and Charlie were just delivering Nate's traveling trunks, but they're leaving." Charlie, Nate, and Ivan descended the stairs.

Susanna's gaze went straight to the boy. How would they have this important conversation with Nate in the middle of it?

Chase nonchalantly pointed with his hat toward the hotel. "I'm just on my way over to the restaurant. Jessie and a few of the other ladies are delivering foodstuffs that Hannah has prepared to some of the homes." He lifted the plate. "Sarah and Shane are there too. Why don't I take your boy with me for an hour or so now that Charlie and I are finished with the trunks?" He looked from face to face. "I'm sure he'd like to meet some children his own age."

Not a bad idea, Albert thought. Sarah, the cutie pie that she was, was sure to befriend Nate and make him feel at home.

"When I dropped Jessie off, Markus was there as well. He's another one Nate would like to meet. They look to be about the same age."

He'd like more time to be acquainted with his son, but right now he had to square things away with Susanna, as best as he could. Maybe his transition to a new town would be easier for Nate once he had a few friends.

Albert crouched down. "Would you like that, Nate? To meet some other boys and girls your age? I think Mr. and Mrs. Logan could use your help. It'll only be for a while."

Nate nodded, his face still a stony mask. He was probably getting used to being passed off like an unwanted chore. Albert promised himself that he'd make it up to his son, if Nate would give him the chance. When Nate put his hand out to Chase, Albert's heart about broke in two.

Chase gave a smile after lifting his gaze off the boy. "Fine then. We'll be back here around eight o'clock tonight."

Seemed everyone knew their need to talk. Albert couldn't bring himself to meet anyone's eyes. "Thank you. Please thank the ladies for thinking of us," he said, gesturing to the food he now held.

He and Susanna watched them walk off. Ivan split off and trotted down the alleyway. Nerves had Albert feeling as if he were seventeen and this was his first talk with a girl. "I guess the only place that affords a little privacy would be my office."

"What about Thom?"

"He's on guard until nine when I take over. Let me run this plate upstairs."

She nodded. When he returned, they started off down the alley. The sun had disappeared behind the far hills. Albert paused to look across the saloon porch to the bank to check on Thom sitting peacefully in a chair with Ivan at his feet.

Albert opened the door to the still-warm jailhouse, envying Thom's peace of mind when his own world was all but falling apart. He didn't bother lighting any lamps, even in the darkening town. He gestured to a chair in back by the stove. "Would you like to sit?"

She shook her head, crossing her arms over her chest.

"Please, Susanna. We can't talk with you looking like a wooden soldier."

Relenting, she crossed the room and took a chair, then arranged her skirt and shawl. The hurt in her eyes was evident.

He took the chair beside her, feeling anything but relaxed. These next few minutes could determine the direction of his life.

"How's Nate taking things?"

"He's confused and scared, even if he's not saying so directly. He hasn't accepted that his mother is gone. Keeps saying she's trapped inside the train and wants us to go get her out."

Her face fell. "That's horrible. I didn't know."

Albert nodded. "I think I have to take things slow and easy."

"I understand."

Did she? Her tone was one he'd never heard before—strong, resolute. He'd better be prepared for the worst. She sounded as if she'd come to a decision. They stared at each other. He wanted in the worst way to spell out this whole horrible mess for her, point by point. But now that Floria was dead and lying in that coffin, that just didn't feel right. Speaking ill of the dead went against the grain. Albert refused to vilify his son's mother to anyone. Even Susanna. He never wanted anything to get back to Nate, and the best way to be sure that didn't happen was to keep quiet about the things she'd done. The boy would have enough challenges coming to grips with losing her and gaining a father he'd never met. As far as Albert was concerned, Floria's past had died when she did, and was now buried in the pinewood box in the cemetery.

If Susanna loved him the way he hoped, they'd be able to get past this. "Susanna, I'm not exactly sure how to begin. Where to start. I know I was in the wrong by not telling you sooner, but I was in an incredibly tight spot."

She crooked her brow.

"I'm still in an incredibly tight spot?"

She nodded.

What did he expect of her? Susanna wondered, working to temper her agitation. They'd never had a formal understanding, but that hadn't stopped the entire town from thinking of them as a couple. She felt for the awkward position in which he found himself, but wasn't it a bed of his own making? He should have been honest with her from the start. This was a betrayal of the worst kind.

Her mother's warning rumbled through her. *Mark my words or else you'll end up exactly like me, penniless and alone, alone, alone . . .*

"What do you expect me to do, Albert? Pretend nothing has happened? Nothing has changed? Pretend this day is like the many that have gone before? Because if that's what you're hoping, I can't—and I won't. I've been searching my heart since leaving you today. Honesty is important to me. Without it, trust can't survive. Without trust, love is impossible."

A burst of raucous laughter sounded from somewhere outside. Probably the saloon. In that instant, Susanna was transported back to the old days in Breckenridge where she'd been looked down upon, mocked, and made fun of—not by everyone, but enough of the young women her own age that made doing anything in town a risk of being teased. Were her friends here laughing behind her back tonight? Was Albert? She'd trusted him, and had been starting to think her mother was just a bitter old woman who'd made a mess of her life.

Albert dragged his chair around to face her. "Please, Susanna. I hope you'll believe I never meant to hurt you."

Could he see her trembling heart? "You never promised me anything either, Albert."

"Don't say that! I enjoyed your company—and let you know I did. That *was* wrong. I admit that. I looked forward to our time together, lunches, walks, spending time with friends. I married Floria when I was twenty-four years old. She was nineteen. We had our differences and went our separate ways."

Susanna struggled to put the pieces of what he was saying into perspective.

"Some things just couldn't be said. It wouldn't be right. I wasn't a free man to court you."

Stunned at what he'd implied, she gaped at him. "Are you saying that up until today"—she poked one finger into the palm of her other hand—"you were still a married man?"

His Adam's apple bobbed. "Yes."

For some reason, since they were living so far apart, she'd assumed they were no longer married. That they had obtained a legal dissolution.

Albert wiped his hand across his drawn face. "That actually felt good. I'm so thankful it's finally out in the open. I didn't know anything about Nate until this afternoon. It's still hard for me to believe I have a son. That's one thing I'm not ashamed to admit."

Yes, anyone could see he was happy about Nate. She tried to stand, but he took her wrist and tugged her back down.

She pulled away and gripped the arms of the chair. "You never thought your marital status might be a problem for me? You never suspected I might have strong feelings about it?" She looked away. What a fool she'd been! "But then how can I be upset. We've never spoken our intentions for each other. Never shared words of love."

"Of course I knew it would matter to you! I've been trying for years to get a divorce. I wanted to have it in my hands before I broached the subject. I was scared. I can't ask you to understand, but I can say that when I came to Logan Meadows, and before you arrived, I was hurting in the worst way. I just wanted to be left alone to sort out my life. That said, I truly believed my past wasn't anybody's business but my own. I wanted to start fresh, build something new and good. I never intended to ever fall in love again. Then you showed up. But by that time, everyone already believed I was single by default. I didn't have a wife, and never spoke of anyone. I just never corrected their unspoken assumptions. If that's wrong, then I'm guilty as hell."

His earnest brown eyes searched hers, forcing her to look away.

"You and I became friends," he continued, his tone not quite so hopeful. "I've wanted to tell you a thousand times, and as a matter of fact I've tried, but you never wanted to listen. After the accident I realized how fast things could change. I was bound and determined to get the ugly mess off my chest, and let the cards fall where they may—trusting enough in our feelings—our love—that you would somehow understand. But you shut me down before I could even get started, like you have many times before."

A spark of anger flashed inside her. He must have seen it, for he hurried on. "I'm not, in *any* way, saying you're at fault for not listening. I just want you to know I had good intentions. I wanted to tell you. I didn't like misleading you."

Susanna's heart jerked painfully in her chest. She'd thought she was ready to hear this, but she'd been wrong. All those times she'd believed he was about to profess his love, he really just wanted to clear the air.

Albert picked up both her hands, rubbing his thumbs across the top. "I want to start fresh. Court you like I've wanted to from the beginning. Get married and build a life together."

She stared at him silently, when she really wanted to pitch a fit, scream in his face, walk out the door, and never return. How could he think anything could ever be the same?

Someone crossed in front of the picture window out front, making the dim interior of the office darken a bit more. Albert glanced up. His eyes narrowed at the man gazing in, probably thinking the office deserted. They were far enough back by the woodstove that they wouldn't be seen without a lamp burning.

Albert straightened. She could tell she'd lost his attention by the expression on his face.

"What?" she asked.

"Nothing," he replied without taking his eyes off the man who meandered on his way.

"Do you know him?" Susanna had been around long enough to interpret Albert's tones and expressions. He felt personally responsible for the welfare of the citizens of Logan Meadows.

Albert shook his head. "No. Never seen him before now. But, never mind him. You were saying?" His eyes took her measure when he glanced back at her.

"I know you, Albert. You want to go see who that is."

His face softened. "Thank you. I do. I'll make a quick walk down the street and check on Thom. This time of evening, between nightfall and darkness, always has me on edge." He looked at her hands, still held in his own. "Will you wait for me?"

She nodded.

"You won't be frightened for a few minutes alone? I'm only going to walk down the block to the El Dorado and come back. Just to make my presence known."

"I'll be fine, Albert." Her heart squeezed as it did every time he was about to risk his life. "Please be careful." There. They were back on familiar footing.

He took out his gun and checked the chambers. Finished, he holstered it and stood. "Always."

CHAPTER TWENTY-SIX

*A*lbert carefully closed the door behind him. He didn't want to alert anyone who might be planning something heinous, like a shoot-out and robbing the bank. The piano music, mixed with the laughter of a group of men drinking in the Bright Nugget, covered the sound of his boots. At the batwing doors, he glanced inside. Several regulars sat at the bar, along with faces he didn't know and some he recognized as new arrivals. Wallace Sadler, the father of the boy that Dalton had helped on the train and whom Dalton had introduced Albert to yesterday, while the man was taking a stroll with his wife and son, sat at a back table alone. Nothing unusual, so Albert moved on as Thom watched his approach.

"Everything all right?" Albert asked quietly. He edged up close and scanned the other side of the street. The guard across the way stationed in the alley between the haberdashery and bakery was just a shadow against the wall.

Thom, not one to wear a six-shooter, hefted the shotgun in his arms. "So far so good. Had a disconcerted feeling about a half hour ago. I've been on alert since."

Albert took a box of matches from his pocket and lit a match, holding it up. An answering signal replied a moment later, letting Albert know that his man across the street would keep a close eye out.

"I had some newcomer look into the sheriff's office a few minutes ago, then start down here. Susanna and I were by the stove, sitting in the dark, so he didn't see us. Gave me a funny feeling as well."

Thom nodded. "Things have been quiet up until now. A group in the saloon is carrying on. Other than that, I haven't seen anyone coming down the street in some time. I missed the fella you're speaking of."

"We can't know everyone. But I can make my presence known to anyone contemplating trouble. I'll walk down to the hotel, but return down the backside of the buildings in the alley. Take a look around there."

When a man tumbled out through the saloon doors and rolled into the street, Albert spun. He had his gun drawn before he recognized ol' drunk Clyde, lying on his back in a cloud of dust. Thom's shotgun was leveled at the man as well.

Kendall, the bartender, stepped out through the saloon's swinging doors, wiping his hands on a bar towel. "You best go home and sleep it off, Clyde. I won't stand for you harassing the clientele, you know that."

Clyde struggled to a sitting position as a horse came up the street and stopped in front of the establishment he'd just been thrown out of.

The rider looked down. "Clyde."

"Dwight Hoskins. The bad penny returns," Thom whispered to Albert. Dwight was the man whose job Thom had taken after solving a cattle-rustling case some time back. Dwight had moved away to New Meringue in disgrace, but seemed to miss Logan Meadows and came back often.

Dwight dismounted and looped his reins around the hitching rail. Just as he was about to go into the saloon, he turned his head and noticed them watching. Albert wondered if Thom was experiencing the same thing: that disconcerted feeling had returned.

"Albert," Dwight called, meandering over to the bank porch where Albert and Thom stood. It wasn't quite dark enough yet to hide the smirk that twisted his lips. He had a standing hatred for Thom, and more pointedly, Thom's Irish blood.

"Dwight," Albert responded. "What brings you to town?"

"Just coming over to offer my help. News of your plight is all over New Meringue." He glanced at the bank, then at Thom. "Also wanted to check on Markus. See how my young nephew is doing."

Albert felt Thom straighten. Dwight knew mentioning Thom's stepson was a sure way to pull his deputy's strings.

"Markus is no concern of yours, Hoskins," Thom said, his grip on the shotgun tightening. "And stay away from Hannah. She has no desire to see you now, or ever."

"That's a pretty strong reaction for just wanting to see Caleb's son, God rest his soul. I do have a right to check on my nephew. What aren't you saying, Donovan? Maybe Hannah finally sees the error of her ways tying herself to an Irishman."

Thom surged forward but Albert grasped his shoulder. Thom's muscles quivered with fury. "Let it go, Thom. He's just trying to get your goat. You should know better by now."

An angry hiss passed through Thom's clenched teeth. "I put up with a lot from him, Albert. I don't mind when it's about me, but I won't have him speaking about *my* family, in *any* way. If you bother Hannah at all, you'll be sorry, Dwight. Do I make myself clear?"

Dwight laughed. Albert wouldn't be able to hold Thom back if the troublemaker kept it up much longer.

"Be honest, Hoskins," Thom growled. "You've ridden over because you're as curious as the next man about all that money."

"I'd be lying if I said different. A million dollars doesn't land in town every day. I'd like to see what it looks like. How's Frank taking the stress? I'm sure he's a mess of nerves. He never is good under pressure."

The bank door opened. Frank stepped out looking calm and cool. He locked the door behind him and slipped the key into his pocket. "I'll answer that question, Dwight. I'm taking the situation in stride. No one has stepped even an inch out of line, but that won't stop me from feeling relieved when the money is finally out of my bank and on its way."

Dwight had the decency to sputter his embarrassment at being caught in the act of besmirching the banker. He coughed into his hand. "Sorry, Frank, I didn't mean any disrespect."

"Only to Thom." Frank's tone had turned as hard as steel.

Dwight rocked back on his heels, and shrugged. "Maybe. You taken to sleeping in the bank these days?"

"I have. An extra layer of protection. Does that surprise you?"

As if knowing he was outnumbered, Dwight took a small step back. "Nope. I guess I'd do the same." He glanced across the street where darkness was now complete except for a lantern here and there. "You have a man in the alley, Albert?"

"We do."

Dwight nodded, as if pleased he'd one-upped Albert by knowing where his second guard was stationed. "I was hoping to get to meet Babcock. I've heard a few things about him."

So, Dwight's real reason for the visit to Logan Meadows was flushed out. "Stick around long enough and you'll get that pleasure." Babcock's name reminded him about Susanna waiting in the sheriff's office. He'd been gone longer than he'd intended already. He needed to get back.

Dwight turned. "Well, I'll be going. Need to wet the back of my throat."

Albert waited until Dwight pushed through the saloon doors. "I'm going to take a quick walk down the street and back. Are you going out, Frank?"

"Just to make a trip to the necessary. I'll be locked up inside before you return."

Albert gave Thom a nod, then walked away. The tension in town was growing. If a gang of outlaws came up against the bank now, his small army of guns might not be able to hold them off. People would be killed. He'd be glad when reinforcements showed up.

At the end of the street, Albert glanced into the hotel window. A few people relaxed in the lobby chairs reading, but paid him no mind.

Releasing a sigh, Albert circled around the building and started back toward his office. On his right, the lights in the community center glowed softly and he wondered who was tending the patients.

A movement in the shadows ahead made him stop abruptly. He edged nearer to the wall of the mercantile. Someone was behind the Bright Nugget or maybe even closer. In the darkness it was difficult to tell. The hum of low voices reached him, but he couldn't make out the words. Drawing his weapon, he proceeded, placing his boots carefully. The dry ground would amplify any sound. Staying close to the buildings, Albert slowly made his way forward.

CHAPTER TWENTY-SEVEN

*P*acing back and forth across the darkened office, Susanna didn't like the direction her mind had wandered. Until today, Albert had been a married man. A married man! That was his wife on the train coming here, not a sister, or aunt, or guardian. No, he'd never kissed her, or whispered love words into her ear, but she'd felt his attraction, and let him see hers. Why was the woman on that train? They hadn't gotten to that question before he'd left to walk the street.

Anger mixed with a deep, abiding hurt threatened to engulf her. What should she do now? Was he just like the men who'd used her mother? That couldn't be. She didn't like to think it of him.

He's a widower now, free and clear. Did that change her feelings at all? The immensity of the lie of omission he'd perpetrated loomed between them. No wonder he hadn't been in a hurry to marry her. What a fool she'd been.

Feeling lower than the day she'd boarded the stage for the unknown, she glanced at the clock behind Albert's desk. Twenty minutes had elapsed. How long did it take to walk down to the hotel and back? Surely not this long. Most likely he and Thom had gotten to talking, and he'd lost track of the time. When he was sheriffing, time could stand still.

Exhaustion pulled at every fiber of her being. Her eyelids felt as heavy as horseshoes, and her muscles ached. All she wanted to do was don her well-worn nightgown and crawl into bed and sleep for a week. Then she would forget about Albert and the mess that had descended. The only thought that brought a smidgeon of relief was the boy. Nate was the spitting image of his father.

Agitation moved her to the window. The street was dark, but across the way, lamps were lit in the upstairs windows of the haberdashery and the bakery. Deciding her exhaustion couldn't be put off another second, she went to Albert's desk. She pushed a few papers aside until she found a blank sheet. Sitting, she picked up a pencil.

Albert,

I'm sorry, but I couldn't keep my eyes open a minute longer and had to go home. At this point, I have to say I don't believe I'll be able to get over this. I think it's better and easier for everyone concerned if we call this goodbye.

Once her words started to flow, it was difficult to stop. Was this what she really wanted? There would be no going back.

Please respect my feelings. It will be hard enough living in the same town without going over ground we have already covered. But please know, I will always be your friend, and want what is best for you. If you ever need help with Nate, you can count on me.

Her hand hovered over the spot where she would usually sign, "With deep affection."

Making a decision, she just signed her name, knowing Albert would notice the absence of her usual affectionate closing and be hurt. She didn't want to hurt him, but she didn't know what else to do. He'd injured her beyond repair and she just couldn't go back to things as they used to be.

She stood, went to the window, and again took in the darkened street. The distance home was very short. There was not wind, or storm, or anything to be frightened of. Tabitha Canterbury's new bookstore, to the right of the sheriff's office, was closed, but Tabitha would be upstairs where she lived.

Her decision made, Susanna squared her shoulders and opened the door. She slipped out of the building and had already pulled the door closed when a man came out of the alley and blocked her way. Her heart bounced around painfully in her chest as she pulled up short.

"Whoa, there."

In the murky darkness, she recognized Dalton's voice immediately.

He stepped back, giving her plenty of room. He glanced over her shoulder. "What're you doing in a dark sheriff's office?" Several seconds of silence passed. "Or shouldn't I ask?"

She straightened. "I'm alone," she answered quickly. "Albert was here a little while ago, but had to go out. What are you doing back here? I thought you were dead on your feet and were going to get some much-needed sleep?"

He stepped forward and dropped his voice. "I'm worried about the money. There's something in the air, and I don't like it."

She glanced over to the place he'd appeared from. "In the alley?"

"Anywhere, really. But, now that I've had a look around, I'm ready to get back to Frank's house. Are you going to your place? Let me walk you."

She was too conflicted to walk with Dalton. Writing that note had been the right thing to do, but it still hurt. "No, thank you, Dalton. I don't mind walking alone. It's just over the bridge."

"Don't be so prickly. I'm going that way anyway, may as well go together." He bumped her shoulder with his. "Tomorrow things will look better in the light of day."

She smiled for the first time in an hour. He'd picked up on her feelings and was trying to lift her spirits. He was right, things always did seem better come daybreak. Amazing, but true. She relented, and they walked together in front of the bookshop, the fresh-cut lumber still scenting the air. "I love this little shop," she said, glancing in the window. "It adds a certain charm to Main Street that's been lacking until now. I hope any new buildings constructed from now on will be as cute as this one."

Dalton glanced down at her, a smile playing around his lips. "I haven't been inside yet, although I have noticed the nice displays in the window. The woman waves to me when I walk by."

Susanna laughed. "I hope Tabitha will be able to make a go of it. I don't know what kind of demand there will be for books in a small town like Logan Meadows." She was careful to keep her voice low.

"Maybe she has deep pockets," Dalton offered in all seriousness.

They were directly in front of the store and Susanna shushed him. "Be quiet. She might have her upstairs windows open."

He chuckled. "What I said isn't a bad thing. Maybe her parents left her a fortune to play with, so she built her heart's desire, not caring if it ever turns a profit."

Before he could make matters worse, Susanna grasped his arm and dragged him forward several steps past any open windows, to the beginning of the bridge. "Stop talking about her," she scolded. "She may hear you. I don't like it when others talk about me, so I do my best to keep to my own business."

He pointed to himself in mock innocence.

Susanna couldn't stop a little laugh from escaping. It felt good to redirect her thoughts to something completely different than her troubles at hand. She went to the edge of the bridge and looked over, something she hadn't done in a very long time. The water splashed over a little rocky ledge, then hurried on its way.

Dalton gaped at something in the stream. "Did you see that trout? Where's my fishing pole when I need it?" He was leaning so far over she feared he might fall in headfirst. She grasped his arm and pulled him back.

"You made that up," she laughed. "You didn't see a fish. Trout don't swim at night."

"What makes you think that? They don't have a little house to go home to when the sun goes down, with a small woodstove and comfortable bed." He turned to face her, tipping up her chin with his finger. His smile faded as he silently gazed into her eyes. Suddenly he looked rather serious. "I like it when you smile like that, Suzie. 'Bout the prettiest thing I've ever seen."

She knew she should put a stop to his flirtations. Gazing up into his earnest eyes, she could almost forget the duplicity she felt from Albert. But instead of telling him they had no chance together, she took two steps back. His hand fell, but he gave her a smile anyway.

Over his shoulder, she spotted Win in the doorway of his livery, a bridle in one hand and a rag in the other. His brows were pulled down as he watched them. Feeling as if she'd been caught doing something wrong, she waved a greeting to Albert's brother. He nodded and smiled in return.

They turned right off the bridge and walked along until they arrived at her house. "Good night, Dalton. I hope you get the rest you need." Frank's house was just a little past Hannah and Thom's on the opposite side of the street.

"I'll be as good as new tomorrow, so don't worry about me. It's you who has been going nonstop."

She nodded, her thoughts straying back to Albert—always Albert. Was he all right? He'd said he'd be back. She hoped she hadn't acted hastily in not waiting for him a little longer. As much as his actions hurt her, she never wanted anything to happen to him.

CHAPTER TWENTY-EIGHT

*A*lbert's head snapped up from his desk when Win barreled through the door of his office at seven o'clock the next morning. His brother's face, uncharacteristically red, made Albert wince. Win smacked his hand on the mahogany desktop, making Albert jump.

"What in tarnation?" Albert snapped. He jerked his thumb to the side, directing Win's attention to the back wall where Nate sat with a plateful of hotcakes and bacon they'd picked up from the Silky Hen ten minutes before.

"Sorry," he whispered angrily, coming close so Nate wouldn't hear. "But I can't help it. Are you just going to sit there and do nothing? Let Dalton Babcock steal Susanna away?" Win glowered at him with a face full of stubble that needed shaving. "Well, are you? Because if you are, you're not the brother I thought you were." It hadn't taken more than a few sentences to bring his ire back up to full force.

So, that was it. This whole mess with Susanna was spreading like wildfire. "Getting a mite personal, aren't you, Win? What side of the bed did you get up on this morning? Surely not the right one."

"Go on and make it into a big fat joke. I'm not the one who's going to be crying in my beer when Babcock up and carts her off."

"I've hurt her badly, Win. That's not something she'll be able to get over quickly, if ever." He glanced down at the folded note he'd read at least twenty times when he'd found it last night after coming in from his check of the town. Whoever it was behind the saloon had skedaddled when they heard him coming.

Win grunted. "That's codswallop."

"And another thing about Susanna Robinson. Nobody carts her off against her will. That woman has a mind of her own, and no man will make it up for her. If she wants to go with Babcock, I can't stop her."

"You can bloody well tell her the reasons you left your man-loving, unfaithful, lying wife behind."

Heat rose up into Albert's face. He struggled not to get irritated with his brother who was only trying to do what he thought best. "How do you know I haven't already?"

"Because I know you! You're too upstanding, you're—"

Albert straightened in his chair, letting Win know with a glower he was coming very close to subjects better left alone. "Keep your voice down! I'm *not* upstanding. If I were, I wouldn't be in the trouble I'm in now. But let me be perfectly clear: Susanna should love me for me, and forgive me for me. Her decision shouldn't have anything to do with Floria's actions. Or my reasons for leaving her. I won't try to gain back Susanna's love by tarnishing the reputation of Nate's mother—even if it is the truth. I could have spoken up sooner, but I didn't. If Floria's immoral ways stay between you and me—Nate will never find out."

Win wasn't backing off. "You damn well—"

"Watch your language, *Uncle* Win."

A look of wonder washed over Win's face, and he seemed to calm down straightaway. "How's the little fella doin'?" he asked. "I still can't get my head around the idea that you have a son—and I have a nephew. That's big, Albert. Really big."

Albert smiled at the sound of wonder in his brother's voice. "I know, Win," he teased. "Actually, I think he's doing pretty good. Chase and Jessie kept him overnight for me. He fell asleep in their buggy, so they took him to their ranch. After supper, they tucked him in next to Sarah, and Chase rode all the way back to town to let me know. Then first thing this morning, Chase brought him into town on the back of his horse. Nate couldn't have been happier. I'm grateful they did so much to make him feel at home." *But from this moment on, I'm seeing to all his needs.*

The starch left Win completely. "That's good to hear," he said in a contemplative tone. "Because he can always stay with me too, if need be. I'm amazed Corey never discovered Floria had a child. After all these years, it's pretty astonishing."

"Well, he only went to check on her when I asked him. It wouldn't have been too difficult to keep the secret, being they lived a distance apart. And she moved twice, putting him through his paces to find her."

Finished with his breakfast, Nate walked over with his cup and plate, a milk mustache under his nose. He still wore the same clothes he had on yesterday at the cemetery. Albert smiled and reached out, taking the boy's empty plate. Nate set his cup on the desk.

"You remember your uncle Win?" he asked. Win smiled, and took a small step toward the boy. "We were at his place yesterday to see the buffalo."

Nate's expression, so much like Floria's, caused a rush of culpability in Albert.

Nate nodded. "Sure. He has the big barn with lots of horses. By the creek with the frogs."

Pride swelled Albert's chest. They'd seen the creek, but not mentioned frogs at that time. He'd have to take Nate down there soon. Hunt up some large bullfrogs. The thought brought a surge of pleasure that chased away the responsibility he was feeling over the boy and how things had turned out with his mother. Surprisingly, Nate hadn't mentioned Floria once this morning.

"That's right," Win said. "You can come over any time I'm there. Play with the barn cat."

Nate darted a questioning look at Albert. His angelic smile was almost Albert's undoing. "That's right. You're going to be spending a lot of time there when I have work to do. You'll pay attention and not get into the buffalo pen, though, correct?"

"Yes, Pa."

Win hid his smile behind a large hand, and Albert could almost swear his brother had tears in his eyes.

Nate looked between them while he balanced on one foot. "Want me to take the plate and cup back to the restaurant?"

"That's all the way at the end of the block," Win replied. "How about if I walk down there with you?"

"I ain't no baby." Nate strolled over to the front window and looked out. "I can walk down the street by myself." He watched a couple of horsemen ride past, then looked at Win over his shoulder, no smile in sight. "But I don't mind if you come along."

"That's a good idea, Win. I have a few more reports to write. Do you mind taking Hannah's dishes back to her?"

With Nate still watching the street, Win leaned in closer. "Not at all, but first I have something to tell you. The reason I busted in here so angry this morning is because last night Babcock walked Susanna home in the moonlight. They stopped to lollygag on the bridge. If the way she was giggling like a schoolgirl has anything to do with it, I'd say she was enjoying herself a lot. I'm telling you, Albert, if you don't do something quick, you're going to lose her." He pointed a finger in Albert's face. "And this isn't the first time, either. He's been friendlying up to her for a few days."

"As much as it hurts me to say this, Win, you have to let it go." He hated voicing the words, but what else could he do? She'd made her intentions perfectly clear in her note. Still, if truth be told, the thought of Babcock walking her home made his insides twist with jealousy. Could one of the shadowy figures he'd seen in the alley last night behind the saloon have been Babcock? Plotting something Albert could arrest him for? The timing was perfect. Oh, he'd like it to be Babcock, yes sir, he would.

Nate sauntered back from the window and stopped by Win's side. He gazed at Albert with an unreadable expression. "I want to see my ma." His voice was shallow, and void of emotion. When Albert didn't answer, his eyes glassed over faster than Albert thought possible, and a moment later a tear streaked down one cheek.

Albert pushed out his chair and reached for his son. Nate hesitated when Albert tried to pull him into a hug, gazing into his eyes. "Are you my pa?"

Win scooped up the dirty plate and cup and backed out of the office, pulling the door closed behind him, leaving the two alone.

"Yes," Albert replied, a deep sadness tearing his gut. "I'm your pa, Nate. I'm not going anywhere."

Another tear slipped out. He dashed it angrily with the back of his small hand. "How come Mama said I didn't have a pa? Then later, she said I did and that I was going to live with him?"

How confusing for the boy.

By now, Nate's small face had crumbled with the grief he'd been trying to hold in. His sorrow had finally caught up with him. It only took a tiny tug from Albert to bring him into his arms. Nate buried his face against Albert's neck, and his body rocked with the first quiet whimper. That was followed by several larger sobs. "Shhh, now. Everything is going to be all right."

"Why?" Nate persisted.

"I don't know the answer to that, Nate. I wish I did. There's no telling why she told you those things. But I can promise you this: if I'd know about you before, I wouldn't have left you behind."

Nate sniffed against his neck, the motion feeling like a stab in Albert's heart.

"Why won't you go to the train and let my mama out?" he asked in a tiny voice. "She's cold and hungry and scared. Then I could go home with her and leave you alone. Please go find her . . . Pa."

What should I say now? I don't know.

"Pa?"

Truth was the best medicine, or a modified version of the truth to ease him into the reality. "Your mother is not trapped in the train, Nate. She died with the others. I'm sorry. I wish I could bring her back—for you." And at that moment Albert realized that he spoke the truth. He'd take what came his way, if he could make it easier on his boy.

The door opened and Susanna entered. Her dress, a cobalt blue, with a tight fitted waist and puffed sleeves, was one of his favorites. It made her look like a princess going to the ball. She was halfway to his desk before she realized Nate was in his arms, and the child was crying. She slowed, then inched to a stop. "Please forgive me for intruding." She turned.

"Don't go!"

A torrent of gladness at seeing her rushed through Albert. He hadn't expected her to intentionally seek him out this soon, if ever. The note she'd left him had said it all. Now, like a miracle, here she was not twelve hours later.

Susanna's face softened as she looked at Nate in his arms. "Albert? Is there anything I can do to help?"

"Can you stay a little while? Just sit here next to me." He gestured to a chair alongside him that he'd pulled up earlier for Nate.

She walked forward and lowered herself into the chair. A moment later she laid her hand on Nate's back.

At the soft touch, the boy lifted his head.

"Nate spent the night with the Logans, Susanna. I'm very, very proud of him." Albert couldn't stop himself from tightening his hold on the boy. How he wanted to take the pain from him. "Chase said he conducted himself with very good manners."

Nate had stopped crying but didn't seem in any rush to move away. His head rested on Albert's shoulder as he gazed at Susanna and listened to his pa's voice. He sniffed and rubbed his eye with a fist, prompting Albert to pull his handkerchief out of his pocket and give it to his son.

Susanna smiled. "That's wonderful news. I'll bet you had fun. And I've brought you and your father some good news."

You forgive me and want to get married? "Good. We could use some."

"I ran into Maude a little while ago. The house is yours if you want. It's ready, and you can even move in today. As you know, it has all the large pieces of furniture that you'll need."

"That's a relief. I've been pondering that for most of the night. This little fella could use some stability in his life."

"I thought you'd be happy." She glanced at her hands. "Well, that's what I came to tell you. I really should be going."

He didn't want her to leave. This simple conversation had lifted his spirits immensely. "Are you on shift with the patients?"

She gave a wan smile. "Actually, I have today completely off. Still, I'm going to check on Julia, see if she needs anything. Later I'll pick up the linen I left at Tap Ling's for Dr. Thorn. The poor doctor is still stretched pretty thin."

Albert narrowed his eyes. "What part of day off don't you understand? You're supposed to be resting. Why didn't you stay in bed for a few more hours?"

"I've never been one to sleep in."

A sad chuckle slipped out and she instinctively leaned forward. He wasn't playing on her emotions, he simply knew the truth to her words. Susanna was always the first to volunteer and the last to go home. Seemed she enjoyed working hard. "Well, I'd think at least one day you could call your own with nothing to do but relax."

When he picked up the note to draw her attention, her eyes widened. "I understand," he said. "I do. I'll respect your wishes. It's the least I can do for all I've put you through." He shrugged. "Just want to say I'm sorry it took me so long last night. It wasn't my intention. Dwight rode in and got to baiting Thom. I didn't want to see anyone come to blows."

She stood, and straightened her dress. "That's all right. I thought it must be something like that."

"I'm glad to hear Babcock walked you home. I don't like you out alone in the dark. I intended to see you home safely myself when I got back."

She blushed. Probably wondered how he knew about her and Babcock. Were they just going to let their relationship go to the wayside?

The door opened again, and Thom came in, Ivan at his side. The dog trotted up and sniffed at Nate, and Albert felt his son relax. A moment later, Nate squirmed down. Once on his feet, he lowered himself to his knees and buried his face in the dog's thick mane.

Thom smiled at Albert, as if he knew just how medicinal that could be. He held a telegram.

"From the Union Pacific?" Albert asked.

Thom handed him the paper. "Just came in. Representatives should arrive on tomorrow's stage."

Albert felt Susanna inching toward the door as business as usual seemed to push her out once again. He raised his brows in question. "Do you have to go?"

She nodded. "I don't want Julia to worry. I promised her I'd visit. She doesn't have anyone else now that her aunt has passed on."

Thom kept his attention on Ivan and Nate as Albert said goodbye to Susanna, feeling like he'd truly lost her. That was something that would take some time to get used to. He'd contemplated what this day would feel like when it arrived. Now he didn't want to live it.

"I appreciate you bringing me the news about the house. If you see Maude before I do, please tell her I'll stop by sometime today and pick up the key." He glanced down at Nate and Ivan, then back at Susanna. "Living so close to other children, and boys in particular, will be good for him."

"Yes, you're right. You have a nice day."

Her tone, light and airy, as if she'd accepted the inevitable and had already moved on, scared him more than he wanted to admit.

CHAPTER TWENTY-NINE

$\mathcal{S}$usanna hurried toward the infirmary, trying to focus on anything besides Albert's words tumbling around in her head. *I hope you'll believe I never meant to hurt you. I'll respect your wishes. It's the least I can do for all I've put you through.* She sighed, pushing away the huge, painful knot of sorrow inside her breast.

He'd looked tired, and a bit old. She prayed their situation wouldn't distract him so much that he lost sight of the troubles at hand. She'd never want to put him in danger. As she rounded the corner, the infirmary came into sight.

Gabe came out the door, a cot hefted in his strong arms. He carried it to a buckboard parked in the shade, and stacked it in the back with others of the same. A patient, an older man, with his hand in the crook of his wife's arm, tottered away, clutching a bag of his belongings.

"Morning, Susanna," Gabe called as she approached.

"What's going on?" She could hear voices within, fueling her curiosity.

"Only one patient left. Dr. Thorn gave the other three their marching orders this morning and they pulled up stakes." He hitched his thumb over his shoulder at the retreating man and his wife. "We're breaking down the place. Brenna, Mrs. Hollyhock, and a couple other women are in the kitchen putting things to right."

"Oh. I best hurry before I miss all the fun."

He wiped his shirtsleeve across his moist brow, and chuckled. "You're right about that. It's coming down a heck of a lot faster than it went up."

She opened the door and stepped into the coolness of the large room, glancing around for Julia. Her friend must be the one patient left that Gabe had mentioned, but she wasn't in her usual spot, and her cot was packed up, too. Susanna started for the kitchen but slowed a few feet away from the door when she heard her name spoken.

"I can't believe how well Susanna is taking the situation. Seriously, a wife and son? I can tell you right now, I wouldn't be if I were in her shoes. I'd dress that sheriff down so fast his head would spin, and I'd do it in front of the whole town. Then at least I'd have reclaimed a smidgeon of my pride. How does one get over such a shock?"

Susanna's feet stilled, and humiliation burned deep in her gut. She *was* the laughingstock of the town. Roberta Brown's voice droned on and on. "Perhaps Susanna's feeling desperate. She's no spring chicken any longer and perhaps—"

"Roberta," Brenna interjected in a steady tone laced with steel. "Don't say another word. I'll have to ask you to leave if you can't control yourself. Susanna would be extremely hurt if she heard you."

"Brenna's as right as rain!" Susanna would recognize Mrs. Hollyhock's voice anywhere, especially as angry as it was now. The old woman's loyalty felt good.

"I'm just stating what everyone else is thinking . . ."

Unable to listen to Roberta for another second, Susanna stepped across the threshold of the kitchen door, a strange-feeling smile plastered on her face. Roberta snapped her mouth closed, and her eyes popped wider than if she'd just seen an apparition.

"I'm touched by your concern, Roberta. The last person I had the pleasure of thanking for looking out for me was Beth Fairington. You're both just too kind."

The dish Roberta was drying quavered in her hands. Susanna's words had hit their mark, and she was glad. She wasn't a victim, and didn't want to be made into one. Mrs. Hollyhock ducked her head as she scraped what was left of the wedding cake they'd been feeding to the patients into a bucket, probably intending to give the remainder to the hogs behind the butcher's barn.

"I *am* concerned, Susanna, even if you don't believe me," Roberta said softly, still trying to sell her point. "I've only spoken the truth. If you have any sense, you won't let that man—"

"Don't speak about Albert!"

Brenna rushed forward and put her arms around Susanna, giving her a brief hug. "Forgive us."

The news had been a shock to everyone's systems, not just hers. Roberta Brown, a reformed busybody of the worst sort if there ever was one, had slipped back into her old bad habit. Working at the restaurant, Susanna had actually become fond of Hannah's mother now that Roberta had opened her heart to Thom and others she'd held at bay for years. Susanna took a deep breath and slowly let it out. Holding a grudge would only hurt herself. "No harm done."

Gabe knocked on the doorjamb and then stuck his head inside the room. "I'm all finished out here loading the wagon. If you don't have anything else for me to do, I'll start returning the things to the households who lent them. That should take an hour or two— or three." He looked handsome as usual with his messy chestnut hair falling into his vivid green eyes. Susanna was always moved at what a sincere and responsible lad he was for his age. Maybe that came from losing his family when he was just a boy. He seemed not to notice the tension that still hung on the air.

"Nothing, Gabe, thank you so much for your help," Brenna said. He was just turning to leave when Susanna had an idea. Julia had been in her thoughts nonstop since yesterday. She was missing her aunt Biddy terribly, and there wasn't anything anyone could do about that. Susanna assumed she was sitting out back in the rock garden. As of today, Dr. Thorn had given her permission to go and do, if she felt up to it. "Can you hold up for just one minute, Gabe? I'll be right back."

He looked perplexed at the request. "Sure, Susanna, I don't mind. I'll wait out front at the wagon."

"Thank you. I'll only be a minute, I promise." She glanced at Brenna who still had a sheepish look on her face. Gabe ambled off, and a moment later the front door opened and closed.

"Is Julia out back?"

Brenna nodded.

Holding her head high, Susanna gathered what remained of her self-respect and left the room, happy to have someone or something else to think about besides her own troubles.

She spotted Julia immediately sitting in a chair among the moss-covered rocks and early spring flowers, her face raised to the sunshine. A gentle breeze moved the branches of the nearby oak and a folded plaid lap robe covered her legs. The sweet little smile playing around her lips was a welcome sight. Susanna wondered what she was thinking about. "Julia, you're feeling much better, I see," Susanna called.

Her eyes opened. "Susanna! You came!"

"I said I would, didn't I?"

Julia's eyes danced happily. "You did. But then Brenna said she'd forced you to stay home and take a day off, so I didn't think I was going to see you."

Susanna crossed the grass, thrilled at how different and strong her young friend looked in the fresh air and sunshine. She'd brushed her hair and let it lay across her shoulders. Her cast, as usual, was cradled by her good arm.

"The moment I awoke this morning, all the things I'd rather be doing popped into my head," Susanna replied. "And visiting you was on the top of my list. How does your arm feel?"

Julia lifted her cast. "I hardly have any pain to speak of. It's just clunky. I can get by."

"Wonderful. How do you like being outside? Are you feeling up to it?"

"Absolutely. I was just thinking about Aunt Biddy and my last birthday." Her smile wobbled, but she forged ahead. "We both dressed in our best Sunday dresses, donned our finest hats, and she treated me to high tea at the nicest restaurant in our town. I'll cherish that memory forever."

She unfurled the hankie in her palm and pressed it to the outer corner of one eye, then waved Susanna closer.

"What?"

"Come over here quietly," she whispered. "I want to show you something."

Julia pulled Susanna down to her level. Pointing east, she directed Susanna's line of sight. "Do you see it? Look though that clump of trees. There's a hawk sitting on the weathervane at the Red Rooster Inn. I've heard that if someone you love very much passes away, they can come back in the form of a hawk, to look after you and give you comfort."

"Aunt Biddy?"

"Yes." The answer was very soft. "I know it's her. The moment before you arrived, I was thinking about her with a heart so full of love it hurt. When I looked up, the hawk was there. It hadn't been there the second before."

Susanna remembered the hawk she'd seen the day of the funeral, hovering above the graves. *Could what Julia thought be true?* "She's come to check on you. And to tell you she's fine. Not to worry."

That seemed to please Julia, and she smiled. "I'm not daft."

"I don't think you are."

Susanna stood and Julia set the blanket covering her lap aside. She stood too, stretching out her muscles. "Mrs. Hollyhock has invited me over for tea whenever I feel up to it. I think I'm ready today." Her happy expression subsided, and she jerked her gaze away.

"What is it? What's wrong?"

"Nothing."

Susanna plopped her hands on her hips and gave Julia a withering stare. "Spit it out right now, young lady. You're as transparent as a newly washed window. I can see something is troubling you."

"I'm just worried about where I'll go now." She glanced over to the now-empty building.

"Susanna?"

At the sound of Gabe's deep voice, she swiveled around, as did Julia. He'd retrieved his hat in the wagon and held it in his fingers. He was tall and broad of chest, and incredibly nice. Handsome too. As far as Susanna knew, he wasn't sweet on anyone in Logan Meadows. "I'm so sorry to keep you waiting, Gabe." Susanna looked between the two young people. "Do you know each other?"

"Sure," Gabe said. "I've been in and out since the train accident."

Julia nodded a bit shyly.

"Of course, of course." She struggled to hide her smile. These two would make a darling couple. "Since you've been cooped up for days, Julia, I thought it would be nice for you to get out and see some sights. Gabe is set to make deliveries of the cots and such back to their rightful owners. I'm sure he'd wouldn't mind if you rode along. He could show you around and point out things of interest. You haven't seen anything of Logan Meadows since you arrived except the inside of the infirmary."

"I couldn't," the girl choked out. "I have to figure out where I'm going to go. I can't just sit here and pretend nothing has changed."

"That's easy. For now, there are rooms open in the hotel. You can stay there temporarily until we figure out what your next move should be. As a matter of fact, Gabe can drop you there when he's finished."

Gabe just stood there.

"Well, what're you waiting for?" Susanna gathered up Julia's lap blanket, took a gentle hold of the girl's good arm, and escorted her around the building before she chickened out. "Gabe has work to do and we don't want to hold him up any longer than we already have."

When they passed Gabe, his face pinker than the early blooms of shooting stars amongst the rocks, Susanna continued to hide her pleasure at playing matchmaker. He turned and followed along behind without an utterance of complaint.

CHAPTER THIRTY

One hour past noon, Dalton stood guard in front of the bank when a broken-down wagon rumbled across the bridge, two men on the front seat. Dalton stepped to the edge of the boardwalk and gripped the wooden post next to his face. When he realized who he was looking at, he felt more relief than he had since they'd locked the money trunks in the bank's vault. Pat Tackly!

The missing guard looked like he'd been roughed up and tossed into a dirt pit. When the wagon was within twenty feet, Dalton strode out to meet it. "Pat! You're alive!" The old man driving the rattletrap of a rig pulled it over to the side of the road.

Albert must have noticed the reunion in the street because he exited his office and hurried over in time to hear Dalton's words. "This Pat Tackly?"

Dalton nodded. Pat swayed, still looking weak. "What happened?" Dalton asked. "Where've you been? We've searched high and low for you."

The old man smiled, while the tremors of old age made his head softly bob. "I found this fella stumblin' down the road toward town and offered to bring him in the last couple of miles."

With his sunken yellow cheeks, and the nasty cut across his brow that was crusted over, Pat wasn't a pretty sight. "Pat?"

"Don't know exactly. I guess I was knocked out awhile. I woke up in a thicket patch in a pitch-black night with a pain in my head hurting so bad I could hardly see. I found the tracks, and started walking—in the wrong direction." He blinked in the bright sunshine and looked around. "What happened? Is the money safe?"

Dalton gave a wide smile. "Sure is. It's locked up in the bank."

"And Evan, what happened to him?"

"He's under the doctor's care, hanging on to his life by a thread," Dalton said. "He hasn't woken up. We're waiting on representatives of the bank to get here, to tell us how to proceed."

"So Evan never came around at all? Or said a thing?"

Dalton shook his head. "No. Nothing."

"How'd you get the money out?"

"Blasted the roof off," Dalton said.

As best he could in his weakened state, Pat looked Dalton up and down approvingly. "Ya done good then, Babcock. With me and Evan out of the picture, all the responsibility fell to your shoulders. I'd like to meet the bank owner, if I could," he said, "then I'd like two full plates of food."

"We'd be happy to oblige." Albert's tone was much more accommodating than Dalton had ever heard it.

Dalton helped Pat off the wagon as Albert went into the bank for Frank. He gave a quick scan up and down the street. He didn't want to be caught off guard. A moment later, Frank stepped through the door, his face concerned.

He put out his hand to Pat and they shook. "I'm glad you're alive, Mr. Tackly. Truthfully, we all had just about given up hope. Mr. Babcock said you're the head guard and in charge of the shipment of cash. I want you to know, the money is securely locked in my vault, where it'll stay until a proper way to transport it is worked out."

"It's a pleasure to meet you, Mr. Lloyd. We'd be in a real quandary if Logan Meadows hadn't had a bank. I guess for now, I can breathe easy knowing that the money can stay just where it is."

Frank smiled, then nodded at Albert. Seemed to Dalton, an unspoken meaning passed between the two men. Dalton didn't appreciate being kept out of the loop, and he let his expression mirror his feelings.

"Babcock," Albert said, "why don't you take Pat down to the restaurant and get him something to eat. I'll take over your shift until you get back."

"You have your boy to look after," Dalton replied cynically, still bent out of shape at how the sheriff had duped Susanna. "This is my shift. I'll fill Pat in with all the information when I'm relieved."

Albert shrugged. "Suit yourself. I'll just gather Nate up from inside and we'll head on down to the Silky Hen. I don't mind having a bite myself."

Now that Julia was taken care of for a while, Susanna intended to complete her last task quickly and then lose herself in the new bookstore. She entered the laundry house and tapped the bell.

Giggling came from the back room. An instant later, Lan raced into the counter area, a long piece of ribbon trailing behind her from one hand. When Tap Ling's young daughter saw Susanna, a smile curled her lips and she sprinted around the counter and hopped into her arms.

Her mother, Bao, was next to appear from the back room, her face a glossy pink. She stopped short when she saw Susanna standing there with Lan in her arms.

"Oh, Miss Robin-*son*, you surprise me!" She laughed and gave her daughter an I-will-deal-with-you-later look. Lan wiggled out of Susanna's embrace and dashed off once again into the back room.

"I hope she did not get you dirty," Bao said, looking over Susanna's dress. "That child keep me running."

"No, no, she's fine. I love that she's so comfortable with me. How're you? Are you keeping up? I'm sure everyone and their mother wants to have their things washed."

Bao fanned her face. The petite woman only came to Susanna's shoulder and her arms and wrists were as thin as a child's. "Yes. But Mr. Ling work hard."

Susanna knew that well. She also knew Bao worked just as hard by her husband's side. For the last four months, they'd been in the process of trying to bring the rest of Bao's family over from China. "What is the news on your sister and mother? Will they be arriving anytime soon?"

The happy expression slid off Bao's face. She glanced away, clearly upset.

"What? Has something happened?"

Bao walked to the front door and looked out as if checking to see that the coast was clear and they wouldn't be interrupted. "I no want anyone to hear," she said softly. Bao's regular speech was quite soft already so Susanna had to bend forward to hear what she was trying to say. "New law. Say no more Chinese."

"What? I haven't heard of this."

At Susanna's outburst Bao grasped Susanna's wrists and pulled her close, shushing her. "We not want more people to know. Law pass, say no more immigration from China. People who come after 1880 get sent home."

Fear streaked up Susanna's spine. Tap Ling had been in town longer than Susanna, so he was in no danger of being deported, but Bao and Lan had made the voyage last year to reunite with Mr. Ling.

"Oh, Bao! I'm so sorry about your family not being able to come—but more, I don't want anything to happen to you, or little Lan."

The woman bowed her head, dejected.

"It's not right! Maybe Albert can—"

"No! Promise you not speak of this to anyone. I am sad about family, but more, we do not wish to draw attention to us in any way. We work, eat, and stay out of sight. I don't want family split up."

Susanna took her friend's work-roughened hands between her palms. The strong lye had chafed them so much they were almost raw. "I understand. Your secret is safe with me. How horrible to live your life worried about deportation. I just don't understand people, I really don't."

Tap Ling came out of the back room, his hands filled with the laundry she'd dropped off Saturday morning. The items were pressed and folded in perfect squares. "Miss Robin-*son*, hello. Lan say her friend Miss Robin-*son* is here for her things."

Susanna chanced a quick look at Bao. "Yes, thank you." She went over and retrieved the heavy stack of bedding and towels as Mr. Ling gave a small bow and hurried away.

"You want help?" Bao asked. "That heavy."

Susanna shook her head. "No, I can get this." She gave her friend a long look. "Try not to worry, Bao. People love you. Things will work out." But as Susanna left and headed straight to Dr. Thorn's, she wondered if she was trying to convince Bao or herself. Her thoughts strayed to Albert, and the danger he'd perceived last night, and now this trouble for the Lings. Seemed she wasn't the only one in Logan Meadows who had problems—and deadly ones at that.

CHAPTER THIRTY-ONE

Wanting to get the move over with before the railroad men showed up and demanded all his time, Albert borrowed Win's buckboard from the livery and pulled it around the back of the sheriff's office where loading the wagon would be easier. He and Nate emptied as much of the smaller stuff as they could without help, then went and fetched Win to help load the sideboard, the only substantial piece of furniture Albert owned. The bed and dresser stayed with the apartment and was owned by the town for whoever held the sheriff's job. The last to go into the wagon were Floria's trunks. A burning curiosity needled Albert's mind, but not enough to move him to open that can of worms yet.

With everything in the wagon, Albert lifted Nate up onto the high seat, then climbed up after him. Gathering the wide leather reins, he pulled the team around to return to the alley road the way they'd come, then hit Main Street. "How do you like the town so far, Nate? Is it what you were expecting?"

The furrowed brow Albert was coming to know relaxed. Nate looked up into Albert's face. "Fine."

The boy didn't say much. Most of the time they sat in companionable silence, which didn't seem to bother Nate at all.

"I think we should'a stayed there. I liked lookin' out at the road."

"That may be, but above a jail and next to a saloon is no place for a boy to live. The new house has a family with children across the street. That'll suit you better."

"I don't want to play with no kids. I want to stay with you."

A surge of emotion squeezed Albert's throat. It stood to reason. He'd just lost his mother and probably thought he'd lose his pa next. Albert glanced down at the brown hair combed to the side and the boots that didn't yet reach the wagon floor. His son was a handsome lad, one he wouldn't trade for all the money in the world.

"Didn't you have fun with Sarah yesterday? And Markus? They seem like nice children."

"Sure." He shrugged. An echo reverberated when the wheels of the wagon hit the small bridge over Shady Creek. Nate's face lit up like Christmas. "I'd sure like ta go froggin'. More than anythin'."

Albert hid his smile. "I feel the same. We'll get to that just as soon as everything settles down in a few days. I still have business with the bank and train, but after that, we'll spend a day, or two, rounding up as many frogs as you want." Albert made a pointed decision not to look to the right, up the road to Susanna's small, three-room place.

"And fry 'em up in egg and corn batter?"

Albert had to laugh at that, surprised he'd remembered. "Yes, exactly that."

That got the boy's attention. "I can't wait. Ma hardly ever let me go froggin'. And she never tried herself. You will, though, right, Pa? You'll try to catch some frogs, too?"

"I will, son. As a matter of fact, I'm looking forward to it."

After crossing the bridge, it was only a short distance to Maude's rental house opposite Brenna and Greg Hutton's. He pulled the horses to a halt and set the brake. He knew their neighbors were home because he could hear a few voices coming from within. Still, he didn't feel inclined to knock on their door. People were still judging him. And why not? They loved Susanna, and were loyal to her, and he was glad about that. She'd need all the support she could get. Never before had he felt such censure in Logan Meadows, but he knew he had it coming. Things would ease up in time.

He climbed off the wagon, but before he could reach up to help Nate, the boy had crawled over the seat and jumped out the back into the dirt. Albert stifled his reaction to scold him, and tell him not to do that anymore. They'd get used to each other soon enough. May as well let the boy ease into it or else he'd have him bucking the reins from the get-go.

Albert looked at their new home from the street. "Well, what do you think? Can you be happy here?"

"It's yellow."

Albert almost chuckled. "It is. Anything wrong with that?"

"Yellow's a girl color."

"Says who?"

"Says Becky Cook. She has yellow dresses, ribbons, and dolls."

"Who's Becky Cook?"

"My friend. We play every day."

"I see." *Not anymore, poor little guy.* "I can live with yellow if you can, even if it is a girl's color." Albert went to the tailgate and dropped it down. He muscled the first trunk into his arms and carried it to the front porch. Taking the key from his pocket, he unlocked the door and pushed it open. Greg had lived here so recently, the house hadn't had a chance to get musty.

His new life. Without Susanna. He never thought it would come to this.

Nate scampered in, darted past him, and ran into the kitchen. Instantly he was back, looking into both bedrooms. "Where's the toilet room?"

Floria was sure to have had one of those pull-flush toilets in her house that he'd heard so much about. Some folks around here were thinking along those lines as well. "Outhouse 'round back."

When the boy's eyes lit up, Albert laughed again. "You like that?"

"Sure. Lots of lizards."

Nate stilled in the middle of the living room, his gaze glued to the watercolor portrait of a staunch-looking woman hanging over a brown corduroy couch. Her dark, beady eyes accented her narrow face. Her scowl would scare any little boy and perhaps some men as well.

Nate backed up until his legs touched the rectangular maple coffee table in the center of the room. Albert walked past and lifted the painting off its hook, leaving a dark square outline on the wall where the green wallpaper hadn't faded. "This can go under my bed for now."

When Albert returned, his son was still where he'd left him, round eyed, and smile gone. "She looks like mama. Can we go to the train now?"

Albert didn't see the resemblance at all, but that didn't mean Nate hadn't connected with something in the woman's expression. Albert remembered back to his childhood, when he was a boy and his favorite uncle had unexpectedly died from influenza. The priest had advised his mother to be sure her small boys spent some time viewing the body before the burial. Give them time to come to terms with the reality of losing their uncle. It was healing, and showed them that death was something real. After which, they wouldn't misunderstand, or think that their beloved uncle was just away and might return.

Nate hadn't had that opportunity. The last he'd been with his mother she was alive and well. No wonder he was so confused. It was time for the difficult conversation Albert had been dreading.

"Nate, have you ever had an animal that died?"

Nate's chin dipped down, and he avoided looking into his father's eyes. Perhaps he understood more than Albert thought.

He nodded. "Oldie Judy."

"Oldie Judy?"

"Mama's yellow cat. One day a dog took after her and chased her into the street. She was old and could hardly see nothin' anymore. A wagon ran right over the top of her."

Albert sat down on the sofa and pulled his son up next to him. "I'm sorry to hear that."

Nate's lower lip trembled. "Mama and Nana put her in a shoe box lined with leaves from the garden. I held the box while Mama dug a hole next to the rose bushes." His lips pulled down into a small frown as he recounted the tale. "When the hole was really deep, she put the lid on and set the box in the ground. We all helped put the dirt on top and Mama and Nana cried."

Nate's eyes glistened with unshed tears.

"I see." Shame for not being there for his son when he needed support pricked at Albert's conscience.

Nate shrugged.

"Then you know that Oldie Judy was dead, and she was never coming back, right? That's why your mother put her body in the box, so it could turn back to . . ." Maybe Nate didn't need quite that much information.

Nate nodded even though Albert hadn't finished the sentence.

"Well, it's the same with your mama. Yesterday in the cemetery, her body was in the casket that was lowered into the ground, but her soul is now in heaven, with Oldie Judy. I'm sure she's sitting somewhere in the sunshine with her cat asleep on her lap." He wasn't sure if animals went to heaven, but right now Nate needed something he could understand.

Nate gazed up at him listening. "And she's petting her warm fur?"

Albert nodded. "I believe so." He'd not been gifted with the strong virtue of faith like his mother had, but he did believe in the hereafter and heaven and hell. He attended church and said prayers now and then, even if it was just a glance up to the Almighty from the back of his horse. He had no experience speaking about God, especially with a son he'd just met. One who was grieving for a mother he'd just lost. "So then you understand that once her soul is up in heaven with God and Oldie Judy, it can't ever come back down to earth. You won't see her again until you die, and go to heaven, too."

Nate was avoiding his gaze once more. Albert wanted to be

sure his son had caught the jist of the conversation, without bela-boring the fact. "Right, Nate? You understand?"

He nodded. "Then I can pet Oldie Judy, too, even though she's dead."

Warmth flushed Albert's face as he gazed at the small person huddled by his side. "Well, not actually, son. In heaven she'll be alive. Here her body is . . ."

Nate lifted his face to Albert's. "I understand, Pa," he said, pat-ting Albert's leg. His confused expression said perhaps he'd made matters worse.

Albert sucked in a deep breath for having conquered the dif-ficult topic as best he could. Nate understood well enough for now. He wouldn't be talking about the train, and getting his mother out, any longer.

A rapping on the doorjamb drew Albert's gaze from Nate's face to the open front door. Greg Hutton, the schoolmaster of Logan Meadows, stood on the porch—one that had been his just a few days before.

"Are you renting the place, Albert?"

Albert couldn't tell if that was a smile or not. He hadn't seen Greg since the cemetery, and knew he was most likely full of ques-tions. "We are."

Nate stood, the sadness on his face replaced with curiosity.

Greg gave Nate a hospitable smile. "Well, welcome to our street. Can I give you a hand with the things in the wagon?"

Again, a surge of emotion moved Albert. He'd felt he was being judged by most everyone he saw. So far, most had treated him fairly.

"I can use a hand." He turned to Nate. "You stay out of trouble while we unload the wagon." It felt so natural, speaking with his son, as if he'd known him all his life.

Once back out on the road, Greg stopped him with a touch to his arm. "I'm sorry, Albert. If there's anything I can do to help, please let me know."

Albert wasn't sure of his meaning. The end of his and Susanna's relationship, or the death of his wife? It was a strange situation he was in. He decided he could live not actually knowing for sure. "I appreciate that, Greg. I'm just thankful to find this house empty and ready to be occupied. I'm taking it one day at a time."

Greg nodded. "That's all you can do. How old is your son? Will he be coming to school when we start back up?"

Albert let the April breeze waft over him, easing his heavy heart. It felt good, and calm. One way or the other, things would work out. They always did. They may not be to his liking, but then, he had to take the bad with the good. He smiled when he noticed Nate, his head barely over the bottom of the windowsill, watching them from the living room window. A blessing, to be sure.

"To tell you the truth, I'm not quite sure. I don't even know my own son's birthday yet. If he's of age, and capable enough to keep up, then I'll send him. As soon as I think he's settled." The sincerity in Greg's eyes bolstered his confidence.

Greg gave him a winsome smile. "Good. I was hoping you'd say that. You know, children are a lot more resilient than us adults. Give him a few days and he may surprise you."

"I sure hope so. Nate's having a difficult time accepting Floria's death. I'm not really sure how I should handle it."

The smile slipped off his friend's face. "He's young. And the accident is still so fresh in his mind. He's probably tussling with the fact that he was almost killed, as well. Give it time, Albert. Don't rush him. With your love and support, he'll come through, and be all the stronger for it."

If only he could believe that. Of all of the recent happenings, his worry over the boy, and his lack of knowledge, was what had his gut in a knot. He didn't want to make things worse than they already were. Albert reached into the back of the wagon and pulled the remaining two trunks to the end of the tailgate. He took one and Greg took the other.

Nate was sitting on the couch looking at a book that had been on the coffee table when they arrived. His eyes lit up when he saw the trunk Greg had in his arms. "That's my trunk," he all but hollered, jumping up. "Can ya bring it into my room?"

Albert cut an apologetic look to Greg. As soon as Nate started school, he wouldn't be directing his teacher around quite like that.

Greg just smiled. "Sure thing, Nate. I'd be happy to."

Albert set his load down in his own room and hurried to Nate's.

"Nice room you're going to have." The room was bare except for a small dresser and bed. "Where would you like me to set this?"

Nate took a sweeping look at his four walls. Cupped his chin in his fingers, tapping as he thought.

"How about Mr. Hutton puts it anywhere for now," Albert suggested. "Then as soon as we have everything inside, we'll find the perfect spot."

"Sure!"

Greg set the trunk by the wall, then went to the window that faced the back of the house. "Have you looked out here yet, Nate? Over that slight rise is a pond. My boys hunt salamanders down there."

Albert laughed at the excitement Nate could hardly contain. Yes, moving here had been a good decision.

The rest of his belongings came off the wagon much faster than they'd gone on. In fifteen minutes, he and Greg had everything inside, including the sideboard, which they found room for in the kitchen. The place came with its own set of brown-and-white Johnson Brothers dishes that were much nicer than the ones Albert owned. A few were chipped, but that wouldn't bother him and Nate. He left his own dishware packed up and shoved the box under his bed next to the dour-faced woman.

After some arranging, Albert and Greg glanced around satisfied. "I enjoyed living here," Greg said, a gleam of sentimentality in his eyes. "This is where Brenna and I fell in love. When she was nursing me back from my case of measles," he added quickly.

Albert slapped him on his back. "I remember that. You were sick as a dog for almost two weeks."

"Yes. I'd rather not remember *that* part of the past. I don't know what I would have done if I hadn't had a tenderhearted neighbor who wasn't afraid of hard work. She not only nursed me, but took care of her children, and taught school in my absence. I knew if I didn't snag her when I could, I'd regret it for the rest of my life." He glanced out the open front door to his and Brenna's house across the narrow dirt road.

Albert heaved a resolute sigh. "I hope this house holds as much luck for me as it did for you." He couldn't see Susanna forgiving him anytime soon. And Babcock was poised to swoop right in and pick up the pieces of her broken heart.

"Have faith, Albert."

Albert shrugged. May as well. He didn't have any answers.

"I best be going," Greg said. He gave Albert a stern glance. "Keep your chin up. Susanna will come around. She just needs a little time."

Albert gave an agreeable nod, even though he wasn't sure that what Greg said was true. "I appreciate the help more than you can know, Greg. And the friendship. I'm feeling pretty much like a leper these days. Say hello to Brenna."

As Greg descended the porch steps, Albert wondered at how fast his life had changed. In the span of a heartbeat, just like the train accident.

CHAPTER THIRTY-TWO

As the day was drawing down, Susanna went about her errands knowing this was the last free time she'd have to tie up the loose ends still on her list, after which she'd head home to fix a light supper. Tomorrow, she'd start back at the restaurant, since all the patients at the infirmary were gone. There was still the question about Julia. If only Susanna's home were a mite larger, she'd be happy to take the girl in. As it was, she hardly had room to turn around in her thimble-sized cottage.

The afternoon sun glinted off the shiny glass of the haberdashery's front window, and the soft call of a mourning dove drew her attention to the cemetery. She glanced at the path that led to the church. She wanted so badly to shed this cloak of sadness. She wasn't a quitter, or a victim. She couldn't have traveled by herself with such an attitude. The path up to the cemetery was deserted, and most everyone in town was inside preparing to close up for the evening. She had every right to walk right up there and look at the graves. And, by golly, that was exactly what she was going to do.

It took several minutes to reach the top. A few mourners scattered around glanced up at her appearance. She proceeded down the row of newly dug graves until she reached Floria's. None had headstones yet, just freshly mounded dirt in a nice even row.

She stood there quietly for a few moments, her thoughts calming. She looked up to see a man a few graves over. He gave her a nod, then proceeded to blow his nose on his handkerchief.

Albert hadn't said much about how he'd met his wife, or why their marriage had failed. Just that he'd been twenty-four and she'd been nineteen. Six years younger than Susanna was now. A tiny seed of suspicion tickled her mind. Had they planned a reunion? Surely, Albert couldn't lie his way out of that. She would have been able to tell. He said he hadn't known about the boy. So many unanswered questions, and Floria wasn't going to share any of her secrets.

The woman was dead. Nate had lost his mother, and Albert his wife. She searched her heart until she found some charity to soothe her aching soul. She'd get through this, just like she had so many other tough times in her life. Thank heavens for her good friends, old and new. Like Julia. She and Gabe had likely finished their deliveries long ago, and the girl must be fretting over her future and where she was going to live.

She'd scoot down the hill and catch Tabitha in her bookstore before she closed. The apartment over the shop had an extra bedroom, and Tabitha had expressed interest in finding a female boarder to help pay off the loan she'd taken out from the bank. Julia didn't have a way to pay rent just yet, but Susanna would tackle that problem next.

Arriving at the bottom of the path, she was just about to go left when she heard voices in Dr. Thorn's waiting room. He'd been absent when she'd dropped off the linen earlier, so she decided to stop in to be sure he'd seen that she'd put the sheets in the proper cupboard, out of sight. Inside she found her friend Nell with Maddie, her blind stepdaughter.

"Susanna," Nell exclaimed. Her jeans and cowboy-style shirt always brought a smile to Susanna's face, as did the hat hanging down her back on a rodeo string. Her thick head of curly hair was as unruly as ever. "I'm delighted to run into you. How're things?" Nell's concerned gaze searched Susanna's face, just as all her friends did, thinking they'd find answers about her and Albert there.

Susanna shrugged. "I'll get through." She smiled, not wanting to dampen Nell's enthusiasm. "Don't worry about me." She knelt down to speak with Maddie. "How're you, Maddie? I hope you're not having any problems, and that's why you and your ma are here in Dr. Thorn's office."

The darling girl who had stolen the hearts of the whole town when she'd arrived last year alone on a stagecoach, smiled happily. Her hair was braided down the back in the way Nell often fixed her own hair, but Maddie's had a pretty pink bow on the end. That was something Nell would never do.

Maddie pointed to her knee. "I fell down and cut my knee."

A checkup for a tiny wound with one stitch? Susanna wondered if something else was going on. After a soft caress of Maddie's cheek, she stood.

"Yes, and we're glad it's tiny," Nell said. "Still, you should have seen Charlie. He was a wreck when he saw all the blood." Nell placed her hand tenderly on her stepdaughter's shoulder, then looked at the closed door to the back room. "Dr. Thorn's in there with the guard they pulled out of the train. He said he still hasn't come around. I guess Albert comes here every day to check on him."

She hadn't known that about Albert. "Right now it's this little girl that has me worried. How is she getting along at the ranch?"

Nell's face darkened "It's been six months since we moved to the ranch. The changes we've made have kept her safe so far, but it's a constant worry. I'll feel better when I find someone to come and watch over her when she's not in school. We're doing it all on our own."

"Any promising prospects after the original tutor took ill and wasn't able to travel to Wyoming?"

"No. And now that Maddie's hurt herself, Charlie's more anxious than ever. With all we have to do, and how active Maddie likes to be, it's more of a challenge than I'd anticipated." She gazed down at Maddie patiently waiting for her turn with Dr. Thorn.

"And with the spring cattle sorting almost upon us, and breaking the new colts, we're determined to find someone."

What if . . . ?

Excitement zipped through Susanna. "What if I told you I may have the answer to your problem today?" Unable to stop herself, she lifted Maddie into a hug, squeezing her as they twirled around. The child laughed with abandon, bringing giggles from both the women.

Nell stomped her boot. "Tell me! Don't keep me guessing."

Julia was the perfect candidate. She was one of the kindest young women Susanna had ever met. And Maddie could help her past the hurt she felt from losing her aunt Biddy.

"Susanna, you're being cruel."

"I have a young patient whose arm was broken in the accident. Her guardian was killed and now she doesn't have a home to go back to, and the relation they were intending to move in with was only taking them in because she had to. Julia doesn't know quite what to do. She needs a place to live. And after her arm is completely healed, a job."

Nell grinned from ear to ear. "She sounds perfect. How old is she?"

"Seventeen. She's soft-spoken and seems to have had a good education. I really think she and Maddie would hit it off, if given the chance. What do you think?"

"I'd like to meet her. I know Charlie will want to as well, and of course, Maddie. Where's she staying now? Hannah's?"

"No, she's been at the infirmary the whole time. Dr. Thorn couldn't set the arm right away since he had so many critical patients, so she's had a bad go of it. Really, today was the first day she's gotten out of bed. I sent her on a mission with Gabe, so she could meet someone her own age."

Nell gave a small laugh. "That was good thinking. The guest room at the ranch is fixed up real nice if she agrees to come out."

"I'll have to speak to her first. See how she feels about living out of town."

Maddie reached up and tapped on Susanna's arm to get her attention. "I've walked to town with my pa lots of times. It's not far at all." Her childish voice held mounds of hope.

At that moment, Dr. Thorn came through the door that led to his patient's room. "Sorry to keep you waiting, Nell," he said, surprise pulling his lips into a smile when he saw Susanna. "I wondered who else was out here. Susanna, you're doing way too much. I found the linen you put away. Thank you."

Dr. Thorn was always so appreciative of any help. "You're welcome. I just stopped in to see if you had any other chores that need doing." *So I can avoid going home where I'll have nothing to do but face the hurtful truth.*

"I sure don't, but thank you." His gaze dropped to Maddie. "Come on, Maddie. Let's have a look at that stitch." He took her hand and led her to the examination table on the opposite side of the room. Lifting her up, he pulled the glass magnifier on his head over his eye, and bent close to her knee.

"This looks just fine, Nell, not ready to be removed, but soon. I see no signs of infection at all. Now, young lady, I'll have a quick look at your eyes, all right?"

She nodded seriously.

Dr. Thorn gently picked up one eyelid, and brought his face very close to hers. Susanna wondered what he was looking for. Pulling back, he snapped his fingers in front of one eye, and then the other. Lastly, he went to the sideboard for something. "Maddie, I'm going to light a match just like I've done before. Don't be frightened. I won't burn you."

"But the ph-phosphorus will smell funny," she said softly.

An endearing smile stretched his face. "You said that long word very well. And that's exactly right."

He gathered a box of matches and returned to the child. He lit a long wooden match and held it in front of her left eye for several seconds, then moved it around to several different positions.

Maddie sat stone still except for wrinkling her nose at the pungent odor filling the room. Dr. Thorn lit another match and continued his examination.

"What's he doing?" Susanna whispered to Nell.

"He does this every few months. You know Maddie lost her sight after the wagon accident that killed her mother. Well, we don't mention this to Maddie, but, Dr. Thorn thinks there's a very slight chance she could regain it someday." Nell gave a heartfelt sigh. "It would be so wonderful if that happened. Not only for Maddie, of course, but Charlie, too. He feels responsible that he let Annie drive to town alone."

Susanna squeezed her hand. "I didn't know."

Dr. Thorn blew out the match and lifted Maddie to the floor. "Very good. Your eyes look as healthy as ever." He glanced at Nell with a shake of his head.

"You take good care, Nell," Susanna said softly, feeling deeply for the family. "I need to get going. I'm sure Julia thinks I've fallen off the face of the earth. If she hasn't eaten supper yet, I'm going to take her to Nana's Place. If you want to stop by there and meet her, perhaps we can get everything arranged this evening? For her, the sooner the future is worked out, the better." She gave Nell a hug, and hugged Maddie as well. "And for you, too."

Before she could exit, Dalton stepped into the room. He removed his hat, and murmured hello to the women, his eyes lingering on Susanna.

"Mr. Babcock," Dr. Thorn said. "What can I do for you? I hope you're not in need of my services." His tone was light, but something about his expression made Susanna wonder.

"No, not at all doctor. I stopped by to see how Evan is, and look in on him." He took a step toward the back room. "He in here?"

The doctor ambled in front of the door. "You can't see him just yet, Mr. Babcock. He's close to coming around, and any disturbance at all might set him back. I hope you understand."

With a perplexed expression, Dalton gazed past the doctor at the door. "No, that's fine," he said. "I can come back another time. By the looks of it, he's not going anywhere soon."

He turned and smiled again at the women. So far, he'd fulfilled his heartfelt promise to keep Susanna's history to himself. A history they'd shared—one that didn't hold any hurtful surprises for either of them.

She thought back on the pleasure of their walk home in the moonlight, and it prompted her own smile—the warmth of which surprised her.

CHAPTER THIRTY-THREE

$\mathcal{W}$haddya say we go out for a bite to eat, Nate, before we return the buckboard to Win? I think we've both worked up an appetite. Besides, we don't have a crumb of food in the kitchen." Nate had been a real trooper. He'd done everything Albert had asked of him without complaint.

"Sure, Pa!" Nate scampered back into his room and returned with the pint-sized, felt cowboy hat, more toy than the real thing, he'd had packed in his trunk. He plunked it on his head and tucked in his shirttails. "I'm ready to go."

Albert chuckled. "Not quite, son, follow me."

Conscious of the time, and how soon he needed to be back at the bank, Albert hurried to the kitchen. It took several minutes working the pump before a moderate flow of water appeared. Taking a dishcloth, he held it under the stream, then wrung out the excess moisture.

Nate watched with suspicious eyes. "What's that for?"

"To wash your face. It's a bit grimy from all the work you've done. You want to look respectable when we go back into town, don't you?"

Nate began backing up.

"Nate?"

The boy was almost out the door. Albert had to do something quick to divert him from making a scene.

"Watch, I'll go first." Albert washed his face, making sure to scrub his forehead, go over his eyes and cheeks, and even around his ears. He dared a glance at Nate who had stopped in the doorway between the kitchen and the living room. "This cool water feels good. Real refreshing."

Albert pumped again, rinsed, and wrung out the cloth. "Your turn." He held it out.

Reluctantly, Nate came forward.

"I think we'll go to Nana's Place," Albert said, deliberately distracting him as he handed him the cloth. "The Silky Hen is always so busy." *And full of my friends.* A nice, uncomplicated supper sounded more appealing to Albert than he liked to admit. Just him and Nate.

Nate rubbed around quickly under the brim of his hat and handed the cloth back.

"Thank you," Albert said, thinking that little bit had only made matters worse. There would be time for improvement later. He went into his bedroom and retrieved his gun, and strapped it on. Nate was already out the door and waiting on the porch.

"Here we are," Albert said, pulling the wagon to a halt alongside the tiny restaurant. If one wanted a bit of privacy, this was the place to come. There was a shop or two around, but most of the businesses were over on Main Street. Albert came here when he had some thinking to do. Or wanted to be alone.

Nate climbed down off his side before Albert's feet hit the dirt. The eager child raced to the door and was about to open it himself when Albert came up behind him and grasped the bent iron pull. They stepped into the dim interior of the almost empty eatery. Albert removed his hat. When Nate didn't, he did it for him. "We always take off our hat when we're inside, son."

Nate smiled, his eyes already following Mrs. Manning, a woman in her late fifties who was waitress and owner. "Yes, Pa."

Albert walked to a booth along the wall. "You sure are polite, Nate. I like that."

"Yes, Pa."

Nate scooted in on his knees, then took up a menu lying on the tabletop. There were three things scribbled in unintelligible writing.

"Can you read?" Albert asked, hanging his hat on the end post of the booth and doing the same with Nate's. He had no idea at what age children began their letters. Floria could have started him.

"No, Pa."

"Okay, I'll read the menu for both of us." Albert took the paper and turned it around. As he was reading, he heard the door open and close. "You can choose from vegetable beef soup, chicken in cream sauce with green beans . . ."

Albert glanced up when a woman softly laughed. "Or beef chunks with . . ."

He blinked. Susanna had entered with Julia, the young passenger with the broken arm. They hadn't seen him and Nate, and took a booth on the opposite side of the room. He swallowed down the surge of emotion that had strangled the words from his throat.

"With what, Pa? I sure am hungry."

Albert jerked his attention back to Nate, who was watching him with eager eyes.

"With potatoes and gravy," he said in a voice he didn't recognize. The door opened again and Dalton walked in and joined Susanna's table. From the way he scooted in beside her, it was evident the two women were expecting him.

Albert pinned his gaze on his boy, willing himself not to watch the goings on across the room. "What sounds good to you?"

Mrs. Manning walked up to the table before Nate had a chance to answer. "Sheriff Preston, it's good to see you." She glanced at Nate and winked. "Why he's the spittin' image of you.

Sure is a cute little thing." No need to explain, everyone had heard about the son he didn't know he had.

Albert tried to find the peace he'd felt a few minutes before, when they'd completed things at the house, and then again in the buckboard on the way to the restaurant. It was a joy to sit across from his son and carry on a conversation. A blessed joy—and he'd not forget it anytime soon. It wasn't right to let his hurt feelings over Susanna show to Nate. The boy hadn't had a father for all these years, and Albert planned to make that up to him starting right now. Between him and Win, they could give him a good life.

Albert forced a smile onto his face. "Thank you, Mrs. Manning. I agree wholeheartedly. It's been pure pleasure getting to know my son."

Nate's face shined so bright Albert almost chuckled.

"Well, I can certainly understand why. What can I get you two to eat?"

He looked at Nate, and gave a go-ahead nod.

The child sat up straight. "I'll have the meat with potatoes and gravy." He rubbed his belly as if he'd already eaten and enjoyed the supper.

"Good choice. I'll have the same. Also bring an extra plate of green beans. Seems I remember my mother telling me I needed to eat plenty of those if I wanted to grow tall." When Nate opened his mouth to object, Albert raised a brow halting the boy. He pointed at Nate. "And give him a glass of milk." Just feeding Nate was going to be a challenge, Albert realized. No more eating on the run, or grabbing something quick. He'd have to take to cooking more suppers at home, and eating breakfast.

"Right away, Sheriff."

Albert watched her walk away, but really wanted to catch a quick glimpse of Susanna's table from the corner of his eye. He wondered how she was doing. Less than a day had passed, and yet it felt like a year since they'd spoken—and it seemed Dalton wasn't wasting any time taking advantage of Albert's bad situation.

He hadn't realized how long he'd been watching their table until he heard Nate's high-pitched voice ring out, "Hi there, ma'am. Remember me?"

Jerking his attention back to his son, he saw Nate sitting on his knees while waving madly at the table across the room.

CHAPTER THIRTY-FOUR

$\mathcal{S}$o you like the idea of watching over Maddie when she's not at school? I'm sure that would mean fixing her meals when Nell and Charlie were out with the stock. It would include room and board. At least it's something until you get on your feet and decide what direction you want to take."

"Sounds like a good opportunity," Dalton chimed in.

The smile on Julia's face hadn't dimmed since the moment Susanna had sprung the idea on her twenty minutes before. They'd gathered the few things she had with her in her travel case and promptly walked over to the restaurant where Nell was supposed to pop in when she was finished with her errands in town. Earlier, as she and Dalton had exited Dr. Thorn's office, he'd invited her to supper. Already hoping to have plans with Julia, she'd invited him along. Susanna had learned he was good at cheering her up.

"Yes. I'm very eager. I can do it, even with a broken arm." She lifted the heavy cast and set it on the table. "This shouldn't prevent me from any of the duties, unless it's climbing a tree. I could even ride a horse if someone helped me up." She gave an enthusiastic laugh. "I don't know how I'll ever be able to thank you, Susanna. You've made it possible for me to remain in Logan Meadows, for a while, anyway. I'm so glad."

Susanna's head snapped up at the sound of an excited, high-pitched voice. Looking across the restaurant, past several other startled diners, she saw Nate in a far booth, his eyes alight with discovery, and glued on her. Susanna tracked her gaze to his father, whose face, colored up with embarrassment, held a slightly different expression than his son's. It was clear Albert had been just as surprised by Nate's greeting as she had.

Her sudden delight at seeing them both was quickly replaced with pain. *He's been married all this time. He had two years to tell me, and he didn't.* It was a grievous breach of her trust. One that couldn't be swept under the rug as if nothing had happened.

Still, even with those circumstances, she didn't want to disappoint that darling little boy. She waggled her fingers back and felt a smile curl her lips. Dalton's face darkened, but he tossed Albert a curt wave. Julia smiled.

"Please excuse me a moment," Susanna said.

Looking none too pleased, Dalton slid out of the booth, then offered her a hand in getting out. The touch of his skin on hers was pleasant.

"I'll be right back." She crossed the room to Albert's table.

He slid out of the booth and stood. "Susanna," he said, his voice a bit gruff. "We're sorry to disturb your supper."

A surge of emotion passed from his eyes to hers. "That's all right. We just sat down." She smiled down at Nate. "How're you, Nate? Settling in?"

"I'm fine, ma'am," he said, totally oblivious to the interplay going on between her and his father. She could feel Albert's gaze. Her stomach fluttered and she was surprised to find herself at a loss for words. After seeing him this morning, the day had dragged by, knowing she wouldn't have another chance anytime soon to seek him out. Not like before when he used to come into the Silky Hen every day for lunch. Oh, to go back to those days would be a joy. But she couldn't. Not now, knowing all that she knew. It was like trying to put a genie back into a bottle when he didn't want to go. She couldn't forget the news from yesterday.

Buck up, dearie, her pride scolded. *He did you wrong. Who knows what he was intending to do once his wife arrived on that train.*

Nate put his hands on the table and stood up on the leather seat. "We moved into that little yellow house you was talking about."

"Were," Albert corrected. "And sit down."

Nate did as he was told, not seeming to notice the correction to his grammar.

"There's a pond out back that has salamanders," the boy went on. The little one had finally opened up. Seemed he liked to talk more than his father.

"There is? That's wonderful." She glanced at Albert, and then back at Nate. "Have you met the two boys that live across the street yet?"

He shook his head, his neatly trimmed chestnut hair swishing this way and that. His little hat on the post at the end of his seat brought another lump to her throat. What a delightful gift Albert had received. About the best in the world. What would it be like to have a child of her own? "Albert, do you have someone to take care of Nate when you're on guard duty again?"

It was Albert's turn for his face to brighten. He almost seemed surprised she'd addressed him. "As a matter of fact I do. I've arranged it so Win and I are never on guard at the same time. If he's at work at the livery when I am, Nate can hang out there—get to know his uncle Win. There're lots of interesting things in a big ol' barn. It'll be good for both of them. Tonight, Win's stopping over to our new place—you know, check it out. Nice that it's so close to Main Street and the back of his livery."

"Things *are* working out well for you, and I'm glad." She was. She didn't wish him ill. She wanted only the best for him and now his son.

"Well, they will be just as soon as we get that million dollars on its way. I'll sleep a lot better once it's out of the bank, and out of town—and Babcock goes with it."

Her eyes widened. Did she just hear what she thought she did?

"I couldn't resist," Albert said. "It's the truth, and I'm not sorry for saying it."

She glanced over her shoulder, wondering if Julia was embarrassed to be left alone with Dalton for so long. "I better get back."

Albert nodded. "Good to see you, Susanna. Thanks for coming over to say hello."

"Bye, Miss Susanna. My ma is gonna get out of the train soon. I just know it."

Shocked, she jerked her gaze back to Albert, whose smile had ebbed away.

"Nate," he said in a voice so soft it could lull a baby bunny to sleep, "she's not coming back. Remember, we talked about that earlier tonight. She's with Oldie Judy." He reached over and rubbed his son's hair. "You'll get to remembering that after a few nights in your new bed."

Mrs. Manning appeared with two platefuls of food. She stepped around Susanna, and set them on the table. "Here you are, Sheriff and Little Sheriff. I'll be right back with a tall glass of milk and a bowl of green beans—for *both* of you."

Susanna couldn't stop her smile. "Little Sherriff, huh? I like that." Nate may have been too engrossed in his mashed potatoes to hear her, but Albert had. His bittersweet smile brought an acute sense of loss.

CHAPTER THIRTY-FIVE

$\mathcal{D}$alton sulked moodily in the alley between the haberdashery and the bakery, trying to keep his thoughts on the bank across the way and not on how Susanna's face had looked when she'd returned from Albert's table. He kicked a clump of dirt from between his boots, wanting this long night to be over. Surely the soldiers from Fort McKinney would show up tomorrow. He hoped the bank men from Colorado would show as well.

Squinting, he saw movement across the way. Albert was over there, but Frank, having contracted some sort of sour gut, had left an hour ago for home in search of baking soda and water. The money situation was weighing on the man. His usually pleasant face, taut with exhaustion, had looked five years older than a few days ago when they'd met. Sleeping on a small cot in his office would knock the starch out of anyone even half his age.

The sky above was clear. The narrow expanse between the two buildings gave Dalton a view of the stars. He wiped a hand across his face, wondering if he was wasting his time with Susanna.

A whistle-like birdcall sounded from up the street.

Alert, Dalton searched through the darkness, his senses fully awake. It had to be close to midnight. Logan Meadows was closed up tight, and the people asleep in their beds. He wondered if Albert had heard it as well. Instructions were to stay split up, making them a difficult target if bullets started to fly.

A match winked for several seconds at the bank, then went out.

Nerves pricked up Dalton's back. It felt like something was about to happen. If outlaws were planning trouble, they might be getting edgy, feeling their opportunity slipping away. With only a quarter moon, cover would be good. Tonight would be better than tomorrow, with reinforcements scheduled to arrive.

Mad at himself for not recommending a few more guards tonight, he quietly cursed in the darkness. He should have suggested stationing Chase Logan and Charlie Axelrose on top of a roof. He'd grown complacent when the interest in the million dollars had waned in the aftermath of the funeral. And what about Pat Tackly? He'd claimed fatigue and was mostly keeping himself holed up in the hotel room Albert had arranged for him. Was the story he'd told them the truth? Had he really been stumbling around, and following the tracks in the wrong direction? Seemed a bit farfetched, by Dalton's way of thinking.

Out of habit, he dropped one hand to caress the stock of his .45 Colt. His guns were ready. With his back against the cool batten and board siding, he slipped around to the front boardwalk, trying to get a better view of the street. If trouble was on its way, he didn't want to get caught unawares.

CHAPTER THIRTY-SIX

I thought I saw a light out here," Hannah said, stepping around the side of Susanna's cottage and into the tiny backyard. "What on earth are you still doing up? And outside alone in the dark?"

Surprised, Susanna whirled around, her hand pressed tightly to her chest. She'd been engrossed in the soft sounds of the night, the brightness of the stars, and completely missed the sound of her friend's approach. The self-absorption of her thoughts had shut out everything except her hurt over Albert, and the decisions at hand.

"Hannah! You gave me a fright! Hasn't anyone ever told you it's not nice to sneak up on someone?" She gripped the shawl around her shoulders and pulled it tight. "You almost gave me a case of vapors. I was just thinking about going inside when you appeared out of nowhere."

"I'm sorry." Hannah approached and gave her a gentle hug. "I forgot about your skittishness. Markus was restless tonight. The little stinker woke up around eleven-thirty from a scary dream. When I went down into the kitchen to heat some milk, I noticed a light out here and was worried. Being you're only a few houses down, I decided to check and be sure everything was all right. I hope you don't mind." She ran her hand down Susanna's arm, no words needed to know what Susanna was thinking about.

"I don't mind. But, if you believed something was wrong, I would have thought you'd bring along Thom—just in case. Am I right?"

Hannah softly laughed. "I suppose. Don't be annoyed if I'm concerned about my dear friend who just might need a heart-to-heart talk."

Gratitude moved Susanna. Hannah was a special friend indeed, one she was truly blessed to have. "Of course I'm not annoyed. I am worried about Thom, though. He'll have my hide if he wakes up and finds you gone. You know he doesn't like you coming down here alone after dark. Even more so since everyone has been walking on eggshells this last week."

"Yes, with good reason," Hannah responded. Her hair flowed freely around her shoulders, a style she seldom wore.

"Did Markus fall back asleep?"

"He did. Took him a while. I snuggled down next to him and we counted sheep until I heard his little snore." The smile in Hannah's voice was evident. "He got all the way up to one hundred and eighty-eight. His little mind is hard to calm down once it's restless. But he's a good boy, a blessing to be sure—and a very good counter."

How simple life could be, Susanna thought, envisioning Hannah and Markus together on the child's bed, wrapped in each other's arms. The warmth of the house and tick of the clock. Thom asleep in the room next door, believing all was fine. *The way life should be.*

For a few minutes, they just gazed at the stars in companionable silence.

"I don't know what to do," Susanna finally said, not taking her attention off the night sky. "Everything's so mixed up. I feel like a pincushion with a new box of needles."

The thin slice of quarter moon gave off a shimmery glow. Hannah turned to face her. "I'm sure you do. It was a huge shock to all of us to learn about Albert. I can't imagine how you must feel. I've heard rumors that the woman, was, well . . ."

"His wife? Yes, yes she was, up until the day she died."

Hannah didn't respond for a good half minute. "I see. Has he shared with you why he left her? Or why he never mentioned her to you? There has to be a reason he's not saying."

"He said they only stayed together for a couple of months. Coming from Albert, the most honest man I've ever known, I didn't have the presence of mind to ask questions then, while we were talking. I just sat there like a voiceless doll."

"You were in shock."

She nodded, remembering the conversation. "Now I'd have a lot more questions for him. I thought I knew him, Hannah. Believed him to be a decent man. I can't help it, but I *still* do. But what man leaves the woman he loves, who he has vowed to stay with until death parts them, after such a short time? What could she have done? What would prompt such a drastic move? I can't make heads or tails of it."

"That's not much to go on, but I'd bet he's hurting as well. That he has some reasons he's not yet shared. His son must be a huge surprise to him. I'd guess he's floundering as much as you are right now just to take care of him. Albert *is* a good man. He must have motives for keeping his history to himself."

"Perhaps."

"How do you feel about Dalton?"

That was a good question. Whenever he was around, she was happy, and felt a portion of herself healing from the pain and humiliation of her past. Like he was somehow showing her that she wasn't the only one to suffer. "I like him."

"Only like? When I see the two of you together, you're always smiling. Susanna, I don't want you to take my words wrong, because you know I love Albert very much. Working together, Thom and him are very close, and he thinks the world of Albert as well. But, the two of you are not married. And from what you said, you haven't even spoken about making your intentions official. There's no crime in enjoying Dalton's company, especially if it helps. You have nothing to feel guilty over."

"I know." And she did know. She'd hardly thought of anything else but the three of them since last Friday. So many feelings rumbling around inside were almost making her dizzy, and she wished she could close the door to her thoughts. "What a mess."

Hannah sighed, her tone full of meaning. "Don't rush yourself. No decisions have to be made right now. Nobody expects that. Take your time. Let your heart rest and recover. A lot has happened."

Anxiety squeezed Susanna's stomach. On one hand, she had plenty of time. On the other, time was fleeting. "That's just it. Dalton won't be here forever. He'll move on with the money shipment when it's time to go. What if after he leaves, I realize he was the one? That I hadn't recognized my feelings for him because of my brokenheartedness over Albert? I'm mixed up, Hannah. One minute I think I want one thing, and a few minutes later, I think another. I'm as fickle as they come."

"What does your heart say?"

She looked up at the stars, avoiding the question. "Look at them, Hannah, how they sparkle and shine. They look happy. I want to be happy, too."

"Susanna?"

"My heart says that my life is changing faster than I'd like. That I'm not in control of anything." She chanced a glance at Hannah. "I'm frightened—and that's not a good feeling."

Susanna had never shared anything about her mother with Hannah. Or her life before coming to Logan Meadows. Even with Hannah, she still felt embarrassed by it. But weren't her mother's words ringing true now? As much as she despised the thought, she couldn't deny it. Maybe it was time she got it off her chest.

"Growing up, my mother, well, she didn't have much of a reputation. She took up with a lot of men, if you catch my meaning. I think somewhere when she was very young she must have been badly hurt. She insisted men couldn't be trusted. She took great pains to instill that into me with her every breath. She'd said that they were liars, and cheats, and they would hurt me. Once the chase was over, they'd move on. That if I ever trusted one, I'd end up alone, broken, and penniless, just like her. Please understand, she had a hard life. I don't pretend it was not one of her own making, but still, she was my mother, and I loved her. Her existence was one neither one of us would want for ourselves or anyone we loved . . ."

The sentence died in her throat. A moment of silence stretched out into the night like a spirit sneaking through the knee-high grass.

"What happened?" Hannah asked.

"When I was a girl, she repeated her words of warning so often I had no choice but to believe them. When she died, I left after I was approached by one of her gentleman friends—expecting favors."

Hannah sucked in a deep breath, but Susanna forged on. Speaking about her past was freeing.

"By the time I arrived in Logan Meadows, the words were engraved on the walls of my heart—not by desire, but by pure dominance. That's why I kept Albert at arm's length for so long. And I actually discouraged him when he was trying to tell me about his past, about Floria. I thought he was trying to profess his love, and ask if we could start courting." Overcome with grief, she turned and grasped Hannah's hands. "How foolish I've been. I wholeheartedly believed that if I never let him speak of his affection, then we'd never arrive at the point where what we felt together would come to an end. That he'd never leave me. It was childish, I know."

"I had no idea about this, Susanna. You've been so close lipped about your past. I always thought there might be something you weren't sharing, but I didn't want to pry. It's not a sin to try to start over."

"I know." *Isn't that what Albert was doing?*

Hannah gave a wan smile. "Now I see that I should have sat you down for a good long talk a year ago."

Susanna wrapped her arms around herself when a chilly breeze ruffled the bottom of her skirt. "I'm sorry, I just can't—"

"Don't stop now! Get it all out, so you can heal from the hurt your mother inflicted on you. Her thoughts were distorted, Susanna. I hope you know that."

Susanna gaped at Hannah, surprised she was laying Albert's sins on her mother's grave. "My mother? Don't you mean Albert?"

Hannah stood close enough that Susanna could see a spark of anger in her eyes. "No, I don't mean Albert! Your problems didn't start with the truth he's kept from you, but with the fear and suspicion your mother drove you to your knees trying to carry. She may have experienced those things in her life, but she had no right to rob you of your innocence. Destroy your dreams of a loving husband, and the desire to build a family of your own. No right at all! I'm disgusted when I think about what your mother did to her daughter's beautiful heart."

Susanna pulled away. Hannah might be right, but that didn't leave Albert off the hook for his betrayal.

"Don't you see?" Susanna went on. "Albert did to his wife exactly what Mother said would happen to me. He left after only two months. They were still newlyweds, for gosh sakes. They'd barely said 'I do.' It couldn't get any more exact if I'd written it myself."

"You may want to consider your life here since coming to Logan Meadows," Hannah argued. "Look at my marriage. It's as solid as a rock. The more Thom expresses his deep, abiding love for me, the more mine grows for him. If that's not enough, look at Chase and Jessie, Charlie and Nell, and now Greg and Brenna."

Seemed Hannah was just warming to this subject. She trooped back and forth in front of Susanna reminding her of a soldier. "Why, Mrs. Brinkley and her husband have been married almost forty years! Think of them when you start doubting, will you? You'd be hard pressed to find one of them without the other. They're always arm in arm. They finish each other's sentences, and practically read each other's minds. Markus even thinks they look like each other." Hannah laughed, the sound a nice break in the tense conversation. "I wouldn't go as far to say that, though. And what about my mother? As exasperating as she can be at times, she dearly loved my father—and he, her. They married at fifteen and sixteen and would still be together if he hadn't died."

Susanna held up her hand. "Please, stop. I hear what you're saying. Now that I've actually spoken the words, I see you have a very good point. It's like their sting has been clipped."

"These are just a few examples. But what they mean is life isn't worth living without love. Have faith in love! Take a chance, and you might be surprised at how well things will turn out. If you do, you'll be filled with joy. I promise."

She wanted to believe. She did. And yet . . . "How can I ever trust Albert again? And if I don't trust him, how can I have faith in love?"

She turned abruptly and faced Hannah. "We could talk about this all night and not come up with a definite answer. You need to get home before you're missed. I don't want an angry Thom hunting me down for a grumpy wife tomorrow. Thank you so much for your concern. I'll consider all you've said."

Hannah gave her a brief hug. "You're right. You're the only one who can decide if you can live with Albert's transgressions. But promise me that if you need to talk some more, you'll come to me. I'm always available. Two heads are better than one when it comes to problems of the heart. And you know, I'll never say a word to anyone."

"Look!" Susanna sucked in a breath as a glittering star streaked the expanse of the dark sky.

Hannah sighed blissfully. "That was worth coming out to see. And you should be pleased. Signs like that don't come along every day."

Feeling so much better, Susanna just stared at the path the star had taken. "Thank you," she said softly to her friend. "For everything. In case you've forgotten, I'll be back at the restaurant tomorrow morning. No more patients to look after, thank goodness."

"What about Julia?"

"Just so happens she got a job that provides her with room and board."

"What! Where?"

"Nell and Charlie have been looking for someone to stay with Maddie when they're out ranching and she's not at school. They've been making do so far, in between trying to find a tutor, but seems Maddie took a spill and that made the decision for them. Julia has already gone out to the ranch with Nell. When school starts back up, she'll take over the job of walking with her into town and picking her up when class lets out, and then watching over her at the house. On her off-hours when Maddie is at school, Julia is free to do whatever she wants, even take another job in town."

"What a wonderful solution for everyone," Hannah said. "Their house is certainly large enough. I'm happy for her."

"So am I." Susanna took Hannah's shoulders and turned her friend around. "Come on, I'll walk out to the street with you and then watch you until you're safely in the house."

With elbows hooked, they carefully made their way through the dark to the front of the house and the small dirt road. "Go on now, and hurry. It must be close to one in the morning. You're going to be sorry when the rooster crows at five."

Hannah gave her a quick squeeze and laughed. "I don't have a rooster."

"You know what I mean."

Hannah started off. "You'll be feeling it as well, mark my words."

Standing on the side of the quiet road, Susanna watched until she couldn't see Hannah any longer. She took a deep, cleansing breath. She felt better. They hadn't answered any of the difficult questions, but sharing her problems had lifted a little of the weight from her shoulders.

Now, she'd better take Hannah's advice and get some sleep or she'd be worthless tomorrow. Her eyelids pulled down heavily. She still needed to fetch the lantern she'd left burning in the backyard.

Turning, she took one step and stopped. Two riders appeared out of the mist from the direction of the fairgrounds—and beyond that, the train station and the tracks that led to Three Pines Turn, the site where all those poor souls had perished. Her skin prickled. Since the accident, the trains had stopped, and the road had been extremely quiet. Why would there be riders at this time of night?

Feeling exposed, she ducked close to the house and stood very still as the riders came near. In the darkness, it was difficult to tell for sure, but neither man looked familiar. Instead of crossing the bridge that would take them directly into town, they weaved their way toward the livery, descended the small incline, and rode into the creek.

What were they doing? Could a man hide his horse under the bridge? Fear for Albert flooded her throat. Dalton was standing guard as well. Both of them could be in danger. There was only one thing for her to decide. Whether she should run through the dark into town by herself, or go for help first.

CHAPTER THIRTY-SEVEN

*A*lbert had been on edge for nearly an hour, not quite knowing what had triggered his uneasiness. He hadn't liked the strange whistle trying to sound like a night bird. He felt exposed, more so because he'd expected Fort McKinney to follow through on the promised soldiers. If they had ridden hard, it was possible they could have arrived today.

He strode up the boardwalk a few feet, scanned the darkness beyond the mercantile and hotel, then turned and started back toward the livery.

He jerked to a halt. Someone was on the bridge. He strained through the darkness trying to see. A lantern on the bookstore porch obscured his vision, and he cursed under his breath. Slowly, he eased back against the wall of the bank and carefully drew his gun from its holster. He didn't want any gunplay. Logan Meadows was known to be a law-abiding town—and he wanted to keep it that way. Folks were not going to be killed in their beds on his watch. Hopefully, Dalton hadn't fallen asleep across the street. It was too late to send a signal.

A woman? When the person from the bridge was within twenty feet, he recognized Susanna. He'd know that figure anywhere; he'd been dreaming about it long enough. He met her when she was almost to the bank, slinging an arm across her shoulders and pulling her under the overhang of the bank's roof. The feel of her against his side sent a heady awareness zipping through him like lightning.

"What're you thinking?" he hissed, almost sounding angry. He wasn't. Truth be told, he was elated to see her, but worried, and more than a mite annoyed she'd put herself in danger.

"Logan Meadows isn't St. Louis, Albert," she replied with her own tone. "It's only a short distance from my house, and you know it." Susanna wasn't one to be bossed around—he'd learned that early on, and it was one of the things that intrigued him about her. He liked her strength and conviction of values.

"Maybe not, but we're not the sleepy little town we used to be, either."

"I was outside when I saw some riders I didn't recognize coming from the fairgrounds," she whispered back, her breath tickling his face.

"What were you doing outside this time of night? You should be asleep in your bed."

He felt her soften. He got the impression she was in no hurry to step out of his protection.

"Albert, please. I'm not a child. I was just looking at the stars and admiring the beautiful night sky with Hannah."

Hannah? Good. She needs someone levelheaded to help her sort out her feelings.

"I heard a noise and saw the horsemen. Worried they were outlaws intending to rob the bank. I had to come warn you—and Dalton."

Under the overhang, they didn't even have the light from the stars or the crescent moon, but Albert didn't need any help to see her face, only an inch away. She could have left off Babcock's name. Did she say that just to hurt him, or did she have feelings for her old friend, more than he suspected?

"I didn't see anything. Which way did they go?" he whispered back, refusing to let jealousy ruin this time alone with her.

"I'm not exactly sure because they didn't cross the bridge and ride into town. It's as if they knew the chokecherry shrub on the corner blocked them from your sight. I think they went down the embankment and rode under the bridge. Can a horse and rider fit beneath it?"

Already heady with the feel of her so close, he was struggling to keep his thoughts in check. He braced his hand against the building behind her head, and daringly placed the other on her waist, hearing the sharp intake of her breath. His feelings were spinning out of control, and desire filled his mind. From what she'd said, the two of them could be in danger of being set upon at any second, but all he could think about was her.

"Albert?"

He jerked his thoughts back to what she was saying.

She tipped her head in question and her skin quivered beneath his hand. "The bridge?"

"Yes, they could. I'm just trying to work through the thought that you ran across that bridge when you believed outlaws were huddled underneath." He brought his hand up to cup her face, the beauty of it in the darkness making his heart seize up. Had he lost her? Could she ever get past the hurt he'd inflicted? Was she still his girl? Would she ever trust him again? "I should be angry with . . ."

Her hair, loose and flowing around her shoulders, was a sight prettier than any prairie in spring. Her familiar scent of lavender tickled his senses and ignited a fire inside him. He fought to remember her note, respect her wishes, but an all-powerful urge to take her into his arms and steal the kiss they'd almost shared down by Shady Creek was winning out.

"Yes?"

Her soft engaging tone was invitation enough. He lowered his head to her lips and gently pressed her back against the building. He felt her tremble, and tenderness surged through him at her timidity. His actions had caused it, wounding her when she should trust. Her warm, velvety lips were everything he'd dreamed.

"Trust me," he whispered next to her lips, as he gently coaxed her on. A moment passed, and then two. He felt a subtle change, and she relaxed. A sigh of pleasure escaped her throat. Before she could tell him to stop, he gathered her closer, kissed deeper, wanting to show her to what depths his feelings ran.

She inhaled sharply and pressed a hand against his chest. "Albert." Her desire-clogged voice brought him to his senses.

Begrudgingly he pulled away, acutely missing the feel of her lips beneath his. They were back to where they'd been the last time they'd talked. Well not exactly. He'd stolen a kiss, and been transported to heaven. "I won't say I'm sorry, Susanna. Even if you think I should."

Her lips looked kissed and a bit plump. "I didn't ask you to."

"We've been heading toward that for two years, but I held back because I was married and I knew you'd never consent to keeping company with me in that way if you knew the truth. Well, I'm not married anymore."

Just as he dipped his head for another kiss, the sound of a man coughing pulled him up straight.

"That's just Dalton across the street," he said when he felt a jolt run through her. "Still, you're in danger every moment you stay out here, especially with what you told me. I don't want you in the middle of a gunfight." He glanced around. "I don't know what I'm going to do with you."

"I'll go inside the bank with Frank."

"He's not there and I don't have the key. Besides, that's the last place I'd put you if I thought there was a chance we were going to be robbed. You can't go back over the bridge until I check underneath."

"This is silly, Albert. I can cross the bridge in one second if I run, then be home in two more. It's just down the street. If there're outlaws, or someone else, under the bridge, they aren't after me."

She took a step away and Albert reached out and caught her hand before she got a foot farther.

"Nothing doin'." Her hand was cool to the touch and he wrapped it in both of his. It brought a fleeting memory of a month ago and the picnic they'd shared with friends after church. She'd had on a flowing dress, one that emphasized her gracefulness. Nobody moved like Susanna. If she wanted to, she could practically float across a room. That day, though, they'd been walking by the stream and she'd slipped on a moss-covered rock. He'd easily caught her before she'd fallen and she'd lain in his arms as natural as could be. Her gaze had drawn him, and he'd almost kissed her then, despite his resolve to be free and clear of Floria before he ever did. And now she wanted him to let her walk home in the dark alone, and so close to a waiting danger? That just wasn't going to happen. "You can get that idea right out of your head this instant. If there are fellows looking for trouble, sometimes they don't care what kind they find."

"Albert, I certainly can't stay out here with you all night. That would set the gossips' tongues wagging more than they already are. I don't need to give them any more fodder."

There it was. The truth of the matter was, she not only felt betrayed by him, but was scandalized and embarrassed. And why wouldn't she? In everyone's eyes, he'd duped her good. Still, in spite of all that, and all the damning evidence against him, she'd just risked her life to see to his safety. Things couldn't be all *that* bad. A spark of hope lingered—or was that just the incredible tingle she'd left on his lips?

CHAPTER THIRTY-EIGHT

$\mathcal{S}$usanna blinked several times to see if she was imagining the smile lifting Albert's lips. The same ones that had just kissed the stuffings out of her. She'd just laid out a portion of her heart. Was that all he thought of her? To smile? She couldn't hold in her irritation. "What's so funny?"

He reached out and touched the tip of her nose. "You." He looked her up and down so long she felt flush under the collar. "Running out here in the middle of the night. And now thinking I'm going to just let you stroll home by yourself as if it were three o'clock Sunday afternoon."

He gave a little chuckle and stepped in her direction, but she quickly pulled away. He leaned in, almost like he intended to kiss her again, but she held him off with a determined hand to his rock-hard chest. She wasn't letting him off the hook—*she couldn't*—even if his kiss had been dreamier than she'd ever imagined all those times as she fell asleep. She resisted the urge to reach up and touch her lips and relive the memory. Instead, she held her ground. "That still doesn't explain your smile. Are you laughing at me too?"

His smile didn't even ebb. "Of course not," he said softly, gently bushing a wisp of her hair from her face. "I'm moved that, deep down, you're still worried about me. Enough to brave the dark night when unseemly looking horsemen you've never laid eyes on before might be right under your feet. You're quite the valiant woman, Susanna. Your spirit is one of the things I love about you."

He said the words slow and enticing, his deep voice melting her insides. He meant to seduce her, she realized with a shock. In all the time she'd known him, he'd never come on like this—and his pull was deadly. She tried to turn her head, but her gaze was anchored to his lips. She was almost defenseless against his charm. If seduction was his aim, he was doing a darn fine job.

· "Your concern tells me a lot," he continued. She shivered when he stroked her palm with his thumb. "You still care. And I still have a chance." His smile had faded and his grave expression spoke volumes. She meant everything to him. His eyes searched her face. "I'm not going to let you go without a fight. It wasn't my choice for Floria to die, God rest her soul, but she has. I'm in love with you, Susanna, and have been since your first few days in Logan Meadows."

"What's going on?" Dalton stepped out of the darkness, one gun drawn. His suspicious tone held a mountain of censure. "I thought that was you, Susanna. But I actually thought you'd be more sensible than to sneak out here in the middle of the night."

"What're you doing?" Albert growled. "We may have some visitors under the bridge waiting for the right moment to make their move. Now you just gave it to them by coming over here."

Dalton never took his gaze from her. She felt Albert's anger sizzle through his body.

How much had Dalton seen? Was he listening to their conversation? She didn't like to think he'd do such a thing, but his tone, and the look in his eyes, made her wonder.

"Get back to your post," Albert said through a stiff jaw. "Standing together like this makes us an easy target."

"Every moment Suzie stays out here talking with you she's in danger," Dalton said, keeping his voice down. "I could hear your whispers all the way across the street."

"That's impossible." Albert shifted his weight. "The sound of the creek alone hides most everything."

Dalton's chin went up as if he were gunning for a fight. If they took to fists, would she be able to break them apart? She didn't know Dalton well enough to read his moods. "The relief guards won't arrive until five in the morning. You can't stay out here with Albert all night."

Susanna's ire rose. Why was he bossing her around? She was about to give him a big piece of her mind, but Albert beat her to it.

"She's with you as well, Babcock, and the rest of the sleeping town. Nothing untoward is going to happen."

Dalton harrumphed.

"There's a chair right there," Susanna said, trying to mollify both. "If I get tired, I can sit." She pointed to the wooden cane-back seat next to the door. "Do you have a better solution?"

Dalton's gaze roamed over her loose hair. "I do. It's safer on my side of the street—away from the bank."

"Over my dead body," Albert said low.

"You're going to forgive him, Susanna? Like he hasn't duped you for the past two years? I wouldn't let him off so easily."

Susanna gaped back and forth, her annoyance at both men growing with each comment. "That's my business, Dalton, not yours." She turned and looked at Albert. "What about the riders I saw? Aren't you worried about them? Shouldn't you do something?"

"Of course I am, and will. But I'm not going to start anything with you at risk if bullets start flying."

It was true, she'd put both Albert and Dalton in danger by coming out here. She needed to get out of the way so they could do their jobs.

"That's why she's coming with me."

"Enough!" Albert's romantically inclined mood had gone all business in a matter of seconds. "I'll take her to the bookshop. She can stay upstairs with Tabitha until morning." Albert's tone said he was done talking with Dalton and with her as well.

Susanna sucked in a breath. She had to admit, it was the perfect solution and she wished she'd thought of it sooner herself, before the heated words had started to fly. Tabitha might be frightened when she first knocked on her door, but there was no help for that.

Albert took her elbow and they turned for the alley. "Stay here, Babcock, until I get back," he said over his shoulder. "We'll go around to the back door. I'll be listening in case any trouble breaks out."

Dalton's expression was sullen as they walked away. Susanna's gaze veered beyond him to the bridge that had always been an attraction for folks in Logan Meadows, not a hideout for outlaws waiting to make their move. Albert's presence by her side, although exciting, brought little peace. All their lives could change in the blink of an eye.

CHAPTER THIRTY-NINE

*T*hom arrived promptly at five to relieve Albert. After a brief rundown of the events of the night before, and as a grouchy-looking Babcock watched from his side of the street, Albert made his way toward his new girl-colored home on foot, looking forward to seeing Nate. As soon as he arrived, Win could get going to the livery, where he'd drop Nate after he and his son had some breakfast. As far as he could figure, Susanna's appearance last night had tipped the scale for the horsemen, if they'd indeed been skulking under the bridge for nefarious reasons. Three people were more difficult to silence than two.

He crossed over Shady Creek, descended the steep embankment on the other side, and peered into the murky area underneath. There were tracks, all right. Two horses, just like Susanna had thought.

The splashing water echoed beneath the ten-foot-wide passage. A fat bullfrog leaped off a flat rock and quickly swam away. Last night, after he'd handed Susanna off to a wide-eyed, and a bit shaken, Tabitha Canterbury, he'd gone straight to the bridge. His anger at Babcock had pushed him forward, and he'd rushed in like a fool. Somehow, they'd come and gone without being noticed. It was a mystery.

"See anything?"

Albert glanced over his shoulder and grunted when he saw Babcock. Charlie must have shown up to relieve him soon after he'd departed. If Albert had any doubts the man had his sights set on Susanna, they'd been wiped away last night. Right now, feeling testy, all Albert wanted was to get home to Nate, after which he needed to hustle back to the office and wait for the bank representatives to show up. The sooner that money was out of Logan Meadows the better!

Without giving Babcock an answer, Albert continued along the side of the creek, doing his best to stay out of the water as he searched for clues. The air was damp, and an occasional spray of water reached his face. There was plenty of room over his head for a horse, but a rider would have to lean over, or dismount. Not a desirable position to be in if your animal was spooked.

He could hear Babcock cutting the distance behind. Placing his boots carefully, he didn't see the moss until he ended up knee-deep with one leg in the ice-cold creek. He cursed, and yanked his boot out. "Go home, Babcock. I can handle this."

"I'm done taking orders from you, Preston. I've had hours to ponder this whole mess. I knew Susanna long before you did. Why don't you back off and give her a chance at happiness? She could never have that here with you now."

Albert swung around. "Susanna is no concern of yours. You'll be gone just as soon as the money is on its way, so don't make things more complicated than they already are."

The two men were a good match in size. The color of Babcock's face deepened. Either one of them slipped or maybe Dalton threw a punch, Albert wasn't sure, but in half of a heartbeat he'd taken a fist to his chin, and they were going at it in the middle of the creek. They fell together into the frigid water and a rock slammed into Albert's side, the pain infuriating him all the more. He threw his balled fist at Babcock's wet face, hitting his mark before his hand slipped off and struck the rocks. Damn that hurt!

"Sheriff!" a scratchy voice shrieked from the far opening under the bridge.

The high-pitched word echoed loudly, making Albert pull up.

"What in tarnation is goin' on down here? You boys quit yer fightin' this instant or I may have ta give ya both a lickin' with a willow switch. I ain't too old ta do it, neither!"

Cold, angry, and with an aching fist, face, and side, Albert dragged himself up off the rocky creek bank after making sure Babcock wasn't going to try a fast one and catch him unaware.

Violet Hollyhock edged her way toward them, a basket of tubers swinging on her arm. She tottered as she came, and Albert hoped she was steady enough not to end up in the stream. The hem of her blue-and-white calico skirt was soaked up a good three inches, and the shawl around her scrawny shoulders was askew.

"Ain'tcha a little old ta be settlin' matters with yer fists?" she asked, her skepticism ringing loud and clear. "I came lookin' for tubers, and found myself at a mad-dog fight instead. Thought I was seein' things."

Babcock slicked back the dripping-wet hair hanging in his eyes. Albert wondered what his own looked like.

"Now what's this all about, Sheriff Preston? I can't imagine ya have a good excuse for actin' like schoolboys. You should be ashamed of yerself, bein' the sheriff and all." Her annoyed gaze raked him over good before sliding over to Babcock. "Sheriff?"

"Nothing I care to go into, Violet."

One thin, barely there eyebrow arched up. "It couldn't have anythin' ta do with Susanna, could it, *boys*?"

"Everything to do with her, Mrs. Hollyhock," Babcock said. He inched forward, but stopped when Albert threw him a glare.

Something cold and wet slid between Albert's shoulder blades. With a sickening shiver, he jerked his elbows back, reached over his head with both hands, took hold of the fabric, and ripped his shirt off in one swoop. A coral-colored salamander plopped into the water and swam away. Albert glanced down at his drenched weapons in disgust.

"Yer boy woulda liked that soft lizard," Mrs. Hollyhock said, watching it float away. She adjusted the spectacles on the bridge of her nose, and then gave them both the evil eye.

"Now, I'm only gonna say this once, so listen up." She shifted her bony finger back and forth between them. "Don't be makin' Susanna's life any more difficult than you both already have. She's puttin' on a good face, but jist barely. You," she said, drilling Albert with her no-nonsense gaze, "have a lot to explain, and make up fer. I'm not judgin' ya, mind you. But I'd walk lightly if I was you where Susanna's heart is concerned."

Babcock had the nerve to smirk until the old woman turned her heated gaze his way.

"I'm getting ta you, Mr. Babcock, so you may as well wipe that look off yer face. If you don't have honorable intentions in mind for Susanna, and are just havin' some fun to pass the time before ya pull out, I won't like that one little bit. That girl's been through a heap of hurt and she don't need any more."

Babcock put up his hands as if Mrs. Hollyhock had a gun pointed in his direction. "I swear, Mrs. Hollyhock, I'd never do anything to hurt her. I only have honorable intentions where Suzie is concerned."

Instantly, Albert saw red. "Her name is Susanna!"

"Enough! Now get home and get changed before you both catch your death."

Violet had begun to shiver and her face was as white as a sheet. He'd never forgive himself if the old woman got sick on his account. As much as he hated to leave Babcock standing, Albert turned and made for the way he'd come in.

CHAPTER FORTY

*I*t felt good to be back at the restaurant, Susanna thought as she pulled a loaf of bread out of the oven with a thick dishtowel, being careful not to burn her hands. She set the crusty, fresh-baked bread on the counter next to the other three she'd made that morning. She arranged the hot pans in a row. Going up on tiptoe, she pushed the window open an inch, letting in the morning breeze to cool them in time for the first customer.

She glanced at the clock. Five minutes until seven. Almost time to unlock the front door, pull up the shades, and turn the sign. The more familiar footing was welcome. She would run the place alone until eight when Hannah arrived. Taking a long wooden spoon, she stirred a large batch of fried potatoes that she'd been browning with onions and garlic, and slid the skillet from the heat onto the side of the stove.

Last night, from Tabitha's upstairs window, she'd watched Albert tromp over to the bridge, gun drawn. He'd glanced beneath the bridge, but nothing happened. Then he crossed to the other side, and did the same. Had the riders somehow slipped out without being seen, or had she been totally mistaken about the whole event, making so much trouble out of nothing? Did Albert think she'd made the entire thing up as an excuse to come see him?

Heat flushed her cheeks and her heart fluttered wildly in her chest as she relived the kiss. *Men crave what's on the other side of the pasture. Once they have you, it won't be long before they're gone, they're gone, they're gone . . .* Her mother's voice burst her bubble of contentment and filled her with uncertainty.

The front door rattled as someone wrestled with the cranky lock. Soon Hannah appeared in the kitchen, looking bright and chipper for the day.

"Well, aren't you the early one," Susanna said, shelving her qualms over last night's adventure. "I wasn't expecting you until eight."

Hannah laughed. She was nicely put together in a soft blue skirt and white blouse with a tall choker neckline. "After our late night, I was worried you wouldn't wake up on time. So, I decided to come in myself, just in case."

Susanna cocked one brow. "Have I ever been late?"

Hannah ducked her head. "No. But there's always a first." She gave Susanna a hug, then leaned back, examining her face. "You look rested. I'm glad. I guess our talk really helped."

"You don't know the half of it," Susanna said, handing Hannah her apron. She should be dead on her feet, and she wasn't. She still couldn't believe Albert had finally, *finally* kissed her, after all this time. And what a kiss! Just thinking about it made her tummy kindle up into a warm mass of honey and an all-consuming tingle that had her wondering what several kisses could do.

Albert wasn't giving up. That's what he'd said last night. As much as she wanted to let his words send her skipping through the room, she had to be practical, remember how he'd left his first wife so quickly. He'd told her he hadn't known about the child, but did that really make a difference? Would he leave her, too?

"You look like the fox that got the last egg. What happened after I left? I can't imagine you went straight to sleep."

Susanna hadn't noticed that after her last comment Hannah had stopped what she was doing and stood, hands on hips, staring at her. "Do I?"

"Yes, you do. You look different. Tell me right now. It certainly wasn't me telling you about my happy marriage. No, that wouldn't do *this*—" She waved her hand around, indicating Susanna as a whole. "No, there is something else going on. Out with it."

So much had transpired last night that Susanna didn't know where to start. Her initial reaction was to keep it to herself, as she'd been in the habit of doing for most of her life—and especially since coming to Logan Meadows. But, hadn't it been nice to share her feelings? She shouldn't be so secretive.

"Susanna? You're being cruel. Tell me right now."

Just as Susanna opened her mouth, the bells above the door jingled out that someone had come into the restaurant. Hannah groaned. "Hold that thought," she said, lifting the coffeepot from the stove and pushing through the door.

Susanna hardly had time to stick a new loaf into the oven to bake when Hannah dashed back in. "What's left to do? Three tables came in at once, and I just have this feeling it's going to be busy."

"Anyone I know?"

"Funny you should ask." She gave Susanna a playful smile. "Albert and Nate at one table. Across the room, Dalton at another. And a third man I don't know. As I was pouring their coffee, they both asked if you were here, and if you might be able to step out and have a word."

Flustered, Susanna slipped into the cold room and returned with a bowlful of eggs. Could she face Albert today after kissing him last night?

Hannah grasped the container of eggs and wrestled it from her arms. "Go on and say good morning. I'll start a batch of scramblers. But only be a minute, mind you, we have things to do."

All Susanna could think about was Albert's lips on hers, and his large hand pressed to her waist. *Scandalous!*

"Yes, all right. I'll just say hello, then come right back." She felt a little foolish asking, but turned to Hannah all the same. "How do I look?"

"Beautiful."

Taking courage, she pushed through the door. She hadn't gone but a couple of steps toward Albert's usual table when she stopped short. A dark bruise marred the lower half of his jaw, and his face was scraped in a couple of places. She glanced across the room to Dalton's table. He smiled but held his coffee mug conspicuously close to his face. As hard as he tried, it didn't cover his black eye.

They'd been fighting!

Nate sat up straighter when he saw her. His shiny-clean face looked rested since she'd seen him last night at Nana's, and his hair was combed. As she approached his table, his eyes jerked toward his pa several times, indicating she should look at Albert. The boy was probably happy it was his pa in trouble for fighting and not him.

"Good morning," she said tenderly to Nate, cupping his face for one brief moment before turning her attention on Albert. She couldn't hold his brown-eyed gaze for long, and felt herself blush. "Looks like you found some trouble last night after all," she said drawing the attention off herself. "What happened?"

"It wasn't last night, ma'am. It was this morning on his way home from town. He—"

"Nate, I'll tell Miss Robinson what happened, if you don't mind. Just give me a chance."

"Sorry, Pa. Don't forget to tell her you was in the creek when you got to fighting. And how a salamander went down your back." He squished up his face and curled his fingers at her as if they were his claws, all the while snapping his teeth repeatedly.

It was impossible not to laugh. He really was a darling. Albert didn't quite think so at that moment. It was evident he'd hoped to keep most of those details between them.

"Fighting in the creek? I'm surprised you told Nate all that." She glanced over her shoulder to see Dalton watching. "With Dalton?"

Albert nodded. "Nate and I aren't going to have any secrets between us. We thought things would go better that way." Father and son exchanged a look. "I can't expect the truth from him unless I give it myself."

That jerked Susanna back to their problem that she'd forgotten about for all of three blessed minutes. Resolve pushed away her longing. "That's a good plan. Nothing like starting off on the right foot. How're you staying awake? You haven't had any sleep."

"Thoughts of you."

She pursed her lips in disbelief, but knew the words were true for her. "I only have one second to say hello and I have to get back to work." She took a moment to really look at Albert, his bruised chin and longing eyes. "Would you like your usual?"

"Yes, and Nate'll have the same."

She nodded, turned, and approached Dalton, who jerked his face away when he realized she was headed over. He gazed into his mug.

"Really, Dalton. I can't believe the two of you."

"I wasn't intending to fight. Somehow it just got started. Anyway, I've learned my lesson." He pointed to his black eye. "I haven't had a shiner since I was thirteen. I'm pretty embarrassed. Especially with the bankers coming to town."

"You're rambling."

"Susanna," Hannah called through the closed swinging door. "These eggs are ready."

"I'll be right there, Hannah," Susanna called back as she shook her head. "Men." Before she could walk off, Dalton caught her wrist. "I know fighting is immature, Suzie, but I'd do it again to get your attention. At least now you know I'm serious. Don't write me off just because you and Albert are making up. Consider what your life could be like if we went back home to Breckenridge. You have friends there, and I have family. I'm serious. I want to marry you."

A chair scraped loudly behind her. Albert was on his feet. His clenched jaw and angry eyes were a good indicator he was about to march over any moment. She held out her hand to stay his advance. "I'll keep that in mind, Dalton. I will. Right now I have to get back to work."

She greeted the third customer, who looked plenty entertained, and took his order. Things today were just heating up.

CHAPTER FORTY-ONE

$\mathcal{G}$usts of wind scattered the dirt in the street and whipped the horses' tails around. Women hurried along the boardwalk with one hand clamped to their skirts and the other one on their bonnets. Frustrated that the soldiers had yet to arrive, Albert paced like a caged wolf, back and forth in front of the El Dorado Hotel. The twelve o'clock stage from Denver was due any minute.

A family of five waited eagerly in the hotel lobby with their bags packed. Every few minutes the husband braved the wind by coming out the door to peer up the street. He'd nod amicably to Albert and then disappear back inside. A lone man, lucky passenger number six, who'd gotten the last seat on the incoming stage, leaned against the outside wall.

Albert's patience was at a breaking point. Someone of importance better be on this stage. Someone who could arrange transport of the money without incident. The torment of guarding the bank and putting up with Babcock had him cranky. After the money was gone, he'd have time to concentrate on winning Susanna back, and to spend with Nate, help him grieve.

Rumbling wheels and jangling harnesses alerted him to the approaching stage. It rounded the corner. The driver pulled the animals down to a trot and finally to a halt in front of the hotel. A cloud of dust billowed out everywhere, made worse by the aggravating wind.

Impatient, Albert stepped forward before the dirt had a chance to clear and pulled open the narrow door.

Empty!

What the hell is going on? I have a million dollars sitting in a two-room bank and no one seems to care.

Angry, he turned on Ralph, who was climbing down from the front seat. The wiry man wore a coat of dust from head to toe. His weary smile faded when he saw Albert's scuffed face.

"Don't ask."

"All right, Sheriff, I won't."

"Where's the banker?" Albert demanded.

Ralph's face turned crotchety. "Don't get testy with me, Albert Preston. You may be the sheriff of Logan Meadows but that don't give ya the right to bite my head off the moment I arrive. I'm the one who just drove a hundred miles, not you." Once on the ground Ralph took a moment to stretch out his back. "You sure got up on the wrong side of the bed today."

"I never got up because I never went to bed."

"That explains it. Now, who're you lookin' for?"

The Cooper family piled out the hotel door anxious to get their baggage loaded. When one of the boys went to climb up the back of the coach, Ralph stopped him. "Just set it here, sonny. I'll load the baggage. We still got some time—'bout half an hour to be exact."

Ralph turned back to Albert. "Who was you expectin', Sheriff?"

Feeling a bit contrite for treating Ralph so shabbily, Albert tried to smile. "Some bankers from Denver. You wouldn't know anything about them, would you?"

"I sure the heck don't. But that don't mean much. They could'a missed a connection somewhere along the way, had one of the team pull up lame, or could'a got sick so bad they couldn't travel. Last I heard, Coloradie was getting some snow. Could'a closed the pass. Any one of a hundred things out there could'a tripped 'em up."

While Ralph was getting the mail bag from under the driver's seat, Albert noticed Babcock riding up the street on his horse. Why wasn't the man home in his bed, asleep? He'd had the same shift Albert had last night. They'd both pulled off at five, then he'd seen him in the restaurant at seven, and now here he was again at noon. Was the man too thick in the head to understand he was supposed to be sleeping so he'd be alert for his next shift tonight?

Anger bubbled within his own tired body as he rubbed his gritty eyes. If he wasn't careful, his lack of sleep would wear him down. Mistakes would happen. Was that what the outlaws were waiting for?

Beth came out of the mercantile with the canvas mail sack and headed for the stage. With a snooty look down her long nose, she handed the bag to Ralph and took the one he held. She scooted off as if interaction with any of them was far below her level. Ralph watched her walk all the way back to the mercantile, and didn't take his eyes from her path until she'd disappeared inside the building.

Ralph turned to him. "Ain't she just about the purttiest little gal you ever did see?" His eyes were glassy and his weathered face took on a faraway look that made him appear years younger.

Albert swiveled to see who Ralph was talking about. It couldn't be Miss Fairington. Perhaps someone else had walked up when Albert wasn't looking. But the street was empty except for Babcock, who'd dismounted and tied his horse to the hitching rail, and a few other men ambling along in either direction. "Who? Beth Fairington?"

The stage driver, who couldn't be more than five feet tall, squinted up into Albert's face. "Whaddya mean who? Of course, I mean Miss Fairington," he said in a quarrelsome tone. Albert's bad mood had rubbed off on him. "A woman like that don't come along but once in a lifetime."

And thank God for that!

"Yeah, I guess you're right, Ralph. Does she know how you feel about her?"

He pulled back as if someone had struck him in the face. "Naw, I ain't fit to wipe her boots." He removed his hat and smacked it several times across his pants creating a small cloud of dust. "Darn this wind. I'm not presentable for a den of varmints."

Albert patted him on the back. "Go get yourself something to eat while you still have time. I see Win on his way down to water your stock, buckets in hand." Nate tromped at his side, face downcast and wind blowing his hair. Win had reported that Nate had withdrawn into himself last night, then woke up with nightmares. He'd seemed fine at breakfast, but now he looked pretty downcast. Albert wished he could help somehow.

Seemed there was nothing to be done except wait, and be patient. Show Nate how much he cared. When Ralph turned around, Albert gave him an apologetic smile. "Sorry I about bit your head off. I'm at the end of my rope and took it out on you."

Dalton looped his reins loosely around the hitching rail and waited by his horse's side. He glanced around. Where was the bank employee? Had he missed him? He'd thought to come before the stage arrived, but didn't want to get in Albert's way any more than he had to. And if he was honest with himself, he wanted to make sure the sheriff wasn't sneaking into the Silky Hen for more one-on-one time with Suzie. She was partial to him, and it wouldn't take much for her to forgive the whole ugly mess. Now that Dalton had come to terms with his own feelings, he didn't want his chances with her to be snatched away so quickly. She needed time to get to know him again, and what he had to offer, then she'd be able to make a better decision. Maybe she was ready to leave this town. Logan Meadows couldn't hold much happiness for her now that Albert had a son to remind her every minute that he'd lied to her.

"No banker?" Dalton asked, ambling over to Albert. He noticed the bruise on Albert's chin had deepened in color.

"No. No banker." Albert started away, presumably headed for the sheriff's office.

"Albert, hold up."

Albert turned and waited until he caught him. "Did the driver know why no one was on the stage?"

"No, he had no idea."

The bloodshot stain of Albert's eyes was almost painful to look at. "You need some sleep. Can't you take an hour or two before tonight?"

"We need to figure out what's going on with this money, Babcock. I don't like having it holed up in our bank, a lure for any roughneck looking for a free ticket. If it hadn't been for the need to get Evan out, we'd have been better off leaving it in the fortified train car out at Three Pines Turn."

"No, that's not true. It's on a deadline to reach San Francisco. They'll be here soon."

"I don't like that you brought this down on our heads."

Dalton took a step closer. He didn't like Albert's tone one bit. "Are you blaming me for the wreck?"

"I have to blame someone and it may as well be you. We need to get that money on its way or find a way to hire a heck of a lot more guards. Problem is, there aren't that many men I know who're good with a gun. Most around here are farmers and ranchers who kill game to feed their families, not shoot at men. Shooting a man takes a whole different set of nerves."

"I hear you on that."

Albert's stance relaxed some, and Dalton nodded. "I just want you to know I appreciate all you've done so far. With the other two guards either gone or incapacitated, I needed help, and you supplied it."

Albert's stony gaze never wavered. "Just doing my job."

He was going to have to eat a little crow to win the sheriff back to his side. They couldn't stay at odds like this and keep the money safe. "We need to work together, Albert. Neither one of us likes the situation with Suzie—"

Albert jerked up straight.

"With Susanna," he quickly amended. "But we can't let that interfere with the challenge we still have ahead of us. What do you say to calling a truce? Just for the time being?"

Albert's stiff body and red, tired eyes spoke for themselves. Dalton wouldn't get too far with him now. A three-hour sleep would do far more to improve his temperament than anything Dalton could say, unless it was that he was throwing in the towel where Susanna was concerned, and that wasn't going to happen.

Best to change his approach and start over before Albert stomped off. Win and Nate had passed by on the opposite side of the street and had arrived at the stage. They dipped the buckets they carried into the water trough to give to the horses. When Nate looked up, Albert waved and smiled.

"How's he doing?"

"We're getting by. Taking one day at a time." Albert ambled off, and Dalton followed. He'd have to return later for his horse. Albert gave a long-suffering sigh. "Seriously, Babcock, don't you want to go get some shut-eye while you still can? Whatever you say isn't going to sway me away from Susanna."

"I know, I know. That's why I thought we could plan what to do if no bank men show up. I've been thinking that maybe they've been murdered."

Albert swung around.

"Don't tell me you haven't been thinking the same thing."

They started up the boardwalk together this time. "I have. Or something like it. You go send another telegram to the bank. Try to get specifics. I want names and dates, if indeed they actually left Denver when they said they did."

"Got it. Do you have anything pressing at the moment? If not, go get a few minutes sleep upstairs in your old apartment. The bed's still up there, right?"

"Are you *still* trying to tell me what to do, Babcock? Because I *still* don't like it one little bit. I'm headed to Dr. Thorn's to check on Evan. See if he's made any progress."

Dalton narrowed his eyes. The sheriff was allowed to see Evan, but *he* wasn't? What was Albert fishing for with Evan? What could Evan know that he didn't? "The longer he lies there, the less likely he'll make a recovery. Has he woken up at all?"

Albert shook his head. "No. And what of Pat Tackly? I haven't seen hide nor hair of him since I left him in the hotel."

"I haven't seen him either." The sheriff turned to take one more look at his son. Down at the hotel, Nate helped Win lug the heavy buckets back and forth. Albert glanced up at the clouds and his eyes narrowed. His words echoed what Dalton was feeling: "There's a storm on the way. It'll be here in a few days at the most."

CHAPTER FORTY-TWO

$\mathscr{M}$onday morning, and groggy from another long night, Albert made his way toward the livery where, by five, Win and Nate would already be feeding the horses. Albert was looking forward to the morning off, a plateful of eggs and potatoes, and a long nap. He crossed the deserted street, leaning into the wind as he eyed the dark menacing clouds overhead. Friday had finally brought a reply from Denver. Knowing the bank representatives had set out on schedule but were slowed down by a snowstorm in the high country helped. At least he didn't have to be disappointed every day when they didn't show up on the stage. Just hold tight until they arrived, that was the message in the telegram. But even if Albert had no choice but to wait on the bank, there were other things he could accomplish. He'd gotten a telegram off to Corey, requesting he find Floria's mother and let her know of her daughter's death. He still had the trunks to go through, but each time he made an attempt, memories made him put the chore off.

As he approached Win's large barn, he glanced up to find Nate lying on his stomach in the darkened hayloft, watching him.

"Morning, Nate," Albert said, a surge of love lifting his spirits. The wind ruffled Nate's hair and sent a few strands of hay dancing in the air. It was a moment before his son smiled back. Nate hadn't mentioned Floria to him again, but Albert wasn't convinced the boy had stopped thinking about her being trapped in the train.

"Hey, Pa." In the dim light, Win's barn cat appeared by Nate's shoulder, and he pulled her into a hug.

"Win," Albert called, stepping into the quiet barn.

"Back here," came the reply.

Albert walked down the row of stalls to the end, finding his brother inside the last one with pitchfork and wheelbarrow. "Storm's brewing outside. You looked out there lately?"

"Earlier. It'll be a doozy when it finally hits."

"There wasn't a soul on the street."

Win took his handkerchief from his pocket and wiped his moist face. "Just finishing up a few things before my shift at the bank," he replied, stretching his back muscles. "I'm going to hire another helper. I liked it when Thom was here. That man's a good worker."

"No, you can't have Thom back," Albert kidded. He leaned against the stall divider, getting comfortable. "You know Nate's in the loft?"

"Yeah, he went up there as soon as we finished feeding. It's my fault."

Alarm snapped Albert up straight. "Whaddya mean?"

"I had a horse colic last night. Before I realized how serious it was, she died out in the pasture, right there with Nate petting her neck. I'm sorry, Albert. It really shook him up. He's been pretty quiet ever since."

Albert grunted, then gripped the back of his neck. There was so much he didn't know about children. He felt lost. How did one get past a violent train wreck and the death of a mother?

Win lifted a forkful of soiled straw and tossed it into the wheelbarrow. "And the soldiers from Fort McKinney?"

"Still expecting them any day. I really thought they'd be here by now. I get the same reply every time I send a telegram. En route." Albert sighed, then took a step toward the door. "I'll go up and get Nate, take him with me to the office and play some checkers until Susanna opens the restaurant. He'll like that."

Win set the prongs of the pitchfork in the soft earth and leaned against the shaft. "Have you told her yet?"

"I thought we had this discussion already."

His brother gave him a stern look. "What's that mean? Yes or no?"

"She doesn't need to know the particulars about Floria, and how she carried on behind my back. Not yet anyway. But, if things do work out between us, which I'm counting on, I'll tell her eventually. I know the truth'll be safe with her. I'm just not ready to voice it."

"I wish you would, Albert. Before it's too late."

"I know you do, Win. I just can't go there yet."

Albert walked back toward the front of the barn. A game of checkers was sounding pretty good as a distraction for him, too. He set a foot on the first rung of the ladder leading to the hayloft and called up, "Nate?"

Susanna had solved her problem by not solving it at all—not yet, anyway. She didn't care if avoiding the issue was considered weak. Saturday and Sunday had come and gone without a mention of the hurtful and perplexing situation with Albert, giving her heart a rest, and for that she was thankful. *One day at a time. That's how I'll get through.* One day at a time and *nothing* more. Between his shifts and worry over the bank, Albert hadn't come into the restaurant, and she hadn't tried to seek him out. Every time she felt herself softening toward him, the enormity of his lie of omission hit her smack in the face and she fell right back on her mother's credo.

Susanna lifted her cape from the peg by the door and fastened it around her shoulders, relieved to have work to keep her mind busy. The wind that had beleaguered the town for the last few days whistled around the eaves, sending a lonely chill up her spine.

Storms! She hated them. They reminded her of her stepfather's heartless prank. The dark room and locked door. The body-filled casket. The howling wind outside. The recollection was as fresh as the day it had happened.

Dredging up fortitude, Susanna pulled her hood over her head and hoisted the basket that held several jars of jam, protectively covered with a towel. She opened the door to the dark morning. Roiling clouds covered the sky and a northern wind rushed inside. Rain and wind were common in April; she just wished the storm would hold off until she made the short walk to the Silky Hen.

Ducking her head, she stepped out and pulled the door closed. Right away, the wind picked up the corners of her cape and whipped the garment around. Clamping down on her hood, she hurried away, knowing the street would be a sea of mud by the time she returned home late in the afternoon.

Within a minute, she was at the bridge. The light of several lanterns on Main Street was a welcome sight, soothing her runaway nerves. Straightening the basket of jams in the crook of her elbow, she hurried on, the glass containers clinking against each other and competing with the sound of the wind.

"Susanna!"

She whirled around. Albert ran toward her on foot, the reins of his saddled horse in his hand as it trotted behind. The brim of his hat took a beating from the wind. He wore his typical black leather vest and guns on his hips. The sight of him brought a burst of excitement only he could create. Her thoughts jumped to the kiss, but she pushed the sensation away and smiled. "Albert."

His gaze jerked here and there as he neared. "Come next to the building so you can hear me," he said, ushering her toward the bookshop, his arm over her back. Something was desperately wrong. She'd never seen such desperation in his eyes. Chase watched them from his post at the bank. Flanked by the wall on one side, Albert on the other, and his horse, too, she asked, "What's wrong?"

"Nate's missing."

Alarm raced through her body. "What do you mean he's missing? It's only half past five."

A deep V pulled down between Albert's brows. Lines she'd never noticed before bracketed his eyes, and he looked haggard, older than he should. She longed to reach out and soothe away his disquiet, but she stayed her hand.

"He was just in Win's hayloft only thirty minutes ago. I went there to pick him up."

"Then he has to be here somewhere, Albert. Surely he's just hiding someplace where he can be alone." She glanced up the street toward the Silky Hen, wondering what Hannah would think when she didn't prepare the breakfast stuffs on time. One thing for sure, the world wouldn't come to a screeching halt if she didn't open up at seven. "I'll help you. Tell me everything you know."

"I'm half out of my mind. If anything has happened to my boy I'll never . . ." He clenched his fist, and his lips twitched. She'd never seen him so distraught.

"Shhh, nothing bad has happened to him, I'm sure. He's probably just hiding away because he's still grieving. He's been through so much in the last few days."

"I've alerted Chase and Charlie to keep an eye out for him and spread the word to anyone who ventures out in the storm. I've searched everywhere I thought he'd go. The cemetery, the creek, Maximus and Clementine's paddock, even though I told him to stay out. My old apartment where I took him right after we buried his mother. I've ridden a circle around the town as well . . ."

"Surely, he must—"

"No. I have a feeling . . ." Albert looked away, as if unable to go on. He shook his head. "He took off on his own. Maybe he's trying to make it back to Iowa. I don't know. But I can tell you, I'm more scared now than I've ever been facing down an outlaw's gun."

Susanna turned and strode up the street with purpose. "Come on," she called over her shoulder, her words swallowed by a gust of wind. "I need to leave this basket of jams inside the restaurant. It'll only take a moment, and then I'll help you any way I can." And she would. She would try to fly to the moon if he asked her. They'd been through so much. They passed Chase in stony silence, the ranchers forehead lined with worry. Nate might be in trouble, and needed her. She wouldn't let him, or his father, down.

CHAPTER FORTY-THREE

Susanna struggled with the restaurant's temperamental lock, every moment a stabbing pain to Albert. On her third try, Albert gently extracted the key from her hand, unintentionally brushing her fingers. A burst of longing ripped through him, making him feel even more disconcerted.

"Sorry," he rasped out, not sure where they stood after her four days of silence. He'd hoped the kiss would start things moving in the right direction—get them talking. All it had done was make him want her more.

With a jiggling twist, the lock gave way.

"I hate this temperamental old thing," she said as he pushed the door open for her. "I'll have Thom replace it. I'm not even going to ask Hannah. One can only take so much!"

Susanna breezed inside. It was dark. He waited by the door as she hurried through the room and into the kitchen. He glanced at the antique Dutch pendulum clock above the wooden sideboard without even seeing the time.

Susanna returned. As he opened the door to leave, she grasped his arm. "Albert, did you check Three Pines Turn? Maybe Nate went out to the train looking for his mother."

"The train! Of course!" Albert's heart thumped painfully against his breastbone. He'd overlooked the most obvious place of all. "No. You're exactly right. That's where he's headed. To release his mother from the wreckage." He looked down at her skirt. "It's only half a mile—a short ride on a horse. Would you consider riding behind me? We'd get there so much faster if I don't have to hitch a buggy."

"Of course."

"You're in a dress. And I've never seen you ride."

"When have I had time when I'm always in this kitchen cooking? I used to be a good rider when I was a girl."

He almost smiled, imagining Susanna galloping across the open prairie with her long black hair trailing behind. "You have a point. Let's go."

It took some doing to get her aboard Dunbar, with the wind flapping her long skirt and cape. His gelding didn't like the idea one bit. He snorted and pranced around every time Albert tried to give her a hand up. Taking his foot from the stirrup, he pointed. "When I pull you up, slide your foot into the stirrup."

Her cheeks went crimson. "Fine, but glance away while I gather my skirt or else I won't be able to get past all the material." A moment passed. "I'm ready."

Determined, Albert reached down, grasped her arm, and fumbled her aboard behind him. Dunbar jerked to the side, and gave a halfhearted crow hop, eliciting a cry from Susanna. Albert still had a grip on her arm but couldn't ride that way. "You'll have to wrap your arms around my waist."

At first, he thought she wasn't going to comply. Then one arm came forward, and then the next. Her warmth seeped through his clothing as she gripped her hands together above his belt buckle. "You ready back there?" he asked over his shoulder.

A thunderbolt let loose, making him flinch and her gasp.

"Yes. Let's go find Nate."

His gelding jumped forward at his first asking, unsure of what was on his back. Usually skittish in the wind, the scent of lightning in the air had him wild-eyed. Now with Susanna's billowing clothing, Dunbar was as unpredictable as a two-year-old on his first time out.

"Give him a minute to get used to you." Albert tried to look behind, but the wind made it difficult. "Feel secure?" Her grip around his middle had steadily increased. They jogged a few more strides until they were out of town. "Here we go, just relax and hang on. It won't take but a few minutes to get out there. I want to beat the rain."

He eased Dunbar into a lope, the sky in front of them as black as night. He had to find Nate before the clouds let go. He must be frightened, and cold. What if they were wrong? What if Nate had gone in the opposite direction and this was just a wild-goose chase?

The once-obscure road to Three Pines Turn, now well-worn from the wagons and buggies that had transferred the injured passengers, flew by under Dunbar's hooves. Albert tried not to think of Nate and how scared he might be. He tried not to think about Susanna and how good she felt with her arms wrapped tightly around his waist. He wouldn't let himself think of anything until Nate was back in his arms.

CHAPTER FORTY-FOUR

$\mathscr{T}$he specter of the train wreckage came into view, and without thinking, Susanna tightened her hold on Albert. In the darkness, with the roiling clouds overhead, flashes of light far off in the distance of the storm on its way, the crippled engine sitting askew on the twisted tracks, the whole scene looked frightening. Dread inched up her spine. She recalled the bodies, at the time of the crash, lined up in a row on the grassy bank.

"Hey, you're shaking," Albert said over his shoulder after he placed one of his hands over hers clenched at his middle. "Nothing to be scared of. It's just a train off its tracks."

Last summer, they'd been caught out in the meadow by a fast-approaching storm. At her strong reaction to the thunder and lightning, he'd wheedled from her a tiny fraction of her fear, but not from where it stemmed. He'd listened intently, and hadn't tried to tell her that her qualms were irrational. The compassion he'd shown had touched her heart.

"I know," she said, laying her cheek against his cool black vest. She closed her eyes for one moment, experiencing what it was like to be close to him for the little time she had left. She'd never felt safer. "When I was a small girl," she began, "my stepfather locked me in the parlor with the body of his dead brother set out for viewing. It was stormy and dark. He made noises like a ghost and thought it funny when I cried and begged for him to open the door. Sometimes I wake up in a sweat, the sounds of those brittle branches on glass scraping in my ears."

She was unaware that the horse had stopped and Albert had his head tipped back listening to her small voice.

He swiveled in the saddle, until he could see her eyes. "I'm so sorry." She could tell he felt her devastation. He cupped her cheek, and for an instant she thought he was going to kiss her, but instead he rubbed his thumb over her cold skin. "I won't let anything hurt you, Susanna. You're safe with me."

When lightning flashed, she trembled, but was able to say, "I know."

Albert reached around and grasped her forearm in his strong hand. "Down you go, easy now. I've got you until your feet hit the ground."

When she was stable on the uneven earth, he dismounted. More lightning crisscrossed the horizon. Dunbar jerked back, and if Albert hadn't had a firm grip on the reins, the horse would have bolted.

"Nate!" Albert yelled above the sound of the wind. "Nate! Are you here, son? Come out so I can take you home!"

She joined in. After a few minutes of calling without any results, he turned to her. "Let's load Dunbar into a stock car and start at the passenger cars. I think that's where he'd look for his mother." He turned and looked at her. "You ready to run?"

She nodded, but still felt flighty inside.

Understanding softened his face. He held out his hand. "It's okay. No ghosts or dead bodies here. It's a thunderstorm that will soon pass."

Susanna placed her hand in his, and they ran bent over to cut through the driving wind. Raindrops began to fall. The stock cars were toward the end of the train. Susanna held her hood on with her free hand and clutched Albert's large hand with her other.

"Nate!" he called forward and back as they ran. "Nate! Are you here, son?"

He tried to hide his anguish, but Susanna saw his mouth twist in pain. Reaching the stock cars, Dunbar didn't hesitate when Albert climbed up into the dark interior and pulled on his reins. The horse hopped inside with loud, clomping hooves.

Standing alone outside of the stock car in the windy darkness, she tried to keep her fears at bay. Branches swayed back and forth in the nearby trees, and debris blew across the ground. The train stretched forward, growing smaller and smaller until it seemed to disappear into the murky dark clouds. For a moment, she imagined she saw a figure standing on top of the train far to the front. Fright made her flinch, and when she glanced back, the image was gone.

Albert jumped out next to her as a flash of lightning sizzled overhead, and within three seconds, a deafening clap of thunder exploded above their heads. The horse snorted and scrabbled on the wooden floor, but his reins kept him firmly in place.

Susanna flung herself into Albert's arms, shaking visibly. She pulled back and looked up into his concerned eyes. "We need to get moving," she said, fighting her fears as she tried to stay calm. Large drops of rain splattered around, and were soon coming down in a sheet.

Albert's gaze softened even more and he took her hand. "All right then, keep an eye out." He looked forward, scanning the darkness. "Nate!" he yelled again. "Come out, son! Come out and let's go home! Nate!"

"Nate," she called, hurrying to keep up with Albert, who'd started for the passenger cars. "Nate," she called again, doing her best to banish the eerie feeling that kept the hair at the back of her neck prickled.

CHAPTER FORTY-FIVE

$\mathcal{A}$ slow panic rumbled around inside of Albert as he made his way slowly down the dining-car aisle. An hour had passed. The rain and howling wind were unrelenting. Searching in the darkness was difficult. He hadn't said anything to Susanna, but it was conceivable that outlaws might be out here. It would be a good place to stay holed up and out of sight. A panicked thought struck him: perhaps someone had taken Nate as a decoy. His breath quickened. He couldn't think that. His son was distressed and had run off. Until he had evidence, he wouldn't entertain that option—but he would keep a sharper eye out than he'd let on to Susanna.

Some articles had been cleared by the porters after the crash, but chairs and dishes were still strewn around just waiting to trip them up. Susanna came along behind him, searching the opposite side of the car. He cursed to himself for not thinking to bring matches to light some of the lamps. Thank goodness Susanna had offered to help. With her probing one side of the aisle as he searched the other, they made much better time. His hoarse voice ached from continually calling out.

"Nate, it's Pa," he shouted again through his cupped palms. "You aren't in any trouble, son. Please come out." His boot struck something hard in the aisle. He bent over and moved the chair blocking the way. "You must be hungry. A big bowl of stew sure sounds good to me. We can sit in the restaurant and watch the storm. You can have as much bread as you want, I promise." His voice hitched, and he blinked away moisture that had gathered in his eyes. *Where are you, Nate? Where are you son?*

He stopped and waited for Susanna to catch up. It was no use. Nate wasn't here. Or if he was, he wasn't coming out. Albert didn't know what he could have done better to help his son grieve, adjust to his new home. He still didn't know why Floria had been on her way to Logan Meadows. It was all such a mystery.

"Albert, I need to poke my head outside and get a breath of fresh air. The walls are closing in on me. You keep going and I'll catch up."

"You all right?"

She nodded. "Yes, I'll just take a minute."

Her hair that had been so prettily fixed this morning was now stuck to the sides of her head, and the bottom of her skirt was a mess, but in his eyes, she'd never looked more beautiful.

"Thank you for your help, Susanna. It means a lot to me."

She gave that quirky little smile that had been reserved for him before he'd messed things up. "Of course I'd help you, Albert. I want to find Nate just as much as you do."

Something had changed between them since her revelation about what her stepfather had done to her. He couldn't name the transformation, but he felt it in his bones.

She laid a comforting hand on his arm, her gaze reaching deep into his. "We'll find him, Albert," she whispered. "I promise."

He nodded, needing more than anything to believe her words. "I'll keep moving forward. Don't be long."

Taking a deep, cleansing breath, Susanna enjoyed the feel of the cool air in her lungs. She leaned against the outside of the dining car and cast her fears to the wind. The rain had stopped. If they could just get past this with Nate, find him alive and unharmed, she'd try to forgive Albert everything. But marriage was a lifelong commitment. She didn't understand why he'd wed Floria and then changed his mind so quickly—after, of course, he'd taken what she had to offer. What had Floria been like? Was she heartbroken when her husband had cast her aside and moved away? Had she decided she couldn't live another day without him and was on her way to try and reconcile? Susanna had so many questions, and no answers at all.

A sound caught her attention. She looked up at the clouds that were breaking up and letting in some morning light. She hadn't meant to stay out so long. Surely Albert was already three cars ahead and wondering where she was. What was *that* sound? She held her breath, trying to discern through the wind's howl the other, stranger, crunching she'd picked up on when she'd been in deep thought. It almost had sounded like a footstep on the gravel.

Albert turned and retraced his steps. Where was Susanna? With her fear of storms, he'd have thought she'd be back quickly. He'd like to get his hands on the cow dung that got a thrill by frightening a child. A burst of anger moved his steps more quickly.

With the aisle now clear of debris, he was able to make good time back to the dining car. He swung out the door and jumped down from the bridge that connected the train—and came face-to-face with the barrel of Laine Sadler's gun.

Albert pulled up short, but held his tongue until he saw Susanna standing between two men, strangers he recognized from the saloon. The way her arms were pulled tightly behind her made him think they were tied or cuffed. He caught her gaze. Her ripped sleeve, the fury in her eyes, and a tiny trickle of blood on the corner of her lip said she'd put up a good fight before she'd been subdued. He'd been right about someone lurking on the train—but it wasn't the outlaw he'd expected.

"Me and my boys have been getting mighty impatient waiting for an opportunity to bust that money out, Sheriff Preston," Wallace Sadler said, stepping out of the shadows and lifting Albert's gun out of the holster. "Now, though, you're going to waltz right in and do it for us—nice and peaceful like."

Laine Sadler let out a bark of laughter. Gone was the sweet prairie dress he'd noticed when Dalton had introduced the family. Gone was the kind and generous glint in her eyes, replaced with a cold hard steel. The wind buffeted her hat and pulled at strands of her hair, her revolver still pointing in his face.

"Who says I'll do anything to help? Guns will be blazing before you get two feet out the door."

The other men looked between themselves. Seemed nobody wanted to be killed before they got their share of one million dollars.

"No they won't. Not if you want to see this little lady ever again." Laine Sadler turned and smiled at Susanna. "If you won't cooperate, we'll kill you now, ride into town, and kill as many townsfolk as we can, then rob the bank. We'll take her with us deep into the heart of Mexico. She'll bring a pretty penny when the men are through with her."

Albert felt Susanna's gaze on him, strong and true. The sound of boots crunching on rocks brought all the heads around. The other two men pulled their guns.

Babcock stepped out from between two cars, the wind battering his hat and coat, his twin colts resting in each hand. His narrowed-eyed gaze went from face to face, skimmed over Susanna as if she didn't mean a thing to him, then landed on Mrs. Sadler. The fool had just walked into a gunfight he couldn't win. Babcock might take down two before he was killed, but he couldn't get them all.

"So, you were going to cut me out just like that?" Babcock said in a half sneer. "I've been trying to hook up with you ever since I came out to the Red Rooster. Damn that old woman and that busybody Beth."

Laine straightened. It was evident she didn't know what to think of Babcock's sudden appearance. He didn't holster his guns.

"Evan brought me in on the deal right from the start. Said he'd sent you a telegram."

"We never got it," Wallace snarled. "You're lying."

"Could be, but I'm not."

Albert watched the conversation bounce back and forth, hoping Babcock didn't get his head blown off right here in front of Susanna. Babcock came a step closer.

"He's a filthy liar," one of the other men threw out. "We ain't cuttin' no one else in!"

"Then go get your sorry hides shot full of holes." Babcock's tone had turned to ice.

More clouds blew away, and the others seemed fidgety as the light of day encroached on their nefarious planning. There was a lot at stake.

"I can get you into the bank and you won't have to worry about the sheriff giving you away. All he'd have to do is say one word and the guards would cut you down. Why risk it? A million dollars is a lot of money. One more split isn't going to make a lick of difference to any of you. You'll still be filthy rich—*and alive to enjoy it.*"

Laine shifted her weight from foot to foot and looked as if she'd just eaten a rotten oyster. "He has a point." She motioned with her gun. "Cranston, tie these two up so we can make our move. We can't wait any longer for Evan. Rumor has it reinforcements are on their way."

One of the men standing beside Susanna didn't look much like an outlaw. He mumbled, "But he's our brother. We can't leave him behind."

"Shut your whiny mouth," Wallace barked. "He should've been prepared when the train hit, like we planned. Then he'd've been able to unlock the door and we'd be long gone days ago. He gets what he deserves."

For the first time since arriving, Babcock looked in Albert's direction. "I'm tying him up. Preston has been a burr under my saddle since the day I arrived." He pointed to the black eye that had yet to completely disappear. "Payback is going to feel real nice."

"I say we kill 'em both now," Cranston objected. "Dead men—and women—can't talk."

"No." Babcock straightened to his full height. "I want the woman. She sets the moon and stars." His gaze drifted to Albert.

Cranston snickered until Babcock zeroed in with a deadly gaze. The man shifted uncomfortably and looked away.

"You, there," Babcock said to the short fellow. "Get the horses ready to go, as well as the sheriff's mount in the stock car." He pointed toward the caboose, and Albert wondered how long Babcock had been hanging around.

It was easy to see Laine Sadler didn't like Babcock taking over. "Who made *you* boss?"

"I did. I'm the one who'll get you in that bank, aren't I? You got a problem with that?" Silence drew out until Babcock shrugged. "I didn't think so. Where's Terrence, your son?"

Laine laughed. "You mean my pain-in-the-neck little brother?" Her eyes gleamed with suspicion. "Seems Evan didn't tell you everything about the Stone family, Babcock—I wonder why?"

"They cut out today for New Meringue," the short outlaw said, as if he'd already transferred his loyalty to Babcock. "We're gonna swing by and get 'em on our ride out."

"They?"

"Him and another brother." A half-witted smile appeared on the man's face. "We're *all* brothers." He shot Laine a dirty look. "Except for our smarty-pants sister."

"Shut your trap!" Laine shouted. "I'm amazed someone hasn't killed you yet."

Babcock glanced between them. "Evan probably figured the less I knew, the better. At least, that's how I would play it. Makes no matter anyway. Now, we'll all go into town together. After we have the money, we'll swing back here, pick up *Suzie* and take care of him." He glared at Albert. "The woman will ride his horse."

Susanna's eyes widened. Albert hoped if Nate was hiding anywhere nearby, he had the sense to stay away. Babcock swiveled his gun on Albert.

"You go with 'em, Cranston," Laine ordered. "Make sure Babcock's not pulling a fast one."

CHAPTER FORTY-SIX

$\mathcal{H}$eart thrashing painfully against his ribs, Nate watched the scene unfold before his eyes. He feared the outlaws would hear the commotion and discover him hiding underneath the dining car on the cold tracks. He'd just decided to go home with his pa when Miss Robinson had come out of the train car and stood directly in front of his line of vision, her once-shiny black boots covered in mud.

He'd hesitated. Seeing her with his pa brought another surge of sadness for his mama. An outpouring of shame followed that, as he remembered she'd been on her way to give him away, to a pa he'd never met. She didn't love him anymore. She couldn't. No matter what she said, Nate knew Mr. Carson was more important to her than he was. She was going to marry him and go far, far away. No matter that the thought cut him like a knife, he still loved her.

He'd come down to the train to release her, to prove to his pa that he was right, that she was still trapped in the wreckage. And to prove to his ma that he was a good son, one she could love if she just let herself. Once that was accomplished, he and his ma could go home, put things back to the way they were before she'd met Mr. Carson. But he couldn't find her. He'd searched everywhere. It was like his pa had said. She was dead. Dead in the cold, hard ground—just like Oldie Judy.

Inch by slow inch, Nate crept backward. Finally on the other side of the tracks from his pa and the outlaws, he tiptoed away. When he was far enough away where he was sure they wouldn't hear him, he took off at a run, his boots splashing through puddles and sinking in mud. He'd seen his pa put Dunbar into the cattle car and wished he were big enough to pull himself into the saddle and gallop the tall dun gelding back to town. That would be faster. A better chance of saving his pa and Miss Robinson.

Where should he cross back under the train? What if they had more men on lookout? When it felt as if his lungs would burst, he skidded to a stop and rolled underneath the train, lying there for a good ten minutes to let his breathing settle back to its normal cadence. He didn't want any harm to come to Miss Robinson. She'd been kind to him. He liked her soft hands and pretty smile.

On his elbows, he crawled forward. He poked his head out, being careful to stay under the cover of the engine. The black clouds had cleared, pushed away by the driving wind. Turning his head, he looked all the way down to where he'd come from, but it was too far to see anyone. Staying close to the ground, Nate scampered away from the train and up the rise to the dirt road he'd followed from Logan Meadows to Three Pines Turn. He didn't stop there, but hurried into the trees and bushes alongside, where he wouldn't be easily spotted. Logan Meadows wasn't that far. Every single moment was prudent if he wanted to save his pa's life. Gathering his courage, he took off at a run.

Nate ignored the stabbing pain in his side. When the buildings of Logan Meadows finally came into view, he stumbled to a walk. He'd made it! The outlaws hadn't caught him. He'd find Pa's deputy and tell him what the outlaws were planning. He glanced over his shoulder and checked his back trail. Pa would be proud if he saved the day.

Nate let out a yelp when a large, rough hand came out of

nowhere and clasped him around the back of his neck. "Now I've gotcha, you little beggar! You're a quick one, I can testify to that."

Fear ricocheted through Nate's body, and he glanced up into a mean sneer and angry eyes.

"Let me go! Let me go!" Those were the last words out of his mouth as the large, unfamiliar man hoisted him up and threw him over his shoulder.

CHAPTER FORTY-SEVEN

$\mathscr{S}$usanna leaned her head against Albert's back, their hands bound together, and a none-too-nice handkerchief stuck in her mouth. A few feet away in the stock car, Albert's horse pranced nervously in place and pulled on his reins.

Albert bucked and strained against the restraints, causing a burst of pain in her wrists each time he moved. His muscles bulged, and then relaxed. The outlaws and Dalton had ridden out five minutes ago, which meant they had probably already reached town. How could she and Albert get away in time to warn everyone? Surely it wouldn't take long to rob the bank. She pushed with her tongue and worked at the sweaty red cloth, trying not to gag at the stench, but the bandanna around her head held it tight.

"Mmmmm. Suuuuuu." Albert shook his head; anger radiated off every inch of his body.

His unintelligible words made his horse prance all the more. He turned his head to the side and laid it against hers, bringing a rush of longing. If only she hadn't been so stubborn. At least he would know that she loved him—before he died. That she'd always loved him. Now, she'd not have a chance to tell him, or kiss him like she longed to do.

Albert twisted, and she stifled her groan. A warm sticky sensation slicked her fingers and she wondered which one of them was bleeding. They had to get free—had to warn the people in

Logan Meadows. She felt the restraints give a little and hope surged into her heart.

With a powerful jerk, Albert ripped one of his hands from their bonds. Blood splatted everywhere when he shook out the pain. One second later, he yanked the cloth out of his mouth and took a large gulp of air. Reaching around, he felt her face. The gag was too tight to pull down so he followed it to the back of her head, and worked the firm knot with his fingers. He fumbled several times before it fell into her lap.

She sucked in a lungful of crisp air. "Thank God! We need to hurry—"

"I know. I'm sure they're already—"

"No. It can't be!"

He worked furiously on the triple-knotted rope holding his other hand to her two.

"I love you, Albert!" she blurted.

He stilled, then awkwardly walked his body around until he could partially see into her face. "That's good to hear, darlin'. And I love you, too." He leaned in, but was only able to kiss her cheek. All the while he kept working the binding knot. "I hope you understand, but right now I have some outlaws to catch."

She felt the bindings fall away. He jumped to his feet and pulled her up and into his arms. The kiss was quick, but ardent. She glanced at his horse. "Go!"

"But what about you? Your fears—"

"Get going, Albert, before I take back my words! I'll be fine." She pushed him toward Dunbar.

With a nod, he untied his horse and jumped out of the car, the horse a ball of fire following in his path. "Stay in the bushes on your way to town," he yelled. "In case we can't stop them before they come back."

Without another word, Albert grasped the saddle horn and swung into the saddle as the horse galloped away.

CHAPTER FORTY-EIGHT

*D*alton dismounted in front of the saloon feeling the sweet tickle of sweat slipping between his shoulder blades. Twenty minutes ago, when they'd first arrived, Frank had exited the bank and hurried down the street to the mercantile. Frank was the only one who knew the combination to the safe, so they'd pulled up to wait on the edge of town until he returned. Dalton sent the two younger brothers, Cranston and the one who seemed afraid of his own shadow, into the saloon, to watch for his and Wallace's approach. Laine Sadler would sit her horse on the other side of the creek, and try not to draw any attention being she was out of her normal dress. She hid her guns in her odd-looking, overly large saddlebag that was just like those of the rest of the clan. Specially made for the heist, he was sure. Her flaps were turned under for fast retrieval of her weapons if the shooting started.

Chase Logan stood at the bank's front door and Thom was across the street. Thankfully, the street was uncommonly deserted. When the banker returned, they'd ridden in. Now, Wallace dismounted on Dalton's right, and the men they'd sent into the saloon ambled out, following a few feet behind. Wallace gave a small nod to Laine on the far side of the bridge.

They started slowly toward the bank talking about the storm. With a thumping heart, Dalton nodded to Chase and sent a quick glance to the haberdashery. The last thing he wanted was for anyone to be killed. Until now, Chase had seemed unaware that the two of them had even ridden up.

Dalton had tried to go it alone, but Wallace squashed that idea instantly. "Just in case you change your mind at the last minute," he had said with a nasty chuckle, "there'll be guns on you from both sides—helping you to keep a level head. Whatever happens, you'll be the first to die."

"Here we go," Dalton mumbled to Wallace. The outlaw gave a small dip of his chin but didn't respond. Dalton stepped onto the boardwalk in front of Chase. The rancher's hat was nonchalantly tipped back and he regarded Dalton with drowsy eyes.

"Babcock, it's not time for your shift yet," he said with a friendly smile. "I'm surprised you'd show your face this early in the day." He chuckled as if his statement were funny.

Wallace and the two others standing at his back had Dalton fidgety. He didn't want to be killed either. "Just wondering if anyone has heard from the soldiers we're expecting from Fort McKinney. I'm getting tired of staying up all night."

"Don't know," Chase said, his hand resting on the stock of his gun. "It's been mighty quiet after the storm. Frank just returned. Maybe he went to the telegraph office when he was out."

Dalton tried to make eye contact, but Chase wasn't making it easy. "You've heard me talk of Terrence, the tyke I helped on the train? This here's his pa."

"Good to make your acquaintance," Chase said. Wallace nodded, and the other men leaned against the outside posts.

"I'll just go in and ask Frank then," Dalton said.

Chase shrugged and Dalton went to step inside, but stopped. He turned back to Chase. "By the way, how's your daughter? That Jane is just about the cutest little thing."

Chase didn't miss a beat. "We think so, Babcock, but she's a mite young for you."

Wallace scowled. When he tried to follow, Chase put up his arm. "Sorry, you'll have to hand over your gun if you want to proceed."

Dalton stepped inside, a voice in his head warning him to take it slow. He envisioned Chase pointing to Albert's sign, as he'd done himself for Seth Cotton. He'd planned to try to get the outlaws inside the small building, where fewer people could get hurt, and then take them on.

Everything that followed next went down so fast Dalton had a hard time discerning it all.

He turned to tell Chase his friends were okay, but felt a gun jab him in the back. Charlie stood from where he'd been crouching down behind the counter. "Get your hands up and away from your guns," Axelrose demanded.

Chase shoved Wallace inside, his gun pressed to the outlaw's side, and pushed him up next to Dalton. The rancher pulled both his and Wallace's guns from their holsters and tossed them out the door. Glancing outside, Dalton saw Thom run forward, shotgun in hand, as the other brothers turned to run. Dalton wondered about Laine, by the bridge, and whether she'd ride in and try to help, or skedaddle while the chance of escape was good.

The entire incident was over in a matter of seconds without a single shot being fired. Feeling a wide grin break across his face, Dalton released a lungful of air. Who had sounded the alarm? They'd been ready for the heist, and had performed the scene like a well-rehearsed play.

Frank stepped out of his office and moved around Charlie. Dalton kept his hands up. He wasn't going to get killed now.

"Someone needs to go untie—"

His words died as Albert stepped through the door, a weapon he must have borrowed in his hand. "Lock 'em up, Thom, Charlie," he called over his shoulder. "Win and Greg have the woman and are already headed for the jail." He looked at Dalton. "Good work, Babcock." A cocky grin spread across his mouth even though his bloody wrists were not a pretty sight.

"Sorry about that. I had to make it at least a little convincing," Dalton said, his hands still raised. "I hoped you'd remember the moon and stars comment from when we were blowing the roof. It was the only thing I could come up with."

Amusement rose in Albert's eyes. "That one almost got you laughed out of the group, but you needn't have worried. I knew before that that you weren't involved. Question is, how did you know about the heist? If you weren't in on it from the beginning . . ." He shook his head. "I can't quite figure that out."

Frank still watched him with suspicion.

"Well?" Albert persisted.

"When you kept going to the doc's to see Evan, I began to get suspicious. When I tried to see him myself and Dr. Thorn turned me away, I figured he must have woken up and told you something that you weren't sharing. I thought he was involved but I didn't know with who. That all came together at the train. I was just surprised that Pat Tackly is indeed totally innocent. He was the perfect suspect."

Albert nodded, then turned to go. "I have someone to fetch back to town." Thom and Charlie, back from depositing Wallace and the others in the jail, closed in on Babcock. Albert chuckled. "You can put your hands down now, Dalton."

That was the first time Albert had called him by his first name.

"But?" Thom looked confused.

"He's on our side, boys. And by the way"—he directed his look toward Thom—"how the heck were you so well prepared? How'd you know they were on their way to town? I tried to get here, but knew it was a long shot."

"The other Preston," Thom answered.

Albert's face went white.

Chase nodded. "The little sheriff."

"Nate? Where is he?" Albert looked about ready to bolt out the door.

"No worries, Boss," Thom said, chuckling. "I'm sure by now he's about finished with his second order of fried chicken. He came scuttling into town, but Dwight, in his thick-skulled, meddling way, and not knowing he was your son, thought he was some half-wild child that had been raised by the wolves by the crazy way he was running toward Logan Meadows. He stopped him, he says with good intentions, and was determined to teach him some manners before letting him amongst proper people. But that didn't slow Nate down. Your boy kicked him in the shins hard enough for Dwight to lose his grip. He scrambled between his legs and was off like a shot straight to the jail, where he found me. Because of his fast thinking, we were ready and waiting for the outlaws."

Albert gave a long whistle, then laughed. "That's a weight off my chest. Good boy. He's learning young." Albert started again for the door.

"Hold up one more second," Dalton said. "If we're all spilling the beans, I need to know how you knew I *wasn't* involved."

"Fair enough," Albert said, turning. "As you suspected, Evan's recovery wasn't quite as slow as I had Dr. Thorn report to everyone. After he woke up, I kept him secluded and handcuffed to his bed. Coming so close to death, he'd had a change of heart and wanted to clear his conscience. He swore on his own grave that you and Pat Tackly didn't have any idea what was planned, but he wouldn't give up his partners—no wonder, since they were all family." He smiled and shook his head. "One of the brothers had worked for the Union Pacific and was in communication with Evan, that's how they knew about the tracks and Three Pines Turn. I'm guessing he's the one waiting with Terrence in New Meringue. If I had had any lingering doubts after your convincing performance out at the train, your comment to Chase about his daughter finalized it in my head. Pretty smart. Good thing Wallace hadn't been in town long enough to learn the names of everyone's children."

Relieved, Dalton couldn't hold back his smile any longer. "Another silly signal, but I was praying it would work and Chase didn't blow my head off. Now, if you don't go fetch Susanna back, I just might do so myself. Never know which way her wind is blowing."

"I do," Albert said, charging through the door. "And I can tell you, a tornado is coming *my* way."

CHAPTER FORTY-NINE

At the sound of thundering hooves, Susanna peered around the trees she was walking through to see Albert galloping her way. The storm had passed, and a bright spring day had taken its place, a little on the breezy side, but still, a vast improvement over what it had been just an hour before. As he drew closer, her heartbeat increased. She'd told him she loved him—and her world had not collapsed. Even though she was nervous, she couldn't wait to hold him in her arms.

He halted a few feet away and dismounted. His eager face made tingles swirl through her body. He dropped his reins and hurried forward, but slowed as he got closer, a somewhat shy look, one she'd never seen before, emerging on his face. He stopped and let her close the distance.

"So, it went well?" she asked, unsure of what to say. "You got there in time?"

He studied her face, then said softly, "I did. Not that it would have mattered much. Nate was under the train. When he heard what was planned, he snuck away and warned the town, even outwitting Dwight, who'd tried to stop him."

He looked so different, so cautious. He'd always been so in command. She had to take a breath to calm her racing heart. "A true Preston."

A smile creeped onto his face. "That's my boy."

They stood together in the road, alone for as far as the eye could see. He held out his hand. The moment she placed hers in his warm palm, he pulled her close, wrapping her in his arms. "Susanna." His voice was tortured, and he buried his face in her hair, which had long since come loose of its bounds, and breathed in deeply. "Susanna," he said again, this time barely a whisper. Leaning back, his lips found hers.

Susanna's lips melded with his, soft and compliant. No hesitation now, her arms slid up his chest until they were wrapped effectively around his neck, giving as good as she got. Their first kiss in front of the bank had been such a surprise, he'd hardly had time to enjoy it before it ended. Not so now. He'd been thinking about this one ever since she'd said "I love you," right before he'd ridden away. He wondered if she'd object if he hoisted her into his arms and carried her under the bushes where they wouldn't be found. For several long minutes they stood locked in each other's embrace, exploring territory that was new to both. Breathing heavily, they finally parted, the light of love shining in her eyes.

"Does this mean I can openly court you? You know my history. You know I kept important issues from you. If I could change the past, I would. So you wouldn't have been hurt. Out of everything, that haunts me the most." He didn't like the uncertainty in her eyes. "I'm sorry."

"Albert, I have things in my past I need to share. Things that may change the way you think about me. You see, I haven't been totally honest with you, either. I've been too embarrassed to—"

He pressed a finger to her lips. "There's nothing you could tell me that would change one wit how I feel. Not one. If your answer is yes, and I can court you, we'll have plenty of time for sharing later. Right now, I just want to hear you say that you feel the same."

He stepped back, whipped off his hat, and hollered as loud as he could up to the sky. "I love Susanna Robinson! And if she'll still have me, I want to make her my wife!"

Laughter burst from Susanna's lips, and Dunbar pranced nervously, the poor horse's eyes wide with surprise.

Feeling very pleased with himself, Albert turned and shouted it again in the opposite direction, loving the happy smile stretched across her face.

He clamped his hat back on. "Well, you never answered my question. You're getting more than you'd bargained for now that Nate's shown up in Logan Meadows, but he's a very good boy. I think you could love him."

She slipped back into his embrace and lifted her face for another kiss, and he was more than happy to oblige. The kiss was gentle and sweet and more than promising. After several long moments he pulled back, his senses soaring. The sincerity and depth to her gaze did marvelous things to his heart. "Well?"

She played with the hair curling around his ear. Red-hot tingles shot down his neck and plunged deep into his belly. Since she was so agreeable, he dipped his head toward her lips, but she held him off with a hand to his chest.

"I say two Prestons are better than one." Her eyes twinkled with mischief as she studied his face. "And I love him already. But, for his sake, I don't want to rush things. He has enough adjusting to do without adding a wedding and a new mother into the mix. He'll let us know when the time is right."

"I totally agree. And it'll give me plenty of time to show my girl around town on my arm, steal a kiss now and then, walk out on Sundays, and take buggy rides. All the things we couldn't do before. I want to have them all."

CHAPTER FIFTY

"Pa, when're we goin' froggin'?" Nate grumbled, standing obediently in front of Albert's highboy as his father combed his hair. He'd asked the same question every day for the past two weeks, but one thing or another had always gotten in their way.

First, the Denver bank had finally shown up with an army regiment of their own, a reinforced stage, and a detailed plan to safely move the million dollars to San Francisco, much to Albert's and Frank's relief. Best of all, they planned to pull out tomorrow. But before that, right after the army detail he'd sent for arrived, the Union Pacific made it to town with a load of new track to lay and fifty workers to do it. Between sending Evan, Laine, Wallace, and the rest of the Stone gang back to Fort McKinney, and the arrival of the Union Pacific and the bankers, Albert had had precious little time for his boy and Susanna.

That was about to change.

He whisked the floppy hair on Nate's head one way, inspected his work with a critical eye, and then tried the opposite direction. "Soon, Nate. The railroad men are almost finished with the new track. In the meantime, another engine is on its way from the opposite direction to hook onto the caboose and pull the train that's been stranded back to the nearest train yard. Once all that's finished, I'll have all the time in the world to do anything you like."

"The tracks will go around the wreck?"

"Yes, sort of. Not around in a circle but alongside and past. This time, a good distance away from the ridge so there won't be any more rockslides, intentional or not." *And hopefully no more deaths.* He flipped the hair back in the first direction again. "I can't get this to work. You need a haircut, and soon."

"But what about froggin'?"

Albert stepped back, smiling down at his son. "If it means that much to you, we could skip the May Day celebration today and go right now." They had plans with Susanna, but she'd made it clear in no uncertain terms that Nate came first. If plans changed because of him, that was fine.

Nate's face scrunched up in deep thought. "I guess we can wait till later."

"Oh, you've seen the maypole we put up and don't want to miss the fun, is that it?"

Nate nodded, looking serious and grownup. "That's right, Pa. We may as well do both."

"My thoughts exactly. Now skedaddle out of here so I can tend to my own beautification. We don't want to be late. And please close the door on your way out—"

Nate dashed out of the room, flinging the door closed behind him. It slammed, rattling the windowpane.

"—gently."

"Sorry, Pa," Nate hollered.

Albert began unbuttoning the top button of his sleep shirt but his gaze strayed to Floria's trunks sitting along the wall still untouched. What was he waiting for? A personal invitation? He'd avoided the unpleasant task long enough. What if there was something important inside? Something that needed tending? He should just do it and get the chore off his mind. Most likely it was a bunch of clothes and shoes, but two trunks? That seemed excessive, even for Floria.

He pulled one across the floor to his bed, then sat, the mattress dipping with his weight. Lifting the latch, he opened the finely built travel case, and rested the top back on its hinge. Just as he'd thought. Clothes. He just looked, not wanting to touch her belongings. It seemed intimate, and it had been many years since they'd been such.

This was ridiculous. Nate would get impatient to go. Albert picked up the corner of the top dress, and looked below. Another garment. He repeated the process. So deep inside, he finally had to lift the top articles out and set them on his bed. Two pairs of fancy boots and some satin slippers lined the bottom along with two reticules, shawls, and a few unmentionables. The money he'd sent home for her support hadn't been put in the bank.

Finding nothing of importance, he lowered the lid, replaced the trunk and brought the other over.

A crash from the kitchen made him flinch.

"Pa? You almost ready? I finished the dishes for ya."

Albert couldn't stop a smile at the surge of love Nate's little voice created. "I'll be along shortly, Nate. Give me a few more minutes. Thanks for cleaning up."

"No problem, Pa!"

Resigned to finish his task so he could stop dwelling on it, Albert opened the second trunk. At the conglomeration of things, papers, envelopes, and very personal items, he sat back in surprise. This looked like everything she might have in the world. On the top was an official-looking envelope stamped with the Louis County seal of Iowa and addressed to Floria. Taking it, he extracted the contents and gazed at the long-awaited divorce papers. Dated two months ago and signed by Floria Brooks Preston.

His heart pounded in his chest and he took a moment to grasp what all this meant. In the same section was a thick envelope containing a tintype of him and Floria the day they married. A flood of emotion washed over him at the pretty smile on her lips. She held the small bouquet of primroses he'd picked and tied with a ribbon. They both looked so young.

"Pa?" Nate was on the opposite side of the door. He needed to hurry.

"Give me five minutes more, son. We're still going to be early, I promise. I'm just doing a few things I've let go. Can you do that?"

A second passed. "Sure, Pa." Nate's tone wasn't quite as chipper. After the frogging failures, Albert didn't want to let Nate down again. He'd go through this trunk when his son went to bed tonight. It would take several hours. As he went to lower the lid, his gaze caught on a letter dated March first, two months ago. His curiosity got the better of him. He lifted the envelope, postmarked from California, and pulled the letter out.

My dearest Fluflu,

I'm counting the days until your glorious arrival. The moment can't come fast enough to suit me. My family is anxious to meet the woman who has tamed my heart and ways, and will soon be my wife. They are thrilled we plan to settle with them in California and to have me back on the west coast.

Just as he'd thought. Floria had needed a marriage proposal to get the divorce done.

Stay safe, my love. You're a very brave woman to travel to the Wyoming Territories by yourself with only the help of your young nephew. If I could be there, you know I would. Your tenacity and spunk are two of the things that drew me to you, as well as your beautiful face, and, oh, so many charms.

Nephew!

As much as I like the boy, I do feel your older sister is sound in seeing to the boy from here on out, since you alone have borne this obligation since your dear brother's death.

Floria was an only child. She hadn't even been willing to claim Nate as her own. He felt sorry for the man she'd been traveling to meet—another fool, just like he'd been.

You deserve a little freedom to see the world before we're blessed with children of our own. Please give Nate a hug for me, and tweak his cheek as I like to do. Tell him we will come and visit often. It's endearing how at times he slips and calls you mama.

Poor Nate! His mother had planned to give him away like a puppy that no longer fit into her life. Maybe it was best that Floria had already passed. If not, he would be tempted to do something he'd regret.

"Pa?"

Disgusted, Albert flung the missive into the trunk and closed the lid. He quietly carried it to the wall, then crossed the room and opened the door. Nate's eyes went wide at the sight of his night-shirt and pants.

Albert scooped him up. "Have I told you today how much I love you, son?" When hot prickles stabbed at the back of Albert's eyes, he buried his face against Nate's neck. "Because I do, Nate. Life is so much sweeter since you arrived. I can't imagine a day going by without seeing your smiling face. You're my boy, and I couldn't be prouder." He gave him a good squeeze, meaning every word from the bottom of his soul. "I love you."

Nate clung to him like a tick. He didn't say anything, but the strong beat of his heart said he'd heard every word his pa spoke.

268

CHAPTER FIFTY-ONE

$\mathcal{S}$usanna turned when someone called her name. Shifting her basket of goodies to her other arm, she smiled at Win, who hurried in her direction. His normal overalls had been replaced with a pressed shirt and new-looking nankeen trousers. Was he seeing someone special and keeping it secret? The names of several unmarried women popped into her head. She'd yet to speak with him since the day of the Stone Family Flub, as the event was now commonly called. Actually, it wasn't funny at all. With so many deaths attributed to the train wreck, they had much to atone for. Shrugging off a shiver, she smiled at Albert's approaching brother. She liked Win. He was kind, and a bit shy.

"Susanna," he said, a wide smile on his face. "Let me carry that for you."

"Oh, you don't have to—"

He waved off her objection, bringing a whiff of pomade to her nose from his neatly parted and slicked-down hair. "It's the least I can do for the woman who'll be my sister-in-law someday soon."

She liked the way that sounded. Laughter from the festival grounds drifted over, adding to the celebratory feel of the beautiful day. Fluffy white clouds floated slowly in the vivid blue sky high above the happy-faced folks as they walked toward the park, their arms laden with foodstuffs and blankets.

"Well, when you put it like that, all right," she replied, handing over her basket.

"You're headed to the festival, I presume?"

She nodded, smiling at his silly question. Seemed he was nervous about something. "Of course, isn't everyone? I can't think of a better way to put the past to rest than a springtime celebration." They fell into step.

A buggy rolled over the bridge and then passed them by with Mrs. Hollyhock and Beth Fairington, and Gabe at the reins. Susanna waved.

"See ya there," Violet called, waving back.

"Susanna?"

Win's suddenly serious tone made her look over at him.

"I'm pleased you and my brother mended your fences. I was more than a mite worried you were falling for Dalton Babcock. Thank goodness Albert finally opened up with the truth."

Truth? What did he mean?

A horrible sinking feeling almost toppled her. All she'd done was recognize that she didn't want a life without Albert and had accepted she could forgive him anything. And had. He hadn't shared any more of his past than she already knew. Susanna's feet slowed to a stop. The moment Win looked into her eyes he realized his mistake.

"What do you mean?"

He blinked several times, then looked away.

"Win, you're not going anywhere unless you tell me what you meant by that comment. What else is Albert hiding?"

"Nothing."

"Win?"

"It's not for me to say, Susanna."

The beseeching expression on his face wasn't going to work.

"I thought Albert had told you," he said, relenting. "That was why you two had made up. Don't ask it of me, please."

"Oh, I'm asking right now, Win! You better believe I'm asking! And, you're going to tell me." She'd never been more serious in her life. The beauty of the morning evaporated into thin air. "What horrible secret is he hiding now? Another wife?"

Win's face blanched. "Of course not. It's nothing like that, as a matter of fact, it's the opposite."

She plopped her hands on her hips. "Neither one of us is going anywhere until you spit it out."

He nodded, then looked around to make sure no one would hear what he had to say. "You have to promise not to tell him I told you, and you can't tell anyone else neither."

"Oh, for heaven's sake, Win, why would I tell anyone?"

He took a deep breath, but just stared at her.

"Win! I'm not getting any younger."

He put his head close to hers. "What Albert wouldn't tell you is that Floria was a no-good, pretty-faced trickster. She'd been jilted the month before Albert came into her town and wanted to get back at the man who'd wised up before it was too late. So she married Albert, a strapping, young, and new-to-town stranger. Floria was very beautiful, and she drew him into her web just like a spider. It wasn't but a couple of weeks before she began carrying on where she left off with that other fella behind Albert's back. And when I say carrying on, I mean *carrying on.*"

Susanna sucked in air, unable to take her eyes off Win's face. Fury burned in her heart.

"My brother didn't understand his bride's constant mood swings, because he didn't know about the other scoundrel yet. One minute she loved him, and the next she didn't. He tried to make it work. Then one day he caught them in his own house, and they weren't just having tea. That's the day he moved out, but not before he went a few rounds with the interloper. After she played him the fool, he knew he couldn't remain in that town. He decided to start over where he could have a clean slate. Even before he met you, he's been trying to get that she-cat, double-dealing . . ." He swiped a hand over his face. "*Her* to give him a divorce, but her temperaments changed faster than a jackrabbit runs. I was worried about him, and didn't want to see him set out alone, so I came along. Being the younger brother, it's my job to look after him."

She could only imagine how hurtful the betrayal must have been for Albert. "But why didn't he tell me? I was having a difficult time understanding how a man could leave his wife after only a couple of months. And to think I've been feeling sorry for the wrong person—*the harlot!*"

"I wanted him to—I begged him to—but he didn't want to tarnish her memory, for Nate's sake. You know how things get out." His face actually colored up. "And when they do, people talk. Albert never wants his son to know about his mother's misbehavior. He planned to tell you eventually, just not yet. I think seeing her again—even dead—has him reliving the pain. Give it a little time."

"That's because he's honorable, and good, and—"

"What's going on over here? Plotting my demise?"

Susanna gasped. She whirled around, her hand plastered to her chest. She'd been in such an angry fit, wanting to scratch out Floria's eyes, that she hadn't heard Albert and Nate's approach. When Albert's gaze met hers, love rushed through her. She could picture him a younger man, betrayed, upset, wondering what he'd done wrong. It was a good thing that jezebel was already dead, because if she weren't, Susanna just might kill her herself for hurting Albert so.

Albert cocked his head. "What's got you riled? I know that look . . ."

She smiled, corralling her anger. "Just something Win told me he heard from *Miss* Fairington. How her pie'll beat mine to smithereens in the contest this afternoon."

Well, it was true—a year ago.

"Hi, Miss Robinson. Hi, Uncle Win," Nate said, clutching Albert's hand as if he'd been doing it his entire life. His face was scrubbed clean and his hair combed.

Albert smiled. "Her pie, or anything else, can't hold a candle to you." He lifted his elbow and Susanna slipped her hand through, praising heaven she'd found such an honorable, steadfast man to give her heart to.

"I'm liking this courting stuff more and more," he said, leaning in to give her a too-long-for-propriety's-sake kiss on her cheek that sent a bevy of tingles racing up her spine, after which he looked down and winked at his son. Win just grinned like the town fool.

The celebration was in full swing when Albert whispered in Susanna's ear. "Will you excuse me for a minute, sweetheart?" He'd spotted Babcock, Pat Tackly, and the bankers arriving at the edge of the grass field, and wanted to make sure everything for their departure tomorrow was solid.

"Of course. I can't keep you all to myself the whole day, even if I'd like to. But only if you'll buy a ticket." She smiled at Hannah and Jessie, who were helping her arrange the cakes on the table for the cakewalk they'd have at the end of the day. It was a fund-raiser for the two memorial plaques they intended to have inscribed. One for the cemetery, and one to put out at Three Pines Turn, where the train's engine would remain for the time being, after the rest of the train was gone.

He pulled some coins from his pocket. "I planned to already, and actually, I'll take four." He leaned in and kissed her cheek again, never tiring of the feel of her soft skin.

"Albert, if you keep kissing me, you're going to start people's tongues wagging."

"I can't help it. I'm making up for lost time."

He straightened, his gaze snagging on the train depot off in the distance. It was difficult to believe so much had transpired. The accident and deaths brought sadness, but also a burst of joy for Nate and Susanna. "I still can't believe Laine and Wallace, along with little Terrence, planned to brace themselves and ride out the crash in the passenger cars, thinking they'd be safe. But when Terrence snuck away, they had to go in search. All three of them could've been killed. They risked his young life, as well as their own. All because of money."

"Don't think about that today, Albert. This is a celebration." She took the devil's food cake Hannah handed her and set it on the end of the row.

"I know. It's just that it could have been Nate."

Turning, she wiped a smudge of chocolate frosting from her thumb onto her apron and hugged his arm close. "Thank God it wasn't. I'm embarrassed how well Laine fooled me. I thought she was such a nice woman. She even lied to Mrs. Hollyhock about their past and going home to help her father."

"If there's any consolation at all, it's with Evan's confession, and all the other evidence, they'll all taste the end of a rope, excluding Terrence, of course."

He looked across the crowd to the maypole in the center of the clearing where the children waited in anticipation for the dance, or whatever it was they did when they scampered around, to start. Long colored streamers were wound tight, and wouldn't be released until it was time to begin.

"Looks like Nate's doing fine."

Susanna stopped what she was doing and turned to look. Nate, along with Markus, Sarah, and several others, were running around the maypole in a single-file race. Penny, Brenna's oldest daughter, watched, her hands placed protectively on Maddie's small shoulders, as the blind girl smiled at the happy sounds.

Julia was sitting with Mrs. Hollyhock's group, and waved. Susanna waved back.

"Of course he is, Albert," she said. "He's such an agreeable little sort. He comes up with the funniest things. Now go on, before Dalton gets away."

Albert ambled away, smiling at the relaxed townsfolk having

a good time. He edged his way into the group of men and nodded to Babcock. "So, everything's set for the big move tomorrow? No last-minute changes."

The head man, as reed thin as a person could get, wiped his mouth with his handkerchief. "We are. Thank you for your assistance in this matter, Sheriff. I've left bank drafts with Frank to pay your men for services rendered."

"Anything for stopping the robbery?" He'd said it tongue in cheek, remembering that last year Charlie Axelrose had received a substantial reward for bringing in the outlaw Tandy Smith. It couldn't hurt to ask.

The man's eyes opened wide. "No. None of the outlaws were wanted. I'm sorry, but you're out of luck."

The look Babcock threw him almost made him laugh.

"And what about you, Dalton, you pulling out with them? Are you going to finish the job you started? I've had this sneaking suspicion you might change your mind at the last moment and stay behind. For whatever reason, I can't imagine."

Dalton grinned like a pesky raccoon with his hand in a sugar bag. "You'd like to know wouldn't you, Preston? Well, I won't keep you in suspense any longer. As much as I know you'll miss me, I *am* finishing the job. Not only that, but I'm kind of excited to see what kind of trouble I can find out in California. That's actually where the Stone family originated, and I'm escorting little Terrence back to his *honest* aunt and uncle, since his parents are dead and all his other relatives are incarcerated."

There it was. He should be relieved, but he wasn't. Somewhere deep inside he'd hoped Babcock would stay. Good lawmen were difficult to find, but he'd never tell him that. "That's good of you. Are you going to tell Susanna goodbye? She was wondering about that yesterday."

Dalton glanced across the gathering to the cake table. "I don't believe I will. The last time I left town, I didn't say goodbye either. I think she'll understand."

At the sound of a single fiddle, everyone turned. In the clearing, where the fun was about to begin, Mrs. Brinkley's oldest grandson held a polished instrument under his chin and warmed up as Frank Lloyd unwrapped the maypole ribbons. Albert could see the excitement on Nate's face all the way from where he stood. "I'll catch up with you men later," Albert said. "I'm going to go join my family."

The sun had set, and tired picnic goers began their trek home. Susanna packed away her dirty plates, as well as the cold oven pound cake drizzled with honey that Nate had won on the cakewalk. He'd wanted to eat it right then and there, but Albert said since they had eaten so many picnic types of foods already, that they should save it until tomorrow. Too tired to argue his point, the child had collapsed on the ground at his father's feet until Albert hefted him up to carry him home.

They arrived at the split where Susanna would go her way and Albert, with a sleepy Nate in his arms, would go theirs. Albert turned toward her house and kept going.

Susanna grasped his arm, and pulled him to a stop. "What're you doing?"

"What's it look like?" Albert said with a crooked smile. "I'm walkin' my girl home." Even his hair was mussed under his tipped-back hat.

"No, that little tyke is tuckered out. He needs to be put to bed right away."

Albert looked down into her face. "Nothing doing. Remember what happened the last time I missed my chance to walk you home?"

Nate lifted his head, still wreathed with a little crown made from leaves. "What're you all whispering about?" He looked around, then rubbed one eye with his fist. He jerked, as if he'd remembered something. "Put me down, Pa."

"You have enough energy to walk?"

"Sure. I want to do something."

Albert set him on his feet and watched him scamper away toward the bridge. Albert groaned. "He's been wanting to go froggin' in the worst way." He gave Susanna a tired look. "But it's late now—and I don't have one ounce of energy left. On my next day off I'll spend the whole day under that bridge with him." He placed his hand over his heart. "I promise."

Susanna couldn't hold back a quiet laugh at her handsome champion who appeared worn through. "Do you want me to go get him?" The sky was putting on a pretty show with its pink and golden clouds, and the night birds swooping here and there.

"No, you're just as tired as I am. Besides, Nate may put up a fight. His powers of persuasion are very effective. I know."

Before Albert had taken two steps toward the bridge, Nate came up the bank and walked toward them with a happy little spring in his step. Looked like he wouldn't be going to bed anytime soon. Clutched in his hand was a clump of clover and several puffs of dandelions. He cupped a hand that needed a good scrubbing over top, trying to keep the seeds from flying off.

Albert hunkered down. "What's all that, Nate?"

Nate stood there for a few seconds just looking at the funny little bouquet he'd picked. "Since it's May Day, and we all got nice leaf wreaths, I'd like ta take something special up to mama's grave." He dropped his eyes to the ground as if he were asking something he wasn't supposed to. He swallowed. "I know she's not coming back, and the next time I see her will be in heaven with Oldie Judy. I know, Pa. I understand. You don't have'ta worry over me no more."

Albert wrapped Nate into his arms, all the while looking up into Susanna's eyes, promising her a lifetime of love. Reaching out, he took her hand and drew her down into their embrace.

"Sure we can, son. We'll go right now. I love you. And Susanna loves you, too." He kissed Nate on the top of his head, then found Susanna's lips.

Warmth, love, anticipation, and thankfulness all blossomed in Susanna's heart at the same time. She'd been given such a precious gift, one that she would care for to her best ability for the rest of her life. And what fun it would be doing it.

ACKNOWLEDGMENTS

When I sat down to put ink to paper, so to speak, for the fourth book of the Prairie Hearts series, my mind was an open slate. All I knew was that it would begin with Greg and Brenna's wedding, characters from book three who still needed their happy-ever-after. Little did I expect what was in store. Albert and Susanna's long-awaited journey basically wrote itself, much to my delight, and kept me—the author—guessing all the way to the end. I hope it does you as well.

As always, I have many people to thank for their expertise, love, and support along the way. First, to Maria Gomez, my awesome editor at Montlake, for her enthusiasm and friendship. She makes every day a pleasure. To my amazing developmental editor and friend, Caitlin Alexander, for her remarkable suggestions, for keeping me on track, and for steering the ending to just the right place. To my loving husband, sons, and daughter-in-law, for the fantastic brainstorming session that came up with the premise for this story. To my dear sisters, who have indulged my crazy imagination since I was a small girl. To all my wonderful author friends, whose support and companionship in this business is essential.

To the Camp 18 Restaurant situated along Oregon's historic Highway 26, for their delightful collection of antique railroad cars, resembling the train that plays a large role in this story.

To the Lord, for the charming life He's given me. And, of course, to my readers, to whom I'm always eternally grateful.

ABOUT THE AUTHOR

*U*SA Today Bestselling Author Caroline Fyffe was born in Waco, Texas, the first of many towns she would call home during her father's career with the US Air Force. A horse aficionado from an early age, she earned a bachelor of arts in communications from California State University-Chico before launching what would become a twenty-year career as an equine photographer. She began writing fiction to pass the time during long days in the show arena, channeling her love of horses and the Old West into a series of Western historicals. Her debut novel, *Where the Wind Blows*, won the Romance Writers of America's prestigious Golden Heart Award as well as the Wisconsin RWA's Write Touch Readers' Award. She and her husband have two grown sons and live in the Pacific Northwest. To learn about upcoming novels, visit her website at www.carolinefyffe.com.